A Vigil for Joe Rose

Stories of Being Out in High School

Michael Whatling

MORTAL COIL BOOKS
VANCOUVER   NEW YORK   LONDON   SYDNEY

A Vigil for Joe Rose
Stories of Being Out in High School

Copyright © 2021 Michael Whatling

All rights reserved. No part of this book may be used or reproduced by any means, graphic, electronic, or mechanical, including photocopying, recording, taping or by any information storage retrieval system without the written permission of the author except in the case of brief quotations embodied in critical articles and reviews.

This is a work of true stories as told by the students themselves. Names and identifying details have been changed to protect the privacy of individuals.

Spot a typo? Send it to: Typo@MortalCoilBooks.com

Front cover designed by Bradley Wind.

ISBN 978-1-7775699-0-7 (pbk.)
ISBN 978-1-7775699-1-4 (ebk.)

2 3 4 5 6 7 8 9

I am especially thankful for those who
agreed to tell their stories because they
thought it might help others. Thanks Alex,
Christopher, Eric, Evan, Geoff, Matthew,
and Tristan.

Contents

Introduction

A FEW YEARS AGO at the annual Quebec Teachers' Convention, I conducted a workshop titled, "Making Schools Safe for Gay and Lesbian Students." While approximately forty teachers attended and the workshop was well received, something telling occurred after the workshop was over. A member of the committee responsible for choosing workshop topics confided to me that including this workshop was not without controversy. While the committee members had acknowledged the "importance" of the topic and the problems that lesbian, gay, bisexual, and transgender (LGBT) students may face in schools, the dissenting opinion was that speaking about such topics was "opening a can of worms."

This work hopes to open the "can of worms" and, by doing so, discover what it's like to be an openly gay student in high school. It has its genesis in my doctoral research. While it is a fictionalized account of being out in high school, in the same vein as what Truman Capote described as the "non-fiction novel," material was gathered through in-depth interviews with students aged sixteen to eighteen. This work is unique as it tells the stories of students who were gay, out, and attending high school at the time of the research.

Clearly, LGBT students are the most marginalized group in schools today. Schools are still one of the most homophobic places in society, denying the existence of homosexuals unless forced to do so—when a gay student wants to take a same-sex date to a prom or a gay student is "fag-bashed."

While these stories take place in the relatively progressive jurisdiction of Quebec, Canada, they serve as a canary in a coal mine and may be useful to researchers and educators in places not yet at this point in the "acceptance" learning curve. Still, much work remains to be done in schools *everywhere* to make them a safer place for LGBT students.

Many of my professional, academic, and personal interests have intersected to form the genesis of this project. In the past, I've taught education courses at both Concordia and McGill universities in Montreal, among them diversity courses that look at race, ethnicity, gender, and sexual orientation. I've noticed that of all the topics covered in these courses, students know the least about sexual orientation, and, while willing to learn about it, have the most apprehension in doing so. Clearly there is still room for work to be done in this area.

While preparing for this project, I discovered how little research in this area allows LGBT students to retain their voices. While I wanted to contribute to the research a deeper understanding of the experience of being out in high school—what it's really like day-to-day—I also wanted a way to represent the findings that would keep faith with participants and their voices. I thought representing findings in a literary way would be appropriate, if not challenging. I strongly reject the notion that intermittent quotes in an academic text, disembodied from participants, could do these gay students and their stories justice.

For literary inspiration, I turned to Capote's non-fiction novel *In Cold Blood*. It served me well, as many nights after reading a chapter or two of Capote's masterpiece, I postponed sleeping to work on these stories. Also, I was greatly inspired by Moisés Kaufman's play and movie, *The Laramie Project*, where researchers investigated the attitudes of townspeople to the death of Matthew Shepard. Stories told in these ways have immeasurable power.

While consisting of individual stories, one for each participant, exemplars to the themes found through this research, these stories comprise one entity under the umbrella of a novel that represents the arc where the protagonists move from the pivotal event of coming out to the ongoing development of their identities as young gay men. Along the way, each of them encounters situations that illuminate the experience of being out in school. I see this type of collection as influenced by the work of Margaret Atwood, although similar in format to some of the works of Alice Munro, Margaret Laurence, and Sherwood Anderson where the stories in the collection form a novel by using the same times, settings, characters, and incidents from other stories.

Let me introduce the stories huddled under this umbrella…

The collection opens with, "Elton John, Uncle David, and Me," a coming out story that depicts that while there may be an imperative to come out, it's losing control of the process that's frightening.

In "The Nail That Sticks Up Gets Hammered Down," Alex is in the early stages of figuring out his identity. For Alex, being gay is nothing special and nothing too momentous happens. Or does it?

"The Holy Ghost" is about experiencing a teacher's homophobia, and the ghosts that arise from the past, exist in the present, and are created for the future.

Geoff, the protagonist in "A Lesson on Being Inseparable," lives completely isolated from other gays, yet is dedicated to teaching younger students about sexual orientation, learning something about himself along the way.

Experiencing homophobia and harassment by other students is the theme of "Episodes in Fear." As harrowing as Matthew's story is, there are clear lessons to be learned by educators that Matthew can even see. Why can't anyone else at his school see them?

Christopher, the main character in "E-mails to My Brother," also experiences homophobia and harassment, from family as well as peers, yet has a different approach to handling it.

The novella in this collection, "The Last Coming out Story," is a postmodern take on the ubiquitous coming out story. How does the president of the school's "Rainbow Club" go from being the most popular student to the most hated? Though not for being gay. "The Last Coming Out Story" rose on the HarperCollins Authonomy website to the Editor's Desk from over four thousand books, receiving over five hundred enthusiastic comments and reviews.

"In case you haven't noticed, I'm gay. Pass the salt," undertakes to show how humour, even in the midst of a serious personal crisis, can be a coping strategy.

The closing story, "Rebel...Just Because," returns to Evan, the same protagonist as in the opening story, who has grown into a self-styled in-your-face warrior against heteronormativity. He's not afraid to "queer" education, for the first time making his school think about students that until then were invisible.

This work wouldn't have been possible without the academic and personal support of the members of my Ph.D. committee: Claudia Mitchell and Lynn Butler-Kisber of McGill University, and Sandra Weber of Concordia University.

Finally, but importantly, Joe Rose was a real person. I went to the same high school as Joe and, from time-to-time, I would run into him at a dance club or on a downtown street. More often than not we'd stop and exchange pleasantries as you do with someone you're acquainted with but don't know well. Among other achievements in his short life, he began the first gay and lesbian club at the college we attended. The insanity of losing somebody in the way he was lost haunts me even today. He hasn't been forgotten. In this novel, Joe Rose symbolizes those who deserve tribute for having blazed the way before us. This work aspires to burn brightly for both him and the out gay students described in these pages.

A candlelight vigil.

M.W.

Prologue

ONE MORNING, a flyer was found in the mailboxes of community workers, social and political action groups, politicians, and university, college, and high school faculty and students, among others, and posted to lamp posts, construction site sidings, and bulletin boards throughout the city where those who would be interested and concerned pass by . . .

Candlelight Vigil

in Memory of

Joe Rose

Tomorrow Night
8:00 p.m.

<u>Meeting Place</u>
Parc de l'Espoir
rue Ste-Catherine and rue Panet
Gay Village

Procession will be along rue Ste-Cathe-
rine to
the site of the loss

Elton John, Uncle David, and Me
Evan's Story—Part I

———————

I HUDDLE over my Tim Horton's coffee and look out the window at November wind and my bike leaning unlocked against a pole. As customers wait in line, they rub their hands together, stomp their feet, and make "brrr" noises to each other and laugh about doing it. Then they take their orders and sit alone at tables like random icebergs in the North Atlantic. They look around, but not at each other—over heads, around people, through them. A few shivering souls look my way, even pause before moving on, but there are no smiles or nods to acknowledge I'm here. Surely they must wonder why it's eleven o'clock on a Monday morning and I'm not in school. But no one says a thing. We've silently agreed to keep each other's secrets—carefully sipping coffee disguises whatever demons we wrestle with alone.

I took off even before the first bell rang. All I remember is riding around for hours. I'd never skipped school before, but I needed to kill time. Now I need time to think and prepare to face this.

Everybody ran up to me and wanted to know if it was true. They were all asking questions I didn't know how to answer. The only thing I was sure about was I didn't want to be there when the shit storm came down.

How quickly things change.

Saturday night everything was going so well it made me think grade eight was shaping up to be my best school year ever. I was with Chantal, my best friend who's in Sec. IV, and her mother at their place—a pretty typical weekend for me. Chantal makes me laugh. She tries to be older, but she goes overboard to the point I've caught her looking skeptically at me over the top of her glasses like she's a sixty-year-old woman. She even dyed her hair from red to matte black.

I brought along Melanie, a girl in my grade whom I just started hanging around with. She's such a girly-girl. She loves clothes and shoes and all kinds of hair and beauty products. She tries to drag me shopping with her, but I fight her off with excuses that I'm waiting for a call for a kidney transplant, or I'm babysitting a sick goldfish. We have the same English class, and we put a lot of effort into passing notes back and forth to each other. Or, at least, trying not to get caught doing it.

It was the first time we were all together and we were having fun talking and laughing. I always have fun with Chantal and her mom—they're like a second family to me. I already told them I'm gay, and they're cool with it, but I hadn't told Melanie yet.

Chantal's mom loves it when I joke around with her. I always call her "Mom," so all night it was Mom-this and Mom-that. Every time I said it we laughed, especially since I made it seem like she really was my mother, even asking for my allowance and to borrow the car. We get carried away sometimes. I love it when Chantal's mom laughs—it's this loud boom that quickly fades into a wheezing noise like she's on life support. Then suddenly it booms again.

Chantal's mom said with a big grin, "You know, if I was your mother I'd get a say in what boys you date."

It was all very innocent on her part; it was something she'd have said to Chantal and me and we'd have laughed about it. But Melanie was there.

"Boys? Boys?" Melanie gave us this weird smile, I guess thinking it was part of the joke. Then she looked over her glasses at me and said dead serious, "Oh, you're gay."

For the longest time it hung there: Melanie putting two-and-two together, Chantal and her mom holding their breath, and me not knowing whether to laugh or run.

But Melanie was cool with it. She told me it was okay. She smiled and said, "Well, I kinda knew."

How could she have missed it? She knows what it's like for me at school with people always asking me if I'm gay. They're not nice about it—they ask with twisted faces that tell me they're bracing themselves for something unpleasant. As unpleasant as a simple "yes" can be. Sometimes they just rudely tell me to my face, "You're gay."

When they confront me, I lie. I say things like, "No, I'm not gay. I'm really not." Anything so they'll leave me alone. I know I show signs; I suppose I have gay mannerisms, at least the kind people always look for. Last year when I started smoking, people got on my case about how I held a cigarette. "Evan you smoke like a girl." They make fun of me because of the way I cross my legs, how I walk, some of the words I use. A few months ago I decided to butch-up my body language and eliminate any signs that could make them think I'm gay; I wouldn't cross my legs; I smoked differently; I changed the way I walked. I tried really hard to be something I'm not.

It didn't work. Everybody still asks me if I'm gay, and I still feel trapped by all the questions and lies. It makes me a very unhappy person. It's raised hell with my sleep. My stomach flips and flops like an acrobat. Cirque de So Gay. I've lost ten pounds, and that's a lot given I've been called "Stick Boy" as much as I've been called "gay." Of course, my mother wants me to go to a doctor, but I'm smart enough not to ask what kind of doctor. Been there. Done that. Almost opened a vein over it.

"I mean, come on," Melanie said. We all started laughing and talking at once. Chantal's mom went Boom! Wheeze! Boom! again. Somewhere in there she was able to apologize.

"I wasn't thinking," she said. "Can you forgive me?"

I could tell she felt bad about it, but it didn't matter. If Melanie was going to be my friend, she had a right to know.

Melanie and I spent the rest of the evening talking: about my life with my joy-sucking parents, about being gay and everything I've been through so far, and about her life as well, her family and their "fun-scapade" getaways, her boyfriend who tears up with happiness every time he sees her. Well almost. I found her to be an open, accepting person. I suppose that's what attracted me to be friends with her in the first place. Deep down I knew whatever opinion she had could only be a positive one. And that doesn't just apply to gays, but people from all walks of life.

It's good to have friends to talk things over with. It feels good to be accepted. I love that there's people in my life who get me.

The thing is, it could've been a lot worse—I'd been through this all before with my parents.

I was twelve, twelve and a half, when I told my cousin, Faith, at a family gathering that I'm gay. We were playing school and she was the teacher. She always played the teacher, and I always had to the student who couldn't do anything right. I hated the game—we'd outgrown it years before, but Faith still loved playing it because she could tell me what to do. She asked me which imaginary girl in class I wanted to be paired with to do work, and I was fed up, so I said, "No one."

"Pick a girl." Faith loomed over me at the upturned milk crate we were using as my desk. I squirmed on the floor and eyed the slightly open door from her bedroom to the hallway.

"I don't want to pick a girl."

When she asked, "Why not?" that's when I told her.

"Right." Faith took the People magazine and the pencil we were using as school supplies from the milk crate, and put them on the lawn chair/teacher's desk. "Don't ever ask me to play some stupid game with you then."

After dinner I saw her telling other people in my family—cousins and aunts and uncles—and at first I could see in their faces that they didn't know how to take it, so they just laughed it off. Then she told her older brother, the older brother told my uncle, my uncle told my mother, and that's when it erupted like Hiroshima 1945.

Quite frankly my parents didn't believe I was gay, they just thought it was a phase I was going through. They sent me to therapy with the idea to change that. I use "they," but I know it was mostly my mother's idea—she's a great believer that psychology cures all. Dr. Phil's her god.

The first time I had to go "see someone," I honestly felt it was an attack from my parents. Both of them sat me down to tell me, a rare unified front—they usually show their love by arguing.

"We've made an appointment with a specialist," my mother said matter-of-factly like it was the time of year for a flu shot. My father nodded.

"I'm not sick," I told them. Two could play this game. With my father there, two-and-a-half.

"I know . . ." my mother said. For a woman who had always been so very certain of everything, she sounded strangely unsure right then. "But it's more a doctor-specialist. Someone you can speak to, someone trained to listen." More like paid to listen.

"It could help you figure some things out. It's the chance to speak to someone about what's going on."

For a moment my father looked like he was about to say something, but one look from my mother and he returned to nodding.

So many questions were rushing through my brain. You're trying to *cure* me from being gay, right? Has *that* ever worked? But the bottom line question was, *Do I have a choice?* Experience taught me my parents, or, rather, my mother always got her way.

"Okay," I said.

They smiled, and my father patted me on the shoulder. For a second I thought my mother was even going to hug me, but I could see in her eyes she thought better of it.

Their words were one thing, but to me it was like they were saying, "No. You're not good enough for us. Go to therapy. Change. You're fucked up." To me this was a big rejection of who I was.

So I said to myself, Alright. To hell with this! I'll play along.

I didn't like the therapist to begin with because right away she said, "Well there's a possibility you *might* be gay, just like there's a possibility anyone could be gay. But in your case it's just a phase you're going through." A phase! Like I was eating only Cherry Garcia ice cream for dessert or had decided not to cut my hair for a year. She totally sided with my parents. She didn't so much as leave the door open a crack to the possibility I might actually *be* gay. It pissed me off she made assumptions about my sexuality so easily.

Her office was in a strip mall, on the second floor directly above one of those cheque-cashing places. The chairs in the waiting room were old Ikea—the cushion sank when you sat on it so your ass was millimeters off the floor. Her office wasn't much better. The walls looked like they'd once been painted off-white but had dirtied to a wet sand colour. The small window at the far end of the long, narrow room was streaked and smudged by patients' hands and fingers as though they'd tried to claw their way out. The big comfy chair you were supposed to sit in and bleed your life out to her was stained dark grey on the arms and the headrest.

There were too many plants for a room that size, and they might have given the place an overgrown-jungle feel if any of them had been healthy. Most of the leaves were brown and brittle-looking.

I'd decided that even though I had to go speak to someone in body, my mind would be somewhere else. I told myself, Whatever goes on in that room, don't let it have an effect on you. I didn't give a fuck, I really didn't. I made myself indifferent to the whole thing. Sitting there, I knew I certainly wasn't going to cooperate with this woman.

The therapist sat in a red, tall-backed, wooden chair. She had grey hair, but it was styled in the same cut girls in my school are excited about when someone shows up with it on Monday mornings. On her it looked like a wig.

For a long time I sat there and said nothing. The therapist tried to get me to talk by sucking up to me.

"I understand you're very articulate. I have the sense you must be mature for your age."

I almost laughed at her. How could she possibly make such judgments given I hadn't said a word?

Silence is difficult for me since I'm a talkative kind of guy. This was close to unbearable. To survive, in my head I ran snippets of conversations I'd have wanted to have with my parents. It kept coming back to questions, and the questions were all about why I'm not good enough the way I am.

Every so often I'd steal a look at the woman to see how my silent-treatment was playing. It wasn't pretty. Whenever I looked at her, she'd always catch my eye and look back at me with an expression as though I'd given her a rash and she was fighting against scratching herself in front of company.

In all that quiet, she abruptly jumped up and ran over to water a ficus near the window, seemingly to drown its last gasps for life.

When she sat down again she said, "Don't you want to get better?" That was definitely a low point in my life.

"A lot of boys experience this. They have homo-erogenous fantasies, but it doesn't mean they're gay."

"Yeah," I finally spoke. "I have those . . . *because I'm gay.*"

She said I was too smart for my own good.

In all honesty, at the time I didn't know exactly what gay was or anything about being gay. I didn't even know anyone who was gay. I had to think back to the schoolyard in elementary school when kids used to say in low voices that the guy who sang in Disney movies was gay. I didn't think I had much in common with Elton John. For one thing, I couldn't sing and I certainly didn't dress like him. Who does? But I've known since day one there's no way I could be straight if that's what everyone else was.

I thought my being gay was normal. I suppose it's the same for boys and girls who know they're straight. For me being gay's just something I've been from Day One; it's the only thing I know how to be. How can I be anything else? Someone else?

As far back as I remember I knew I was different, even before I pinpointed the difference as being gay. I wasn't like all the other boys—I was similar, but then again . . . Action figures. G.I. Joes. They didn't do anything for me. Neither did Barbie. I liked reading and I didn't play sports. I thought to be masculine you had to be athletic, and be good at it. In gym class in elementary school we'd play boys against girls, and the gym teacher would ask one of the boys and one of the girls to be captains. Of course the gym teacher always picked the most athletic and popular boy. Well, whatever "popular" means in elementary school. And, of course, the boy who was captain would never choose me. It's funny how the road to being a walking-talking cliché is paved so early.

Even when I was three or four years old, I had feelings towards boys. It wasn't sexual; it wasn't an I-want-to-do-you type thing. It was just an attraction. I remember my babysitter had two sons, one older and one my age, and I really liked Justin the older son. He was ten and I was seven. He was my first crush. It wasn't sexual, but I was attracted to him—it was emotional. No matter what he was talking about, he had a way of speaking that made it seem like he was patiently explaining something to you, and he wanted you to know what the world was all about, even if he was only telling you in passing about a project he was doing on the migration of Monarch butterflies. I did everything I could to try and hang out with him. I hadn't learned yet to hide my crushes on boys, or that ten-year-olds don't really hang out with their younger brother and his friends.

Like the therapist, my father tried to change me, too: he tried to butch me up. My mother must have put him up to it. Once he even took me to an Alouettes football game. He kept telling me, "I paid good money for these tickets," and all through the game he tried to explain to me they had to measure the twelve yards or the twenty-yard line, or whatever it was. I wasn't paying attention; I didn't care; I didn't have a clue what was happening on the field.

There was a copy of *The Gazette* left on the bleachers, so I picked it up and I started reading Martha Stewart's column, cross-legged as well, and he got pissed off at me.

"Pay attention to what I'm saying. Watch the game."

I put down the newspaper and pretended to be interested. They were expensive tickets after all.

My father was always doing stuff like that to make me "man up";

he was always trying to get me to do something athletic or build something. Once we tried to assemble a birdfeeder together, but we argued all the time. That's when he gave up.

But it's not about sports or birdfeeders. My parents just didn't want to believe I was gay and they tried to do everything they could to change me. I found that totally weird because, the thing is, it isn't like I'm the first person in the family who's gay.

I was in grade five when I found out my uncle had died. I knew my father had a brother, but I'd never met him because he lived out in B.C. He was never mentioned much. He was this mystery to me—an uncle whose name could cause the conversation to stop, looks to be exchanged, and uncomfortable clearing of throats. It was my father who sat me down to tell me, "You know your Uncle David out in British Columbia? Well, he died yesterday."

I was ten years old but I started asking myself some pretty grownup things. I didn't know anything about my uncle, but I knew it was rare to die at that age—people don't normally die in their thirties.

A few days later I asked my father, "Did Uncle David have any kids? Was he married?" That's when my father told me my uncle was gay and he had died of AIDS.

So then I knew two people who were gay, Elton John and Uncle David, although I still wasn't sure what either of them had to do with me. From the way everyone in my life reacted to the word "gay"—my parents, even the kids at school who whispered it—I was sure telling people you're gay wasn't a good idea.

But three years after going through this "gay phase," at least my parents have finally gotten it through their heads their fourteen-year-old son *is* gay and there's nothing they can do about it. They were fighting a losing battle. They could send me to all the therapy in the world and it wouldn't alter my sexuality one bit. For once, my mother wouldn't get her way.

It's not as though out of nowhere they started waving a white flag, but it was almost as sudden as that. One day they stopped talking about it, and when I brought it up, like if I said as a point of interest that so-and-so on TV was gay, they changed the subject.

Now it's like I'm going through the slow torture all over again.

This morning I rode my bike to school as usual. As I was locking it to the bike rack, I saw Melanie standing there. Her hair was pulled back tightly; her hands were on her hips. It was the first time I saw her since Saturday night at Chantal's. I thought, Cool. She's waiting for me. She's *so* going to be my new best friend. But then it registered that something was wrong. Without even saying "Hi!" she said, "I told Ciaran you're gay." Ciaran's her brother who's in my grade.

"I'm not sure, but I think Ciaran told a whole bunch of his friends. I'm so sorry."

I tried giving her a smile to reassure her it was going to be okay, but it didn't convince me, so it had no chance of making her feel better.

She said she was sorry over and over again—I could tell she meant it—but what good was that now? I didn't know what I was angrier about: having everybody at school find out I'm gay like that, or her not keeping my secret. Along with saying she was sorry, she kept repeating, "But I'm not sure," like there was some doubt, like there was some hope it was all a big mistake.

Without a word, I turned away and started walking into school, my legs going weak under me. Just as I pulled open the front door, Mindy Walters, who never liked me, appeared out of nowhere right in front of me as a green wall in an all-wrong Lycra top and still-wet-from-the-shower henna curls and said, "Is it true? Ciaran just told us you're gay." She did her best to put on a concerned face.

My heart started booming: Patump. Patump. Patump. That's when everything began happening so fast, speeding up and becoming a blur.

I didn't stop to answer. I kept walking, leaving Mindy and Melanie behind. I started to shake.

Then Sally Lavigne, who's always been nice to me even though she sometimes screams at people who look at her, came running up to me and cupped her black goth lips with her black nail-polished hand and whispered, "Do you know what everybody's saying about you?"

I didn't stop. I was scared shitless; it was spreading faster than I knew what to do. With the people I told, people like Chantal and her mom, those trustees, I could control it—I told who I wanted to, when I wanted to. Now the word was multiplying exponentially. It wouldn't be long before everyone would know. I feared the harassment would get worse and people would hate me.

Before anyone else could confront me, I walked out a side door, went around to the front of the school, unlocked my bike and rode away. I wasn't even out of sight of the school when my foot slipped off the pedal and hit the ground, and I came close to catapulting over the handlebars onto the pavement in front of me. I barely felt the long scraping of the pedal up my calf.

I still kept going, pedaling faster towards more blur.

So now I sit here under these interrogating florescent lights and drink too many cups of coffee hoping I'll find the answer in the bottom of one of them. I'm angry, more at Ciaran than Melanie really, but I guess I can't even be angry at him. I know Ciaran. He didn't do this because he's mean; he did it because he's fucking naïve and childish. When you come down to it, though, it's not like he made something up about me that wasn't true. It's just he didn't so much as take into consideration this is *my* thing to tell. Knowing him, he probably didn't do most of the telling himself; he probably told his guy friends over the phone last night or face-to-face as soon as he got to school this morning. Then all his little boyfriends probably ran and told everybody they could. Fucking gossips! It doesn't take much to make something the talk of our school.

Now I feel scared when all I've known is being trapped, trapped in my own thoughts and by other people, always asking myself if they know the secret. Not being out's like wearing a mask, only taking it off for certain people in certain situations. One Evan here. Another Evan somewhere else. Most of the time *I* don't even know who I am. I only know I'm gay, but who's the gay Evan supposed to be, because I know from now on that's who I'm going to be to everyone: Gay Evan.

So I sit here coffee after coffee, and cigarette after cigarette. I find no answers. I start to doubt there are any. I know one thing for sure: people will react for better or for worse. If they can't accept it, it will reflect on them, not me. Just as I couldn't change to fit the straight person my parents wanted me to be, I won't be the gay person I'm not meant to be. I'm not my Uncle David, or Elton John, or anyone else for that matter.

I won't wear another mask.

And I'm sure of one more thing: whoever I end up being has to start right now.

When I know school's over, I play the charade of going home like it's any other day. I do homework like I usually do. I make my bed and put away the pile of clothes on the floor. I wait until my mother and father get home from work so we can have supper. As usual, we eat in silence. Even with all that's going on in my mind, I notice the looks my parents exchange, their worried expressions. The unspoken fears they have for me still echo from my uncle's death.

Later I lie in bed and listen to the radio: first some music, then a talk station. It comforts me to hear voices I don't know talking about lives I have no connection to or worries about.

Then I fall asleep.

———————

Just as the bell's about to ring, I walk into school. All at once people come running up to me in the hall. Friends and foes alike. Melanie. Chantal. Sally Lavigne. Mindy Walters. Even Ciaran's there, looking nervous and like he almost regrets what's happened.

Before anyone can ask if I know all the rumours going around about me and if what people are talking about is true, I say, "Yes. I'm gay."

The Nail That Sticks Up Gets Hammered Down[*]
Alex's Blog

Wednesday, November 19, 2008
FAQ

I'm not sure how to jump into this, but I guess I'll start by telling you about myself. I'm 16. I'll be 17 in 3 weeks and I want an iPod for my birthday. Hint. Hint. I like to play video games, and every Friday and Saturday night I play online with my friends. After school I play an hour by myself on my computer or my PlayStation. I also enjoy taking walks while listening to music. I like kind of eccentric music like music from Japan. Most of it I download on LimeWire. I'm a real fan of Japanese culture and I'm trying to learn to read and speak it. I also enjoy chatting online.

I'm a fairly independent person. I like to go by the beat of my own drum. I'm not a big socializer. I tend to have this mysterious air and everyone at school is always asking Megan questions about me. It's kind of like they're afraid of me. I'm not sure why, but they always ask Megan, "Who is that?" I guess it's because there's a lot of new students this year and the grade 9s haven't been at our school that long.

I grew up in the same neighbourhood here in Montreal. I live with just my mom because my parents are divorced. I don't know how to describe my mom. She's an artist, so she's liberal and accepting. She's a good person. She lets me do what I want, but at the same time I have some responsibilities. My relationship with my father is not very strong. He's not a horrible person, but I never got along very well with him. We don't speak much. My mother tries to get me to call him, but I never get around to it. I'm an only child.

---

[*] A Japanese saying.

I go to an alternative school with about 100 students here in the city. It's very multicultural and everything. It's a real small school so there's no clubs or sports. I like that the school's close because I can walk there. At lunch I go home to eat. It's good the school's small and more personal. You don't have to address the teachers Miss La-la-la. You just call them by their first names.

My BFF at school is Megan. She's very energetic and a fun person to be around. She pursued the friendship and since then we've developed a strong bond. I have other friends at school, but I'd say they're more acquaintances. Megan and I still play this video game called Dance Dance Revolution at the arcades. It's pretty fun and pretty physical, too. We go see a movie from time-to-time. Outside of school I have some other friends, but we're not very close. Sometimes I invite those guys over to play video games. But rarely.

School is from 9 to 4. After school I usually go for coffee and do some studying by myself at a rotisserie on rue St-Laurent. I really love their coffee. Then I go for a walk around the neighbourhood listening to my cheap-ass budget MP3. Hint. Hint. It isn't very powerful. Or maybe the headphones are crap. I don't know. As I'm walking around I can hear more of the traffic than the songs. Then it's maybe 7, so I have dinner and do some chatting on MSN. Then sleep. On the weekends I generally come in late, so I sleep in and get up at 1 or 2. Like I wrote already, I'm more of an independent type of person, so I don't enjoy going to clubs and stuff like that. On weekends I also work at the restaurant down my street. I'm the person who answers the phone and gets the menus. It pays for my cell, although I don't use it that much except for Megan's texts. Megan loves to text me at random times just to say Hi. It's pretty funny.

I don't know what else to write about me, so that's it for now.

Thursday, November 20, 2008
School

Last week Andrea asked us to start keeping a journal on ourselves and our last year of high school we can share with other people. Anonymously of course. I don't need people stalking me. LOL. She kept stressing how we should be honest and open about what we write but not to write anything we don't want anyone else to know. I have nothing to hide, but I picked the name Alex anyway.

I decided to do mine online since I'm on the computer a lot, but I just got around to starting it yesterday. We have to keep at least a week's worth. I'm not sure I agree with blogging stuff like this, but it's better than writing it out, I suppose. To me, blogs should be for video games.

I told Andrea my journal's online and gave her the address, and she said OK but I have to watch out that I write English and not "computerese" as she calls it. I think she means don't use chat abbreviations. That's going to be hard for me. I should write it all in Japanese. ☺

So far only Megan's written a comment on mine.

```
Hi Alex. What do u mean I pursued the
friendship? U didn't want 2 b friends with me?
LOL. I'll give u my journal 2 read 2morrow so u
can read MY side of things. We're renting a
movie 2morrow nite, right? Or else. I'll text u.
TTYL. X☺x☺
```

I guess I should explain what I mean about Megan. I wrote she initiated the friendship because she started talking to me first. That's what I mean. But it wasn't really that one sided because I didn't try to ignore her or anything. Sorry about that Megan.

Since I have to do this for school, I might as well write more about that.

I do all the core courses: math, physics, chemistry, English, French, gym. I like them all with the exception of French. I've always had a hard time in French. I'd rather learn Japanese. But everything else is cool. I haven't decided yet what I want to be. Possibly either a doctor or an astronomer. Those 2 roles interest me. But that's years off and I'll probably change my mind. I'm going into Pure and Applied Sciences at college.

The teachers at school are mostly young. They're all good teachers. They're very liberal. They always give us an alternative viewpoint on things, more so the leftist side of things. I mean, my teachers know I'm gay and they have no problem with it.

The students are just like the students you find at any high school, but I don't like that some of them abuse the freedom. Then again lots of teenagers are slackers. When we're given a work period they just talk to their friends instead of getting their work done. They skip classes and if you skip too much you get suspended. There's been a few expulsions for people who've done things like graffiti on the walls. I know some people go to the park at lunch and smoke up. I'd never go. Anyway, that park is sketchy. They're always finding used syringes.

There's a principal, but she's an administrator at lots of schools so we don't see her very often. Instead we have a head teacher, Andrea, who's also my English teacher.

At school I'd describe myself as self-motivated and hardworking. I guess that's what my teachers would say too. I mean, I do my own studying. I pretty much know the material even before the teacher teaches it. I find the stuff we learn's really simple, so I try to get a broader grasp of the subject, like the stuff that's not taught to us.

Friday, November 21, 2008
Being Me

This morning I woke up and found 2 new comments on my blog. One was from my friend TJ in Virginia who I told last night on MSN to read it, but another one was from a complete stranger. I don't even know how he stumbled onto it. Maybe he googled something and it came up. Or it's already getting around the StarCraft chat, although I don't know if he even plays video games.

TJ is the person I play StarCraft with online. He's gay, too. We met in a gay chatroom on the server for video games. We always talk on MSN pretty much every night. Well, less now that he has Guitar Hero. He's 17. He left a comment that was pretty funny. Just one word: Yawn. Well, you can read it for yourself. TJ's like that. If it isn't StarCraft, he doesn't have much use for it. That's usually what we chat about.

The other comment came from some guy who lives in Montreal, too.

```
Hey. I really like what you wrote. I'm gay and I
go to school in Montreal too, but on the south
shore. I'm in Sec. IV and I've been thinking of
a way to tell my friends I'm gay, but I don't
know how they'll react. What if they hate me?
How did you tell everybody?
Lawrence
```

I don't know why he's asking me that. The thing is, I don't consider homosexuality a big part of my life. It's one part, but not the main part. It doesn't really come up very often. It's more of like a passive thing. When it comes up with Megan or my mother, it's not really about being gay, it's more like what guys I find cute. Well, I guess I mean when there's a cute guy, Megan asks me what I think about him. Recently she started doing the same thing about cute girls. I have no idea what that's all about. J/K ☺

I've found guys attractive since I was 10 years old. It's as simple as that. I'd always kind of crush on my best friends. I always wanted to sort of get into their pants. At first I didn't even know what it was. Like I didn't even think about it. It was sort of natural, I suppose. And then maybe around teenagehood I sort of realized I was gay.

Megan was the first person I told actually. I'm not sure why I told her—I think it just came out. Then I told other people shortly after that. Actually I told her on MSN. I was talking about some guy I liked, so I told her. This was back in grade 9. It's been 2 years, so I can't remember the exact proceedings word-for-word. It's not that big a deal for me I'm gay, so it wasn't some huge thing. She was fine with it.

Then I told Aaron. He was my friend at school, but he no longer goes there. And Melissa. She's still there. And then a whole bunch of other people who are in my grade. I told a few of them in person and a few online, and they all took it well. No problems. Well they're acquaintances. We don't really do stuff together anymore. At that time I was more a social type person and I wanted to branch out to more people. This year I'm more into my own thing and I sort of cut off my relations with certain people. I stopped talking to them. On the phone. MSN. I just lost interest. Now I stick with my close friends like Megan.

All the students in my grade know and nothing's changed for me. They all treat me the same way they treat anyone else. And then there's Andrea of course. She knows because I sent her an e-mail about it once. I used to write these online e-mail surveys where they ask you questions like, "What's been your most embarrassing moment?" or "What's your favourite possession?" or "What features on the male body do you find attractive?" I used to send them to all the people on my e-mail list, and I sent it to Andrea, and I guess she figured it out even though I didn't say I was gay directly in the survey. It's like she knows, but she doesn't talk about it.

I find telling people online is a lot easier because it's not face-to-face. You're just behind the screen. People act different when they're online. People are more free.

I told my mom rather recently, only 2 months ago in fact. She asked me as a joke and I just told her. She has no problems with it. Well, she worries I might get HIV. Now she asks me all the time if I have a boyfriend, which I don't. She's even asked me if I have relations with Marc-André who's like a teacher's aide at our school because she thinks he's gay. I mean not like a boyfriend, but like if we're friends. I don't even know if he's gay and I never really talk to him. Sometimes I feel like she's nagging me a bit by asking me if I have a boyfriend. It's assuming I'm lying to her by not telling her something. It's a bit of an annoyance.

I haven't told my dad yet. He hasn't called for a while and I don't see any reason to let him know. I had no plans to tell my mom, but she asked me and that's why I told the truth. As for my dad, I would tell him, I guess, but I doubt he would ask me.

I think there's sort of a trend for girls at our school to be bisexual, like Megan this month, but I don't know of any other gay guys. I'm sure there are, but I just don't know. I don't think people my age are really out of the closet. I guess they're not mature enough to come out yet. I would imagine that the fact most people at school are pretty accepting made it easier for me to come out. Well, maybe they're out like me, but I don't advertise it, and maybe they don't need to advertise it to be out. It would be cool to have more gay students here. It would be nice to have someone to talk to and relate to about everything.

So Lawrence, I think you should do what you think is best. I mean, I don't want to tell you to come out. Just do what you want to do. But online's a good way to go. It worked for me at least.

I guess that's enough for today. It's not like me to tell everyone about all this stuff, but you did ask for honesty Andrea. J/K ☺

Oh, tonight's the 10th anniversary of Dance Dance Revolution, so Megan and I have to go to an arcade tonight.

Saturday, November 22, 2008
Yaoi

Last night Megan and I watched Mambo Italiano on TV. It was her idea. Megan really liked it, but I thought it was just okay. It was kind of funny, but not LMAO funny. I like that it was about Montreal, and the parents' reactions were funny but not very believable. Right after we watched it Megan brought up the idea of walking over to the gay village. It seemed like a way to end the evening, I suppose, even though I'd rather have gone for sushi or something. I'd never been before, but I didn't like it. Lots of bars and clothes stores and saunas. Megan had to explain to me what they were all about. How she knows, I have no idea.

The gay village isn't a place I would go to often. It's not really me. There's too many middle-aged men, and I found it a little too flamboyant. It's very bright and colourful. I'm not into that. I didn't enjoy myself.

I'm not a big fan of movies but I do watch some TV. The few Japanese animes that are on TV aren't very good. Like Yu-Gi-Oh! But I watch them anyway. Sometimes I read this fan fiction from films I like. Slash and Yaoi. If you're wondering, you pronounce it Yowie. It's like these made-up male-male relationships from Japanese animes or movies like Lord of the Rings and Pirates of the Caribbean. Regular people write about them. There's lots of it online.

Megan's the one who loves movies and TV. She's always renting DVDs for us to watch, but it's always something gay like *Queer as Folk* and *Will and Grace*. She's always trying to get me to be *more* gay. It's kind of nagging.

Occasionally I do watch *Will and Grace* by myself since it's on 20 times a day. I think it's okay, but it's too gay sometimes. Sometimes I'm like, "Oh shut up." Sometimes the jokes are too stupid. There's one episode where they're at this gay auction or something, and that girl with the annoying voice says, "This is the only place where I can actually get my hair done in the bathroom," or something like that. You know, "Where I can get a whole makeover." WTF!

TJ likes Slash and Yaoi, too. We have lots of the same interests. But he likes Emo music more than the Japanese music I listen to. He always tricks me into downloading some song or another, so to get him back I always ask him how he's sure it really is Emo since it may not be whiney enough.

This morning I saw Lawrence left a message here to say "Thanks." I don't know why. Like I wrote before, being gay's not a big part of my life. I read his first comment again, and I guess it's not easy being gay at his school if he's afraid to come out. It's not like that where I go. Like whenever someone says, "fag" or something, Andrea or some other teacher will step in and say, "Why should sexual orientation be a put down?" I remember a student at our school called someone else a fag while they were fighting, and Andrea stepped in and said in a typical Andrea way not to use that word as an insult. She's very politically correct and she doesn't respect people who discriminate against others. It doesn't really bother me. I'm not going to say anything or make a big deal out of it because I'm not like some PC thug.

On Andrea's office door there's this poster in French about homosexuality and how it should be taught in schools: "*Démystifier l'homosexualité commence à l'école.*" Well, not taught exactly, but like not put in the closet. Obviously it gave me the impression Andrea was very open-minded about gays. I used to hear "That's so gay" or "You're a fag" a couple of times, but not in the past year, except for that one time that guy called the other guy a "fag." I guess the students matured a little.

About a month ago Project 10 came and gave a seminar for the whole school. Andrea must have invited them. There was one lesbian and one gay guy in their 20s or 30s. They talked about sexual identities and how do we identify as men and women. It was a very interactive. It was basically people asking lots of questions like, "How do you know you're gay?" Stuff like that. "How should you help someone who doesn't know if they're gay or not?" It didn't really affect me in a profound way, but it was interesting. It's always nice to hear discussions about homosexuality or things like that. In class if a debate comes up about homosexuality, it's nice to hear other students' opinions about it.

They told us how to contact them if anyone wants to become involved in Project 10, but I don't see anyone from my school doing that. Well, maybe 1 or 2 of the trendy bi girls. Megan wanted us to sign up, but I don't see myself all involved with "the community" everyone talks about, and becoming some big gay crusader. Anyway, I still don't think Meagan's bi. She's never been with a girl.

Sunday, November 23, 2008
Queer as Folk

Last night after I wrote my blog I played StarCraft with TJ until I went to bed. Before I fell asleep I started thinking about what the hardest thing about being gay is for me so I can have something to write back to that Lawrence guy. But I couldn't come up with anything, and I must have fallen asleep because before I knew it the alarm went off and it was morning already.

The only thing that being gay has done to make me different is it's given me a different viewpoint of things. It's made me more open-minded, I suppose. A little bit more liberal. I can imagine myself being pretty conservative and a lot more close-minded if I wasn't gay.

Before I began writing this entry, I saw Lawrence wrote me again.

```
Hey! I saw Queer as Folk on DVD too. Have you
seen Get Real or But I'm a Cheerleader? They're
more entertainment movies. OMG. Recently I saw
one movie on TV that was really cute. Beautiful
Thing. Did you see it? This British high school
kid falls in love with his jock next-door-neigh-
bour. It's about everything that happens to
them. It was a cute little movie. In my opinion
the ending's the best.
```

Meagan loves *Queer as Folk*. I guess I liked the parts of *Queer as Folk* when it was about Justin in high school. The whole thing of him and the school was pretty good, but I thought the part about that guy who beat him up, Chris Hobson or something, was weird. Like he seemed pretty popular. Wouldn't he get a gang of his friends to go beat him up? He wouldn't just go beat him up by himself. It's minor things like that that annoy me. Like wouldn't he need his friends to help him do it? Like gay bashing is kind of a peer-pressure thing going on.

But I'm not the best person to judge. I have no idea how true it is since I've never encountered those problems.

Oh, and two other people left messages on my blog, one from a kid in Toronto who wrote to say hello and that he was in high school, and another from some guy in Japan, although his English didn't make much sense. I think he likes Yaoi, too, but is more into Manga than I am. Some of it is pretty violent and sexual. I've seen some from Japan, and even though I can't read Japanese yet, I could make out some of what was going on from the drawings. At least I knew enough to read it from right to left.

Monday, November 2, 2008
Meeting Someone

Megan's mad at me. I made some comments about her in one of my blog entries that she didn't like. I've erased it now, so don't bother trying to look back and find it. I stayed at school today at lunch so we could talk, so that's cool. Sorry Megan. ☺

Lawrence didn't write any comments back. I think he's mad at me, too. He e–mailed me and, well, I won't go into all the details, but why should I meet someone I don't even know? No offense.

Once we made up, Megan wrote to say how much she still likes *Will and Grace.* That's so Megan! TJ finally wrote something longer than a one-word comment.

```
Alex u should make a profile on gay.com if you
want 2 meet someone. It's funny I can relate 2
some bits and pieces of Will and Grace. Like I
can see myself in both the serious, ethical Will
and the unethical, totally ridiculous Jack. Also
there's my best friend Christina. We practically
have this Will and Grace relationship. She might
be 20 ft away in a crowd and we just have to
look at each other's face and we know what each
other is thinking. IM me L8R.
```

I never thought that much about a TV show. I don't see myself in any gay movies or shows I've seen. But that's just me, I guess. But I suppose it's a way to know about being gay and stuff for some people.

Maybe I would give the Internet a try to meet someone, but I don't know if I trust it after all I've heard. I've never been in a relationship, but if someone came along who I found interesting, I guess something could happen. Sometimes I think I'd like to meet more gay people. Just to meet people. Not to sleep with them. My mom has some gay friends, but I don't know them personally. She always offers to invite them over for supper if I need someone to talk to, but that would be weird. Like if I need advice on being gay, which I don't. After I told her I was gay, she told me my ex-step-dad had homosexual relations when he was in his twenties, but we haven't seen him in three years. So I suppose he can be considered bisexual. It's funny my mom didn't offer to invite him over for tea.

Andrea answered my blog finally, so I guess she is reading it.

```
You're sharing yourself with the world. No more
hiding in plain sight now.
```

I'm not sure what that means, but she's always saying stuff like that to make you think. It's typical Andrea.

Tuesday, November 25, 2008
Hooking Up on the Internet

Six new messages on my blog. The farthest away was Australia, which is pretty cool, I suppose. Dômo arigato everyone.

And Lawrence wrote back.

```
I've tried the Internet, but that's a really bad
place because everyone's only looking for the
same thing. I chatted with people, and I met a
few, but it was just like hell. I was looking
for friends and trying to figure out who I am
and the guys I met had one thing on their minds.
Like this one guy, I only talked to him on the
main screen, and after we started privating.
Then he gave me his cell to call him. I talked
to him a few times on the phone and then we met.
I was really nervous. I didn't know what to ex-
pect. He was 25. I made sure to meet him at a
public place like everyone told me, so I met him
at a métro station. I guess I took my chances.
He seemed so nice. We talked for a while and
then he asked me, "Can I see your room?" Typi-
cal. I said yes like an idiot. My parents would
kill me if they knew. They were gone for the
long weekend. So we did stuff. Then I thought he
was going to call me, and we could still hang
out together, things like that, but he didn't.
He lives with his parents, and I tried calling
him, but they would always say he wasn't there.
I was only 15. I didn't know a lot of things, so
it sort of takes advantage of the person. Like
you meet someone, things happen, and then after
you don't hear from him again.
```

If I ever met someone over the Internet I'd bring Megan with me to be safe, but I don't think I ever would. I'm not sure I'm the type of person who would go up to someone gay and start talking to them, like at a club or a café. If I really wanted to, I guess I could get friends to start showing me people. But Megan doesn't know anyone except me. I guess I could give TJ my cell number. If he wanted it or something.

Anyway, StarCraft awaits.

Oh! Andrea came up to me in the hallway today when school was over and gave me a handout about a candlelight vigil being held for a gay guy who was killed. She didn't say anything about it or anything. Like there's some uncomfortable thing between us. I feel a little bit uncomfortable about it because we never talked directly about my sexuality. When she left, I read it, but I put it in one of the blue boxes that are right inside the classroom doors.

Well I don't try to be very out anyways. Like I don't parade myself around or anything. I don't do things that are gay just because I'm gay. That's stupid.

Like I've said many times, being gay's not that big a part of my life.

Who Do You Think You Are?
Pages from Joe Rose's Notebook

YOU ASK, "Who do you think you are?" and I can only tell you I'm no different from you. I know you measure me against what you think a man should be, but those are meaningless stereotypes—gay or straight. They're not me. I'm just being myself, whoever that makes me. If you want to know why I don't hide anymore, it's because I accept who I am. Your acceptance would be nice—it's what all people deserve—but I don't need it to live a good and happy life.

If by being out you say, "You're in my face," I say, "Now I'm in control of the attention I'm receiving." Harassing me when I wasn't out was your way of controlling me. But now you've lost that power. I assert myself; I show I'm gay; I make jokes about your heterosexism. It's funny to give hints to people who don't know. I can't believe it when straight people don't see the signs. If my hair's pink now, it's because for so long I've been told to be dull.

I was gay before I came out, but when I wasn't out I couldn't be myself. I'm happy with who I am and I'm enjoying the benefits of being gay—I have more friends now and feel such relief from the time I was hiding away in the closet you made for me.

Sure it isn't always great. Sometimes there's harassment, especially in a school where little is done to stop it. But being gay is like being anything else, and one day homophobia will go the way of racist or sexism or anti-Semitism.

Sometimes you have to put up with gossip, and there can be negative popularity if you have to answer questions all the time like you're the poster boy for homosexuality. While you do have more friends, sometimes the type of friends you have are limited—you have less guy friends, and usually there are no other gay students around whom you can relate to. Sometimes, too, you're made to feel you don't completely fit in with either boys or girls.

When you ask, "How is being gay different from being straight?" I have to say, "I'm just attracted to the same sex." I've known I was gay all my life, well, since I was very young. It was a gut feeling. I know I'm gay like you know you're straight. I'm just not attracted to the opposite sex.

Despite what you may think, being gay's only one part of my life—it doesn't define who I am. I'm happy being gay and I wouldn't want to be straight. Being straight seems boring to me. There's no glitter, I guess. I'm free from gender roles and the heterosexual stereotypes you seem to have to follow. If I were straight, I'd be a different person as I've been shaped by my experiences, both good and bad, and that's what's made me the person I am today. I know I wouldn't be as open-minded.

If you want one word, call me "gay." "Homosexual" sounds too formal. But don't call me "queer" or "faggot," even if you're joking. They've been directed at me as insults too many times.

You ask, "Who do you think you are?" and I can only tell you, "I'm no different from you."

Everyone shines. I just shine brighter.

The Holy Ghost
Eric's Story

FATHER MORRELL sat at his desk staring down at his attendance book while behind him they crowbarred the crucifix off his classroom wall. Two janitors were needed to remove it—it had been bolted there in the day when things were made to survive Armageddon.

Since it was an excuse not to do work, everybody in class watched as one of the janitors shook his head, crossed himself, then took out a bigger crowbar. Everybody except me, and Father Morrell of course. I continued to watch the priest checking and double-checking presences and absences as the crucifix groaned off the wall and crashed to the floor, dusting Father Morrell and his desk with a chalky white powder. He didn't even flinch.

The school hadn't been painted since Christ had died. The absent cross left a shadow outline on the wall, and Robbie Dufresne, always the class clown, nudged me, pointed to it, and called it "The Holy Ghost." As usual he laughed at his own joke. Only then did Father Morrell look up and say, "Quiet down."

It was the last cross to come down at our school.

Removing the crucifixes was a big deal at Our Lady Catholic, as everyone calls it, even though the sign outside says "Our Lady of the Seven Pains Secondary School." Of course the eighth pain is going there. Some teachers and parents had fought for years to stop the school board from getting rid of the crosses, but there wasn't much they could do since the Quebec government had changed all public schools into non-religious ones. It was a lost cause. But that didn't stop the protesters who were outside the school every morning before the 8:15 bell since the crosses started coming down.

To tell you the truth, it was mostly teachers and parents

protesting—students didn't give a damn about it. As I stepped off the bus, I'd never see more than a couple of students holding signs and walking in circles with their parents, and they were mostly kids from the lower grades, grades seven and eight.

I guarantee you my mother wasn't there. She had more important things to worry about than crucifixes. She broke up with her boyfriend a while ago, and although they said they'd stay together until the lease on our apartment was up in June, last month she met someone else, and her ex-boyfriend found out and went crazy and kicked us out. So my mom went with her new boyfriend, and I had to move in with mine. I'm eighteen now, so it's okay for me to be on my own.

But Father Morrell was in front of the school every morning, silently walking up and down with a sign that said, "Where's God?"

Thankfully I'm graduating this year and won't have to go through all the shit that'll happen when the school board finally gets around to changing the school's name.

As the janitors were leaving, the short one mumbled in Father Morrell's direction that someone would return with a vacuum to clean up. The excitement was over, and of course our class didn't know what to do next without being told. Father Morrell closed the attendance book and looked up. "Take out your textbook and read quietly for the remaining time." Everyone groaned. No one wanted to read about history.

I didn't mind. History was one of my favourite subjects. I even liked the classroom with the posters and pictures on the walls of famous events in Canadian history. The Fathers of Confederation in Charlottetown in 1867. Trudeau and the Queen at a desk in 1982 signing the Canadian Constitution. The 1995 referendum crowd under a huge Canadian flag. I believed Father Morrell when he told us we were all linked together because of our shared past, regardless of our race or language or country of origin. We all shared Canada.

Not everyone in class thought so. If you look closely at the pictures you can see someone's drawn moustaches and penises. Once someone used a marker to write "Blow me" on the photo of the Prime Minister. The picture was gone by the next class.

Father Morrell brushed off dust from his sleeves then adjusted his loose shirt collar as though it was too tight, just like he used to do when he wore his priest collar. Habit, I guess.

As long as I've been at the school, I've only known Father Morrell in his priest collar. But at the start of this year, the principal must have told him to stop wearing it, because one day he showed up to class with a regular white shirt buttoned up to the last button. If you looked up at him really quickly, for a moment it looked exactly the same, like the priest collar was still there. The principal must have told him again because the next day Father Morrell came to class with the first button of his shirt unbuttoned. Then he showed up with the second one undone. Now whenever he leans over a student's desk to answer a question, the big heavy cross he wears falls out of his open collar. It's going to kill someone someday. He makes a big production of standing up perfectly straight to put it back inside his shirt, always with a sigh that's quiet like a prayer.

You'd think being a priest he'd be real old, but he's forty-something. Forty-one. Forty-two. The dark brown cardigan he wears on cold days makes him look older than he is. But I think he's okay. For a priest. Back in September when I'd told my mother about the teachers I have, she warned me I might have a problem with a priest teaching me given the Church's opinions and everything. But he's always been cool with me.

This girl sitting at the desk in front of me, Carmen Giorgia, asked Father Morrell if instead of reading could we have a discussion, and everyone started begging him because it meant we didn't have to work.

"A discussion about what?" he said.

"What about same-sex marriage?" Carmen said since, I guess, it was still in the news off and on. But I knew Carmen liked getting a rise out of Father Morrell, so there was that, too.

"No. I don't want to talk about that." He stood up and went to the door and closed it.

"Why not?" Carmen said all innocent with a funny smile, which he probably missed since he was walking back to his desk to sit down again. "It's legal, you know."

"No. I don't want to talk about that," he repeated.

"Come on," someone over near the window begged.

"No . . ." Father Morrell began. But it was too late—he fell for it. I guess the temptation was too much.

"I don't see the point of homosexuals marrying. It's like taking two outlets—one going in and another going in—and trying to put them together. It's not going to create electricity. It's a waste of time."

For some reason he looked at me as he said that. I didn't think he knew about me unless one of the other teachers had told him, so I didn't take it personally. Still this wasn't a discussion I wanted to hear.

The first person I came out to was Miss Marco, my drama teacher. One day just before Christmas break, she asked our class for volunteers to put on a dance show. I went just to try out as one of the dancers, but ended up choreographing the whole show, and after weeks of after-school rehearsals, we became close. I found out she was pretty open.

Everybody loved the dance numbers I came up with. I'm all about hip-hop and the B-boy style. After seeing the show, my friends started calling me "Casper" as a joke because I'm so white, except I spell it with a K. It's more street. I even saw Father Morrell in the audience. The next day he congratulated me in front of the class and told us he thought it had been the best school production he'd seen in years. That made me proud.

Although rehearsals were over, I kept going to see Miss Marco in her classroom at lunch or on breaks to talk to her. She was the only person I could talk to about my life. My mom was going through a lot, and I didn't want to add to her stress.

Miss Marco suspected something was bothering me, but I couldn't get the words out.

"You can always write me a letter," she told me one day. So I wrote her a letter, but in it I told her I was bi even though I knew I wasn't. A week later I just told her I was gay.

She said it was fine and I shouldn't be worried or anything. Positive things like that. I mean, she's straight, but she told me she used to go dancing at gay clubs in the village when she was young. So that was cool.

"We share who we are with those we trust will value it," she said. "I'm honoured you chose me."

One by one, I told some of my other teachers because I was close to them, too. All my teachers love me because I'm not somebody who does shit and makes trouble. They were all fine with it.

My science teacher had a funny reaction though. I'd told her, "You know Miss, I'm gay," and she said, "What? You can't be. You're so cute."

I blushed and gave her a little shrug. "Well, it's not my fault. Sorry."

She still laughs about that. I think she's embarrassed. It was one of those things that come out a lot worse than what you meant.

It was easier for me to come out to teachers first because I get along better with older people. Even my boyfriend's twenty-two. I think it's because I've matured a lot faster than kids my age. Maybe it's because I've lived all my life with my mother, and everything we've been through.

But I never told Father Morrell.

"It's wrong! It's a waste! God didn't create us to be that way."

Everyone sat there in silence looking at Father Morrell with disbelief. A few people looked over at Jasmine Rose, and I could see her face had gone sheet-of-paper white. A few weeks ago at lunch she came over to me in the caf and we chit-chatted about the dance show. We never spoke much before then. Out of nowhere she told me her brother Joe, who'd died this year, was gay.

"I wanted you to know," she said.

After school I went over to my best friend Gabrielle's place, and she told me Jasmine had asked her the day before at school if it was true I was gay. My face must have given away I was kind of pissed she'd talk about me to some random girl.

Gabrielle shrugged. "It seemed important to her."

As Father Morrell spoke, a girl sitting next to Jasmine, whose name I keep forgetting, reached over and gently stroked Jasmine's arm.

Carmen shook her head with disgust and yelled out, "What!"

It was as though that single word was the gunshot at the start of a race. Everyone talked all at once, voices hurried to make their points. "It's not a waste!" "What are you talking about?" "That's not right."

Father Morrell rapped the top of his desk with his knuckles, continuing the rhythmic sound until everyone was quiet.

Again he looked straight at me.

"It's not that I don't like gays. Love the sinner, hate the sin. I'm only trying to explain to you—" But he wasn't able to finish. Again the class exploded as though a storm had broken out in the middle of the room. I couldn't believe he was saying this. It sickened me that a teacher—no, *anyone*—could be so ignorant.

"A sin?" I heard a guy yell out from the back of the class. "The sin's believing in such garbage." It sounded like Brad Ogilvy. He still wears the same "Skate or Die" T-shirt he's had since grade eight. Whenever religion comes up during discussions in English class, he always calls it "voodoo superstition."

I hadn't said a word, so why was Father Morrell looking at me? Then I realized my backpack was on my desk with the rainbow flag facing him.

It was around the time they first began talking about removing the crucifixes that I started wearing my rainbow flag on my backpack. So it's like obvious. Except some kids at school think it's the German flag—I'm always being asked if I'm German.

When I first sewed it on, Gabrielle wanted to know what it was. We were at her family's apartment after school on the balcony. I leaned on the railing and knocked over a row of round, white pebbles probably put there by her little brother. I waited until they hit the sidewalk below before I said, "It's the rainbow flag. I'm gay."

She took my hand and squeezed it. "It's okay. It's who you are." We spent the rest of the afternoon talking about guys we thought were hot.

But then Gabrielle told another friend, and it was like a chain reaction. It got around to everyone. When I found out who started it all, I was mad at first. But what's that going to change? You can't hide who you are forever.

That's one thing about not being out—you're invisible. Then you come out, and suddenly everyone knows who you are, and it's like you're at the centre of a gigantic spotlight. All intense and in focus. But I wouldn't change what happened. It was like Miss Marco said, coming out's the chance to show who you really are to the people you care about. And I chose people whom I knew would be understanding.

Like my mom. Of course I eventually told her—it's not something I'd ever keep from her. My family *is* my mother. I haven't seen my father or my grandmother or anybody like that since I was about seven. I don't remember much about them. I try to hold on to what I do remember, but it's as if they're slowly fading away right before my eyes.

One evening my mother and I were in the living room watching a TV show explaining the female body, the vagina and everything, and I said, "Eww." My mom laughed. "You're not supposed to be 'ew-wing' this," she said. Then she asked me, "Are you gay?" and I was like, "Yeah, I am," and she was like, "That's okay."

I did it on purpose so she'd ask me because I didn't have the guts to tell her right out. I even put up a poster in my room of an actor I found really hot hoping she'd ask. I knew every morning she'd have to go past my room to go outside for a smoke, and she'd see it, but she didn't say anything. I was kind of insulted. Like, Hello!

When I told her I was gay I asked, "Well, didn't you see the poster of the guy in my room?" She said, "I thought it was just an actor you liked." Oh, my God!

Father Morrell had to be blind, too, if he couldn't see his class was in revolt. He knocked on his desk again then put up his hand. "Wait. Wait. Calm down."

But it didn't silence us. If anything, the noise intensified.

"I'm not trying to hurt you," he said as loud as he could without outright screaming at us. I could just make out his words through the wall of voices. "I care about you. You're lost sheep. Listen to me."

Suddenly Jasmine Rose stood up and ran out of the room crying. Everything Father Morrell said made me want to cry too, but I wouldn't give him the satisfaction.

He didn't say anything when Jasmine left.

Students kept on arguing with him. "Sir, you're wrong!" "That's not true." "You don't decide to be gay, you're born that way." It was mostly girls, but you had some guys who were saying things like, "What the fuck!" and "Who the hell are you?" I'm not sure if anyone was agreeing with him, but if they did, I didn't hear them say anything. Even Paolo Sanelli stayed quiet, and he loves to shoot off his mouth and call everyone "fag."

Father Morrell seemed to be getting angrier every time he looked at me. "If someone's gay it's because they were sexually abused as a child."

I thought: Oh, God!

He went on about Jesus, and he even pointed to the ghost cross on the wall, apparently forgetting the crucifix wasn't there anymore.

"With you lot, I'm like Saint Willibrord among the pagans." He fiddled with the cross around his neck, twisting it so the chain started closing up around his throat.

As he spoke, I pushed my backpack towards him, right to the edge of the desk, as far as I could before it would fall off.

He slammed his fist down hard.

"Listen to me." He was yelling at us. "You people don't know what you're talking about. You're young. You want everything to change. But if you had to, none of you would stand up for what's right. You know nothing. You can all shut up!"

And that's how it ended—everybody stopped talking all at once. As sudden as a clap of thunder.

Then the bell rang for morning break.

As I picked up my backpack to leave, other students pushed past me and rushed up to his desk to tell him, "Why were you saying that?" and "You shouldn't be saying stuff like that."

Carmen Giorgia demanded Father Morrell tell her why he wouldn't respect the Quebec Human Rights Charter. "It's only been around since the seventies," she said. I could hear in her voice she knew she had the upper hand and wasn't going to let go now. He started to explain again what he'd said during class, a bit calmer now, not as loud, but he was only repeating what he already told us. It was just more bullshit.

Pissed off, I went to Miss Marco's classroom with the friends who'd been with me in history class, and we told her everything that happened. Everyone kept telling me over and over what a jerk Father Morrell was and how he shouldn't be a teacher.

"If he's going to talk about that," Miss Marco said, "he shouldn't talk about it in that way."

We wondered to each other why a priest was still teaching us anyway.

"He's always talking about God. It isn't religion class."

"Try to understand what Father Morrell's going though," Miss Marco said. "Show compassion. This hasn't been easy for him."

"He's a teacher," I said. "Shouldn't *he* understand what *we're* going through?"

She didn't disagree.

Back home, I tried to let it go, so I put on some music to dance, but that was that. I just sat there until it was dark and my boyfriend came home from work.

The next day things were back to normal. Everyone else in class seemed to have forgotten, and Father Morrell acted like it never happened. He still went on talking about God every chance he had, but he didn't mention gays again. He spoke softly now, and sighed a lot, and he let us get away with things he never would have before. And I never saw him outside the school with his "Where's God?" sign again.

A week later, as I was walking to the door at the end of another one of Father Morrell's classes, I passed Jasmine Rose. She looked right at me, straight in the eye, as if to say, "What are *you* going to do about this?"

She hadn't forgotten either.

I should've done something. I really should have. But what could I do? Whom should I have told? The principal? The school board? Other teachers? Should I have walked up and down outside holding a sign?

They'd have believed me, for sure—thirty witnesses guaranteed that—but that wasn't it. The more I thought about it, the more I knew what happened would be dismissed as a war of opposites, too easily reduced to a student versus a teacher. Liberals and conservatives. Another fag against a priest.

You see, I listened in his history class.

That's the funny part. With how much Father Morrell hates gays, it's ironic how I'm one of his favourite students. I never gave him a day of trouble; I had the highest marks in the class; I never came in late. I worked hard and paid attention when he spoke. I asked him respectful questions, not the kind some students asked as a joke or to make him look stupid.

A month ago he'd asked me to represent our school at the province-wide history challenge in June. That surprised me.

"With your marks and your skills in both French and English," he said, "you have nothing to worry about." He told me to stop by at lunch, and when I did, he helped me fill out the registration form, and he showed me pamphlets about the competition, and the train, and Quebec City. It was pretty exciting. I'd never been out of Montreal.

Just before I went to go eat, Father Morrell said to me, "I know you'll be a success in life, Eric. You're a credit to the school and me. I'm proud to have you as a student."

I thought it was really nice of him to say that.

But I guess a month ago is a long time. "The world can change in a flash," my mom always says.

So I decided that for the rest of the year I wouldn't do anything he told me. I wouldn't answer if he spoke to me or called on me or asked me where my work was. He'd have to forget about the history challenge. My grades could go to hell as far as I cared, and I wouldn't give a damn.

Father Morrell could look right through me like I wasn't even there.

A Lesson on Being Inseparable
Geoff's Story

As HE WALKED TO SCHOOL, checking every so often to see if the music CD he burned on his computer the evening before was still safely in his coat pocket, Geoff Mueller smiled knowing that again he'd slipped in another ABBA song. His friends would laugh at him: he had the reputation of being a music Nazi because he wouldn't let anyone else touch the CD player in the band room where they hung out at lunch. The running joke was that the music his friends listened to—Simple Plan and Nelly Furtado and Rihanna—was garbage, and what he liked—oldies from the eighties—was the best music ever.

The sun was still not up. From out of the dark he saw the headlights of a car coming towards him, and, as it drew nearer, Geoff recognized his neighbours, Mr. and Mrs. Turner. The couple waved to him as they slowly drove by. They were always up first thing in the morning, out for a spin in the convertible they bought to celebrate their fiftieth wedding anniversary. Of course Geoff waved too. Everybody waved at the Turners; they were the oldest and friendliest people on the street. It crossed Geoff's mind that while others may keep the tops of their cars down in summer to bask in the sunshine, the Turners seemed to do it for the opportunities to wave back.

Geoff couldn't imagine the suburban street where he grew up without the Turners. They radiated a joy you couldn't help but feel. On holidays their children and grandchildren descended on their house, filling it with a happiness that overflowed onto the lawn and throughout the neighbourhood.

He couldn't count the times he saw the old couple gardening together or sitting together in lounge chairs on their deck reading newspapers or magazines or hardcover books. Whenever his mother spoke of the Turners she always mentioned they'd met in high school so long ago, and yet had spent only a night or two apart in all the years they've been married. Geoff thought he didn't know the meaning of the word "inseparable" until he knew them.

He sighed and checked his pocket again. He had so much to do that day, but as much as he liked to grumble about it, he loved being busy. He loved all the activities he was involved in; he wouldn't give up any of them for the world. And there were so many. To start, he was responsible for picking and playing the background music for the daily news that ran during homeroom. He knew it sounded more glamorous than it was. It was only a slide show, a PowerPoint thing shown on the TVs in all the classrooms, school announcements and advertisements for volunteer jobs and community service. He always made a point of including different, random types of music, often staying up well past midnight choosing songs and burning them onto a CD. Every so often another student would come up to him in the hallway and say, "Oh, that was great music you picked today." He really liked that part: the attention. Still other students would come up to him and complain their homeroom teacher hated the music. He found that frustrating. He had certain people in mind when he picked the songs, or people would request he play something for them. Like last week he'd played Arcade Fire because some grade tens had told him were going to see the concert. When he saw them later and asked if they heard the songs, they said, "Oh, really? Our teacher turned the sound off."

After school Geoff had band practice. There were over a hundred people in concert band: students from grade nine, ten, and eleven. He played the sax, the alto-sax actually—it wasn't the same thing he always insisted when people asked what instrument he played. He'd taken up the flute one summer but he had almost passed out trying to hold a note. It nearly had stopped his interest in playing an instrument right there. But he was glad he persisted. Now he felt proud that people—his music teacher and even his friends—were noticing he was getting better.

He was also involved in various activities like plays and variety shows, but they were over for the year. He missed them. It was during Christmas break that some random girl and her mother had come up to him in the mall and said, "Oh, my God! You were in that variety show. You were so great." He'd blushed and quietly said, "Thanks."

He'd been thrown off by that kind of attention at first, but he had to admit it was really cool.

With all there was for Geoff to do in a given school day, he always arrived early, at times waiting and shivering for the janitor to show up and unlock the front door. And every morning the man, shaking his head with disbelief, would greet Geoff with the same old joke: "Catch any worms?"

Some winter mornings Geoff found himself watching a mini-snowdrift grow up around his feet, not knowing that school had been cancelled for the day since he'd left before they'd announced it on the radio. Eventually, when no one else came, he'd walk home, careful to make perfect footprints in the snow, imagining himself some sort of explorer, the first to venture into the uncharted territory of his neighbourhood on a quest for a cup of hot chocolate.

So that was his day. Oh! And attend classes, too. With everything he had to do, he often forgot that was part of his school day as well.

That morning he felt the nervousness in his stomach, slight, but enough that it gave him a thrill. That day was going to be different. Somewhere in all he had to do, he had to find the time to go to the mall and buy Mark a gift. He couldn't show up at his birthday party without one. Well, not if he wanted Mark to notice him. No boring class could take away from the excitement he was feeling, the excitement of believing something is possible.

He patted his coat pocket again. The CD was still there, safe and sound. He smiled to himself the last few steps to school. Things were going great; he was really enjoying his final year of high school. His involvement in school activities was paying off. He had more friends than ever; he was busier than he had ever been; he felt appreciated for all his talents. Moreover, he felt good about the person he was becoming.

And if Mark wasn't enough, the day promised to be even more special: it was the first day he was going to teach the Changes and Choices unit to the grade sevens.

"Okay, quiet down," Mr. Mackay said to the class. Geoff was amused by how quickly the grade sevens fell silent. In a grade eleven class, Mr. Mackay would still be waiting to be noticed, left standing at the front of the room like part of the fittings and fixtures. All eyes were looking forward, darting between Mr. Mackay and the mystery guest.

"This is Geoff, he's in grade eleven," Mr. Mackay said. "I've asked Geoff to give today's class, so let's welcome him and treat him with the utmost respect."

Geoff smiled at the students and walked over to Mr. Mackay's desk where his notes were; he had spent the last two weeks writing and re-writing them. Actually Mr. Mackay had never *asked* him, he'd volunteered. Well, perhaps not quite volunteered since every grade eleven student *had* to do some sort of community service. Geoff had heard about this particular job on the school's daily news, and it seemed like fun. He felt he'd prefer it to some of the other community services he could have picked, like coaching sports, or fundraising for Christmas baskets, or organizing a Senior Citizens' tea. Those things just weren't him.

People described Geoff in two ways: always happy and loves to talk. If there was a class discussion, Geoff would certainly jump in and add whatever was on his mind. He considered himself pretty well informed about things—he read the newspaper and watched the news on TV every day. He loved it when people listened to him, and even if they didn't agree and would start to argue their opinion, he loved how he could think of things to say in reply, logical things, things to make them understand his point of view. He felt people respected him for that.

Geoff could tell Mr. Mackay was pleased, if not pleasantly sur-prised, when one day after school he'd appeared at the man's class-room door and said he was there to help teach the grade seven sex ed. unit. Geoff had known Mr. Mackay from being a student in his history 414 class the previous year.

Mr. Mackay told the tall, enthusiastic young man that in his five years teaching the unit, no one had ever wanted to help out. He ex-plained how the topics included contraceptives, safe sex, relationships, and sexual orientation, and right away Geoff asked to teach the part about sexual orientation. Mr. Mackay could have anticipated that; he'd seen Geoff develop over the last year as the school's only out gay student, a popular, sociable student who took part in almost every ex-tra-curricular activity there was.

The last time the two had really spoken was a few days before Christmas on Karaoke Day when Geoff had stolen the show. Mr. Mackay couldn't help but smile when he thought about how the boy loved karaoke. He'd made it a point to go up to him at the end of the day and shake his hand. Some students looked down their noses at such activities. Mackay hated that. Teaching school at the best of times was difficult; he thought it was spirit-raising activities like variety shows and plays and karaoke days that gave the school its soul. He believed students like Geoff nourished that soul.

"Today we're going to start talking about sexual orientation," Geoff began. He'd rehearsed with Mr. Mackay what he'd say and what activities they'd be doing in class. On his own, he'd researched material for the unit, going to the library and scouring the Internet. Mr. Mackay gave him books and articles he thought he could use. "There's a video," Mackay had told Geoff who had taken it home and watched it: it showed some kids in some anonymous American school who came out to their parents and were kicked out of their homes, lost all their friends, and were beaten up for being gay. Geoff had never known such rejection. He didn't doubt it existed; he just hadn't experienced homophobia in his five years of high school. Surely, he felt, it was becoming less and less common. He had to admit that from time to time he had a fear in the back of his mind he *could* be attacked like Matthew Shepard, or, even closer to home, Joe Rose. Logically he knew it was more the media's influence than anything he could put his finger on at his school, a side effect of consuming too much news. But, in reality, he'd never even been called a name, never mind being threatened or fag-bashed.

Geoff felt if anything like that happened to him, he was confident his friends would back him. And his family. And teachers like Mr. Mackay.

The worse he'd known was occasionally hearing friends call something "gay." Whenever they said, "Oh, that's gay!" Geoff made a point of telling them off: "I don't like it when you guys say that." Or he made a joke about it: "So this book has a gender now?" That movie? That song? He knew they were probably thinking, "Oh, my God! Okay. He's going on about that thing again," but they usually stopped. Geoff felt his friends respected him enough that they stopped for him.

"Look," he'd told Mr. Mackay the next day. "We can't show this video. Like no one's going to want to discuss it. They're all going to live in fear about it, and if they're gay, they'll never want to come out after seeing it." So he'd presented the teacher with some stories he found on the Internet about high school students who came out and were accepted for whom they were. "We can use this instead. It's not the whole picture, I know. We can talk about some of the bad things that do happen to some kids when they come out, but I think the class would get more out of something positive than just gloom and doom." Mr. Mackay couldn't help but be impressed with how seriously Geoff took the job.

Hands flew up across the classroom as the grade sevens asked Geoff questions all at once: "How do gays have sex?" "How do people know they're gay?" "Is it true gays have sex all the time?" It took Geoff all he could to quiet them down again.

He wasn't nervous at all; he loved being on stage; he loved performing even though he was aware of the stereotype some people have that actors are gay. He thought of the movie *Jawbreaker* where one of the main characters fixes up another character with a date but warns, "Oh, he's an actor, so I can't promise total hetero sex." But he wasn't going to stop what he liked doing and was apparently good at just because of what other people thought. And even though this wasn't exactly like being in the plays he'd been in, he thought of it that way. The wide-open-eyed faces in front of him were his audience.

"We're going to start off with a bunch of true and false questions. You can put your hand up when I ask if you think it's true or false and we can talk about it. Okay?" Geoff had to smile when he saw the thirty heads nod agreement.

"First question: Gay men are anti-women and lesbians are anti-men. Raise your hand if you think that's true."

Most of the class threw up their hands. Geoff paused for a second, a bit taken aback by the overwhelming consensus in the room. "I'm not sure you understand the question," he said. "Do you honestly think gay men are gay because they hate women?" Slowly some hands began to fall.

"Yeah," one boy in the front said. He didn't make eye contact when he spoke; he looked down at the pencil he was rolling across the desk's surface. Geoff was ready to tell the boy what he felt, then, remembering what Mr. Mackay had said about making them think rather than handing them things on a silver platter, he asked, "Well, can you explain that?"

"I heard from my parents that gays are just afraid of the opposite sex. Didn't something happened to them when they were younger to make them like that?"

Another student, a blond boy whose hair was gelled into a shark fin, said, "But lots of gay men have women as friends. What's up with that? I mean, if they're supposed to hate them."

A girl dressed in black sitting next to the window put up her hand. "I think they just *like* the same sex. Not hate the opposite sex."

And so it went. Geoff continued with the activity as he'd planned, stopping at each question to provide explanations where needed or to ask the students to clarify their answers.

Then Geoff asked them, "Would you feel comfortable if your friend told you they were gay? Would you still be friends with them? How many of you would?" Most of the students raised their hands, and, when they discussed their choice, most of them told him they'd be fine with it. When he asked who wouldn't be comfortable, he heard comments like, "I wouldn't talk to them for a while, but I guess I'd get used to it," and "Wouldn't people start thinking you're gay, too?"

"When you have black friends, do people think you're black?"

"But if you have a gay friend they might start hitting on you," called out a red-haired boy in the back.

"Do your friends hit on you now?" Geoff asked.

"Well . . . no . . ." the boy said hesitantly.

"Are you attracted to every girl, so you hit on every girl you see?"

A perpetually bored-looking girl sitting next to the red-haired boy said to him, but loudly enough for everyone to hear, "Trust me, you're not that good looking." The students laughed.

"But what if your teacher's gay?" asked a girl wearing a Jonas Brothers T-shirt. Geoff spotted the requisite High School Musical notebook on her desk. God they're young, he thought.

"What about it?"

"Well they could hit on you, too."

"They'd lose their job if they did that."

A boy with longish curly brown hair sitting near the girl who asked the last question said, "They're here to do their jobs and not to try to hook up with you."

More laughter.

One by one Geoff answered the questions they had. He kept reminding himself of the goal he and Mr. Mackay had discussed: to get them thinking. He held himself back a couple of times from just blurting out, "No! You're wrong!" especially when he was asked if gays were sex addicts and had sex all the time. Instead, Geoff said, "Well if that was true, it would be very difficult for them to go to school and hold down jobs." It didn't take long for Geoff to realize they wouldn't believe him just because he said so—they needed to understand the logic in his answers. When he made that connection, he could see in their faces a that-makes-sense expression that made him smile. As young as they were, he felt they were pretty smart.

Class was almost over—there was only another ten minutes left. Geoff was about to assign them their homework—write one page about how their day would be different if they were gay—when a girl wearing glasses in the second row asked him another question.

"Are *you* gay?"

Mr. Mackay had warned Geoff that would probably come up. "Some students have this immature notion that if you speak about gays in a positive way, you must be one." The man had looked unwaveringly at Geoff, skepticism crossing his face. "How will you go about answering that? It's your decision and there's certainly no expectation you tell the class more than you want to. We're not looking to put you on display here like the only panda in the zoo."

Geoff had told him he'd think about it.

But he hadn't decided what to do, and now, faced with the question, faced with a room full of eager grade sevens who were just forming their opinions of people different from them in ways that may affect them for the rest of their lives, he felt there was only one answer.

"Yes I am."

He could see Mr. Mackay at the back of the class, a worried expression on the man's face, poised as if ready to leap into the discussion before something bad happened. But Geoff was okay. He smiled at his former teacher, reassuring him he knew what he was doing, even though it felt like inching towards the edge of a cliff in the dark. There was remarkably little reaction from the students to what he'd just said. Geoff wasn't sure if they'd accepted what he told them matter-of-factly, or if they were still processing it, wheels turning. "Any other questions," Geoff asked.

Hands waved urgently in the air. There was a chorus of "Me! Me! Me!"

"Do your friends know?"

"Of course," Geoff said. He told them how he'd come out to his grade a year ago January on a school ski trip. He liked to say there was no big long story to it: Geoff and the three other boys in his class sharing a chalet had been getting ready to head back onto the ski hill when one of them had asked jokingly if he was gay. They were always making jokes like that. Geoff had said, "Yeah. I am." Their response could best be described as, "Oh. Okay," although one of the boys said, "So, you're gay?" as if checking to make sure he heard what he thought he had. Beyond that they were fine with it.

But that was the thing—when he told his other friends upon returning to school after the trip, they, too, were mostly indifferent. Geoff attributed it to kids that age being wrapped up in their own lives. The friends he was closest with had listened to him, had even asked a few questions, for sure, then had changed the conversation to their own pressing issues, *their* dramas-du-jour.

When he was with his friends, being gay didn't come up that often. That was what Geoff liked about his friends: it wasn't a big deal for them. When it came up, it came up, but usually it didn't. So the bottom line was nothing had changed among his friends, except now they were really nosey and were always asking him, "So, did you meet anyone yet?"

"And I told my family," Geoff added. "Everyone took it fine." He'd had his doubts, you didn't know how people were going to react to something like that. When he'd thought about it later, he realized it had been a calculated risk but the odds had been well in his favour.

"It would have been really out of character for them to react any other way than the way they did," he told the class. "My friends are nice people, not judgmental type people at all. That's one of the reasons we're friends, I guess. Nothing's changed. I'm still good friends with everyone I told. And my mom and dad love me. What changed there?"

"How do you know you're gay?"

"Good question. Do you want a *straight* answer?" Geoff waited until the student who asked the question nodded her head, although everyone seemed to have missed his little joke. "Cause I like guys." Geoff said, and *then* they laughed. He saw Mr. Mackay at the back of the room smiling, any signs of worry had disappeared from his face.

"When you decided to be gay did you do it because you knew other gay people?"

"Well, let's get one thing clear. You don't *decide* to be gay. You just are. Like, did any of you decide to be straight? Like did you wake up the morning you were going to be gay and then at the last minute you decided to go the other way?" A few students laughed.

"And to answer your other question, my mother has some gay friends and I have a cousin who's lesbian, but we never see her because she's been living in Ireland with her girlfriend." He didn't tell them all the details; they didn't need to know everything. Like how he really didn't know his mother's gay friends from work other than to say "Hi" to, although they had come over to dinner a couple of times. And he only found out recently he had a lesbian cousin when he overheard his parents talking about how she'd broken up with her girlfriend and was thinking of coming back to Canada. As sad as it was, Geoff had to laugh at his father's take on the situation. For some reason his father had the idea that Ireland was so small she *had* to leave for fear of running into her ex on the one street that country apparently has.

"And no one can influence you to be gay or make you gay. Look at it this way . . . almost all gays and lesbians grew up in a home with straight parents. *That* didn't make *them* straight."

"Do you have gay friends and go to clubs and everything? I heard gays have the best clubs."

Geoff wanted to say he wished he had some gay friends, but, instead, he simply said he didn't know of any other gay students in school. "So, no. I don't." As far as clubs went, Geoff told them he didn't go to clubs being only seventeen and without an ID. "Drinking age is eighteen," he reminded them, wagging his finger. Not that it stopped anyone in his grade, he thought.

"Do you have a boyfriend?"

Silence.

For the first time all class, there was no quick reply.

Geoff could feel his heart freeze for the briefest of moments. Having been so ready to answer whatever they asked, he was now at a loss as to how to respond to *that* question. If there was one thing about being gay that he felt put him at a disadvantage from everyone else, that was it. He found it difficult to meet people. Well, *gay* people. He'd never been in a relationship, had never even met someone his own age who was gay. The big problem, he knew all too well, was so few people came out in high school, you didn't know who was gay. He was at a large high school with tons of students, he couldn't be the only one who was gay. Sure he heard rumours, but at one time or another wasn't everyone rumoured to be gay? Geoff felt he was seriously dating-challenged because he had absolutely no gaydar to speak of. The truth be told, he didn't even know how to begin to meet someone.

It was so different for everyone else at school who hooked up with someone one day, then seemed to move on to someone else the next. The whole fish-sea thing. And usually just in time for the next party at a house where the parents weren't home. Everyone straight, that is. The school drowned in talk about who liked whom, and who was going out with whom, and who had broken so-and-so's heart. Geoff had to admit it was all lost on him.

There was birthday Mark in his French class, of course, but he didn't know if Mark was gay. It could just be wishful thinking. Geoff felt there'd be nothing more awkward than going up to some boy in his school and saying, "You know, I really like you," and then he says in return, "I'm *really really* not attracted to guys." That had to be the most embarrassing situation in the world. He thought Mark was a nice guy—more than nice—and he didn't want Mark to think that since Geoff liked him, he was going to constantly be hit on. He didn't want Mark to stop being friends with him. Professing his love, or any variation on it, just might do that. No matter how brave you'd have to be to do it.

Geoff had confided in a few of his friends about his feelings for Mark, but they hadn't been very helpful. "What you have to do," one advised him in a serious, conspiratorial voice, "is draw a penis on his birthday card. He'll get the hint." His friends were like that. In French class whenever Mark went up and did *une orale*, one of his friends would wink at Geoff, while another coughed loudly to make sure Geoff was paying special attention (which he was), and another play-acted looking dreamily at Mark who was intent on his French pronunciation and conjugations, oblivious of his admirers. Geoff would feign annoyance at his friends' antics, but he did have to admit they were funny.

He wasn't one-hundred-percent sure, but he felt Mark liked him, too. Well, not just *liked*, but *liked-liked*. Mark was one of the students who complimented Geoff on the music selection for the daily news. It had only been a few days since Mark had stopped at Geoff's locker at morning break and told him he liked the music that morning. "I'm not much for retro," he said, leaning against the locker next to Geoff's. There was something about the way Mark leaned that thrilled Geoff. As Mark spoke, a stray chunk of his thick, dark hair kept falling across his eyes, and every so often his hand would move up to brush it away. Another thrill. "But you should make me a CD. I'd love to hear some more," Mark said.

A very good sign, Geoff thought, although, when he thought about it later, he decided he had no intention of making Mark a CD. It was too intimate. Too boyfriend-girlfriend. Well, too boyfriend-boyfriend. Geoff knew how much of himself he put into those CDs. The songs you choose reveal so much about yourself. That was the whole idea of a mix CD. What if Mark thought the lyrics were directed at him? It would be difficult finding songs that didn't have something to do with love. Why in the world had Mark asked him such a thing?

But Mark seemed to go out of his way to be nice. Last week Geoff had been sitting with him at lunch, just the two of them at a table together in the cafeteria, and Mark had said out of nowhere, "It's my birthday." He told Geoff he was having a party that weekend. "Consider yourself invited." Geoff had been excited at first, then, when he realized he was going up North that weekend with his family, disappointed. He spent the rest of the day questioning if it was always going to be like that: wondering about someone, getting closer to him, allowing himself to hope this could be it, then somehow being let down.

Geoff was not one for being depressed, but that day had been an exception. As was his nature, by the last bell he'd started telling himself, "Obstacles are only problems to be solved." He just needed to figure out a solution. Or start praying.

After school Geoff had been surprised to find Mark waiting for him. "I decided to change the party to next weekend." Geoff's response was an ear-to-ear smile. How else should he acknowledge a miracle? Mark went on to add, "Well, a whole bunch of people couldn't make it this weekend." Geoff barely heard him he was so happy.

"No I don't have a boyfriend," he told the grade sevens. Then, not missing a beat: "Why are you going to set me up?" They laughed again.

"Do you want to get married?" a boy called out from the back of the room.

"Well, not this week." Another thing he hadn't thought of. Give me a chance, he thought. First he'd have to find a boyfriend and at least kiss someone. Walk before you run, he told himself. For a second his mind flashed on what did Mark think of marriage, but just as quickly he told himself Mark probably wasn't even gay. It was just something he was reading in that wasn't there. No use being carried away. No use making a fool of himself.

A girl in the front row, eyes open with hope as she looked up at Geoff, asked him tentatively, "Are you sure a hundred percent you're gay? You're cute."

More laughter. "Yes," Geoff said, laughing as well. "I'm hundred percent sure." She half-jokingly feigned disappointment.

The bell rang, and Geoff quickly told them he'd be back the following week to continue the unit with them. He wished them a good day and started gathering his notes from the teacher's desk when he heard the students clapping. He looked up and saw Mr. Mackay walking down the aisle towards him, clapping as well. "Thanks, Geoff. Good work! You did a great job!"

<hr>

It was already dark when Geoff finally made his way home after band practice; they had worked on the plan to record a CD of the final concert of the year. He had even convinced the band to play an ABBA song. For the first time they'd asked him to put on his ABBA CD just to hear how it was supposed to sound.

Darkness came early that time of year, but Geoff noticed the days were already starting to get longer. It would soon be spring. Then grad. Then he and his friends would go off to college and their separate ways despite pledges of never losing touch.

He liked that time of year; the lengthening days always seemed so hopeful to him: soon the dark would give way to the light. It fed his optimism—he needed that. On his walks home from school he always tried to find something positive to cling to; he almost felt in shock having plunged from the social cacophony of friends and acquaintances and teachers into the silence and solitude of the walk home. He could only pinpoint two times he felt loneliness: last year when everyone went on the Europe trip and he didn't go because he had appendicitis, and walking home from school.

He was tired; he was barely able to keep placing one foot in front of the other. The downtown commuters in their cars started rolling past him and down the street, no doubt happy as well to be almost home. Geoff couldn't wait to eat dinner and then spend the rest of evening listening to music in his room. Eighties music, of course.

He was happy how his day had gone; he was proud of what he did with the grade sevens; he seriously felt they understood the points he was trying to make. Mentally he started going over all the things he had to tell them next time: the help line numbers; the support groups for gay and lesbian youth in the front of the Changes and Choices guide; the homework assignment he never had time to give them.

He stopped dead in his tracks—he'd forgotten to buy Mark a birthday gift. "Oh, well," he thought as he started walking again, "there's always tomorrow after school," although he knew that would be cutting it short. For the tiniest second he allowed himself to believe a gift was all it would take to make Mark see what Geoff so wanted him to.

He found it funny the grade sevens had wanted to know if he had a boyfriend. He was confident he'd prepared for every possible question, and he really felt he had. Except that one. They weren't unlike his friends who kept asking him if he was going to bring someone to grad.

For the last month or so, everyone in his grade was buzzing with talk of graduation. They were already planning dates and limos and hotels, even though it was still months away. If he was honest with himself—and that walk home after school in the dark tended to make him so—*that* prospect seemed out of reach. Whom did he know? Between then and grad, what were his chances he'd meet someone who was gay and that person would like him enough to want to go to the grad with him?

So he answered all who asked by saying he planned to go alone because he didn't want to start trouble like that kid in Ontario who sued his strict Catholic school so he could take his boyfriend to the prom. Of course, Geoff didn't think for a moment his school would stop him if that was what he wanted to do.

"You'll meet someone in college," a friend told him out of nowhere one day. He still didn't know why she said that; he never spoke about it to his friends. Instead he just silently witnessed the couples walking down the hallways hand-in-hand, and their secret kisses in stairwells, and their hurried goodbye hugs and pecks outside classroom doors seconds after the period bell rang.

None of that had ever bothered him as much as it did when the grade sevener asked him that question.

Right then Geoff decided he would burn a CD of some of the music he liked for Mark's birthday gift, just as Mark had asked. He'd start making it as soon as he walked into the house. In those last steps home, he began choosing which songs to include, songs that would express what he was feeling. Songs that would show Mark he cared.

As he reached the driveway to his house he saw Mr. and Mrs. Turner returning from walking their dog, their pre-dinner ritual. From passing cars and front windows, everyone on the street who saw the Turners waved at them as they strolled to the cul du sac at the far end of their street and back again, arm-in-arm on cold evenings like that one, or holding hands and swinging their arms carefree on warm summer days.

Geoff waved at the couple, too. And, as always, together they waved back.

Truly inseparable.

Episodes in Fear
Matthew's Story

Leaving Home Again

Matthew waits for the bus to pull out and head towards the Canadian border. He looks through the tinted window at his mother, the ends of her long black hair flailing in the wind. Many times Matthew has heard her tell people with pride that she hasn't cut her hair since she was a girl on the reserve, though what she doesn't like to add is it was the nuns who had forced her to cut it.

"I'll miss you," she says again. Matthew barely hears her above the bus's idling engine. "Your father will be waiting for you at the bus station," she yells. He nods, and her face contorts into the look he has come to know all too well in the last few weeks.

"He won't hurt you now," she says, or whispers, or mouths for all he knows—he only sees her lips move as the luggage compartment is slammed shut. She says it a dozen times a day. Two dozen. A hundred times. Matthew knows who "he" is—she doesn't have to say his name anymore. No one does: the lawyers, his mother's boyfriend, his grandmother. "He" lost the right to have a name, Matthew supposes. Matthew wonders if the word "he" will ever mean someone else again, like the boy next door who he finds cute, or a friend at school, or the old man at the post office who hands him letters and packages from his father in Canada. His father's always sending things; he never calls. Matthew can count the times he's heard his father's voice on the phone, his slight French Canadian accent a surprise and a treat amid all the American drawls. His father uses "he" too.

The bus's doors close. There's the sound of gears meshing into place, then the engine groans from idle and the bus starts moving. Matthew looks at his mother one last time—a small woman standing alone in sadness. Her mouth forms the words, "I love you," and he gives her a smile and a wave goodbye. He doesn't want to go back to living with his father, to leave her, but he wasn't given a choice. For his parents, this is the only solution. Matthew hopes it will stop the memories that bleed into his dreams.

He doubts he will see this part of the States, this place, again. He's going back to Canada, back to his father, back to his father and his father's boyfriend and their home. His father's gay, and, even though his father's gay, Matthew finds it so difficult to tell anyone he's gay, too.

Knowing

The first time I can remember was this feeling I had, and I knew what it was because I'd look at other guys and think they were good looking. I can remember waiting with my friend, Lucas, for the métro—it was summer and we were going to another friend's house. We were probably about ten or eleven. Lucas was a bully who all the other kids at school feared. He liked to protect me and he told everyone he was my cousin, even though he wasn't, because there were kids who'd always beat up on me. I remember waiting for the métro and just listening to him talk, and he brought up the subject that because my father was gay there was a chance I could be, too. Lucas always used to hang out at my house, and he was okay with it and everything. That was just his way of thinking, and I was young then, too, so I thought the same thing. And then I wondered, "What would happen to our friendship if I was gay?" I never asked him because the métro came, but I thought about it a lot after that. And that's when I had this moment of epiphany where it hit me: "Gay! *That's* what I am. *That's* what I'm feeling."

A New School

Matthew burns himself some toast for breakfast, and his father asks him how things are going at school. His father's boyfriend has already gone to work.

What can Matthew say? Should he tell him again how bad it is? He already has. "So people *know* you're gay at school?" his father kept repeating in disbelief. "Yes," Matthew kept answering, even though that wasn't the point at all. But for his father there was no other point.

Should Matthew tell him how he feels safe at home, but, then, walking to the bus stop each morning, it starts, a feeling in his stomach that gets worse as he stands waiting for the bus. Then boarding the bus, and having the feeling build and build. And on the ride to school, having to put on this shell, this mask, this whole other personality. He purposely looks depressed and angry like he's had a big argument at home and people had better watch out, hoping against hope they'll leave him alone. When the conversation finally circled back to the harassment, his father said, "You've dug your own grave, now lie in it. I told you, you shouldn't have come out there."

So Matthew smiles and says, "It's okay," and "School is school," as though that explains everything.

In a way it does.

School is school and school is a shit hole. Matthew knew that from the minute he walked into the building. The first thing he noticed was how run down the place was. The bulletin boards were cut up and covered with graffiti. The hallways looked dirty, like they washed them but it wasn't doing any good. There were very few lights. The school he went to back in the States had just been built, and everything was clean and new: the desks were in perfect shape, the walls were bright, the bulletin boards had posters and notices inviting students to become involved in all kinds of sports and after-school activities. In that school, there had been over twenty clubs and every single sport. Matthew en-joyed watching the cheerleading competitions—it was all new to him. Both schools have a large student body, but Matthew's new school has more students than desks for them to sit in. You'd think with so many students, there'd be school spirit, but his first week there Matthew asked at the office about clubs, thinking he could join one to get to know other students. The secretaries looked at him as if he asked where they kept the solid gold blackboard erasers. It's like his new school doesn't want to waste any of the students' time.

He's trying to fit in. In the first few days he meets Amy and they sit together in history class in the back corner and talk. Because they get into trouble a lot for "disturbing others," they start writing notes back and forth. In one note, Amy tells Matthew she's bisexual and that eve-rybody at school knows and they're cool with it. He feels a sense of trust with her and writes back he's gay—he wants her to know, he feels it's a part of who he is. He knows if Amy is going to hang out with him, she'll eventually see he's gay, especially if he has some gay friends or a boyfriend. Matthew's happy to have someone to hang out with at school so he's not alone.

Then Amy starts telling people Matthew's gay. When he finds out, she tells him not to worry because everybody's cool with it and they won't say anything. But it spreads, and before long everybody knows.

That's when the harassment begins.

The Welcoming Committee

Matthew sits outside the principal's office, in the open, clearly visible to all who walk by. Teachers and students give him looks that ask, "What have you done?" or "Who you ratting on?" He's been waiting for nearly an hour. Finally the door to the principal's office opens and Matthew's told to come in.

Matthew explains how it happened: "It was after the bell. I was walking back to my locker and I saw a group of boys at their lockers, so I went around them. They stopped me as I was walking past. They pulled me back by my backpack, and pushed me up against the lockers. They said I was looking at them and they asked me if I wanted them. One of them said, 'You want to suck our cocks, don't you?' and he grabbed himself through his baggy pants. They kept puling me off the locker and then pushed me back against it. Then they punched and kicked me."

He points out the marks on his body.

The principal says, "We'll do everything we can to deal with the situation. Don't worry."

He smiles and Matthew feels relieved knowing it will end.

On the Reserve

On weekends he stays on the reserve with his grandmother. She spoils him, making special dinners like sausages and corn bread and gravy, and she takes him shopping for the things his father forgets he needs. At supper she tells him about his aunts and uncles, his mother's sisters and brothers. Tonight she tells him about his aunt who became a Jehovah Witness and left the reserve with her husband and never spoke to the family again. His grandmother tells the story with pain, and Matthew puts his hand on hers as she speaks.

Later she takes him to the Super Bingo up the highway where they win $143. They treat themselves to cokes and hot dogs and greasy homemade French fries from Fadee's chip stand. They eat, laughing at how small their good fortune is.

Good Advice . . . You Just Can't Take

Classes are over for the day. Matthew goes to talk to his morals teacher. Even though he spoke to the principal, nothing has changed. Maybe she can help. He knocks on the classroom door and she looks up from her correcting. He doesn't know where to begin. He starts by telling her he's gay, then about the harassment and the principal.

"I can't even walk down the hallway without somebody yelling 'faggot' and shoving me into a wall. It happened at least three times today alone. I'm called a name at least twenty to thirty times a day—some days I can't even count how many times. They say it when teachers aren't around or low enough so teachers can't hear."

She offers solutions. "Don't look directly at them," she says, like they're an eclipse or a pack of wolves. "Look elsewhere," she says. He's not sure what he can look at. The walls? The lockers? The floor? She tells him ways to get out of situations—they all involve him standing up to them. "Show them you're not afraid," she says. He's not sure he can do that—well, he *knows* he can't. Anyway, how does he not look at them yet stand up to them at the same time? As he leaves, his teacher tells him college is a whole other world and a lot more open. She says coming out in that school wasn't a good idea.

The Writing's on the Wall

It's lunchtime. Matthew makes his way to his locker to put his books away. The hallways are empty—the other students are already in the cafeteria eating. It takes Matthew longer to reach his locker because he knows where their lockers are, where they hang out, around which corners they might be. He avoids those areas. Every day he finds another, more roundabout route back to his locker, or from one class to another. He reaches for the combination lock out of habit, but as he looks up he sees spray-painted across his locker, "All fags die!"

He goes to see the principal and asks him to come and see what they've done. "I don't have time for that," he says. "Go ask the janitor for some cleaning solution and a rag to remove it. You don't want the other students to see it, do you?"

Matthew scrubs his locker clean. When he's finished his punishment, he goes for lunch.

Loosening Jars

I was in my room on the Internet and my mother was in the living room with her boyfriend. I could hear the TV, the occasional footsteps to the kitchen for a drink or snack during a commercial, a sentence or two as they discussed the story on *Law and Order* or the plot being hatched by a player on *Survivor*, the sound of their laughter accompanying the laugh track of a comedy show. They love their TV.

I was chatting online with people I'd met through the personal ad I placed on PlanetOut looking for a friend. People from all over: Canada, the United States, Mexico, Europe even. Some were my age, some older. Recently I'd added Rob to my MSN Messenger—he was thirty-three and seemed like a nice person—he lived in the same state I did. I liked how he was interested in what I wrote him and how he'd always help me out with advice. He used to e-mail me every day just to say, "Hi."

I had questions. "Is what I'm feeling gay?" "What does being gay mean?" "What's it like to be out?" "What would it be like to be my age and out?" I was looking for someone older, thinking they'd know their lifestyle and would be able to answer me based on their experience. I didn't want someone my own age who was as confused as I was, so I purposely chose chat rooms where older men went.

One night, just before I typed my usual "nite" and "ttyl," Rob wrote, "Do you want to meet me?" I didn't answer—I turned off the computer and went to bed. It excited me to think if I were going to meet him, he'd be the first gay person I'd know. Well, not including my father, of course.

Every night my mother would come to my room and say "Good night" to me. That night she kept standing at the doorway and wouldn't leave. "Can I ask you something?" she said. "We've always been honest with each other, and we've been through a lot together." She waited for me to say something, so I nodded my head. Then she asked me if I was gay.

I said, "no." I acted angry. I changed the subject and asked her what she was watching on TV—I knew if I did she'd forget what she just asked. Before she turned off the light she said, "It's only natural I want to protect you until you can protect yourself."

I know I was being harder on her than I should've been and I wasn't being honest. If she asked, she was probably ready to know. I just wasn't ready to tell her. I was scared. I didn't know what jar lids would twist open if I said, "Yes." I mean, I didn't think she'd stop loving me. I knew my mother well enough to rule that out. But I'd be unique—I wouldn't be like everybody else. I was afraid she'd say it was wrong.

All the signs were there anyway. I used to collect pictures of Zac Efron and Jesse McCartney and Cody Linley. What boy my age does that and isn't gay? I no longer had any guy friends—I only hung around girls. I did have a girlfriend the year before, but we only went as far with each other as the shopping mall.

I'm smaller than most guys my age. It's a family curse. My fake girlfriend used to say my face was "too pretty," which is embarrassing. My black hair, my big brown eyes, my full lips. I can check off one-by-one from which parent I inherited each of my features. Should I hate them for being the way I am?

That's when I realized those jar lids weren't as tight as I liked to think.

New Boy in Town

He tries to act more masculine at school. He watches how he walks and moves and sits and holds a book. In class he doesn't look at anyone in case they feel uncomfortable and read something into it. Especially other boys. He keeps his eyes focused on his desk. He has a new technique to go from class to class: he sticks close to teachers as he makes his way through the dark halls—human shields—although he seldom talks to them or acknowledges why he's walking alongside them. He assumed the dispassionate air of someone who's simply hopped a trolley car that will take him from one point to another.

They have to wear uniforms at his school, but he sees how the boys wear theirs and how they're different from him. Instead of tucking in his white shirt, he now keeps the tails out. Teachers yell at him to "Tuck it in," all day, just like they do to them. He rolls up the sleeves to his elbows. He convinces his grandmother to buy him pants, still in the requisite school navy blue, but many sizes too big. He keeps his running shoes untied, long laces flopping around as he walks.

He'll try this straight-boy act and maybe they'll leave him alone.

Batty Man

They've taken to calling him "batty man" and "sodomite." At first he doesn't know what they mean, so, in a way, it doesn't bother him, but he knows it can't be good. Amy explains it to him as they try to eat their lunch. It's the same every day. No matter where Matthew sits, they sit at the next table and throw food.

"Batty man"

"Sodomite."

When it first happened, he looked around for help. A lunch lady. A teacher. Someone. But he learned quickly that at this school you're on your own. Just last week a girl from another school walked right in and smashed a girl's head against a table, putting her in the hospital. Some women in the kitchen came out and tried to stop it, but it was over by then.

Today Amy has had enough. She throws food back at them and says, "Why don't you leave him alone? Why do you care? It's not your life. What does it have to do with you?" They listen until she finishes, then they start throwing food again.

"Batty man"

"Sodomite."

Matthew and Amy finish their lunch in silence.

Judging Books by Their Covers

He thinks he might find answers in the school library. He'd like to read an advice book or a book on famous gays and lesbians, anything to learn more about other people like him and what they've gone through and how they've handled it. He laughs at himself. He knows he's getting desperate if he's actually going to the library.

He asks the librarian and the man gives Matthew a weird look and says, "There's nothing like *that* in *this* library." Matthew feels as if the man is annoyed by his being gay in his presence. On his own he finds one general book on sexuality. The cover shows a man and a woman embracing fully clothed. The woman looks up at the man with undying love. Matthew doesn't bother opening it.

Climbing Down Off the Cross

"I don't get it," Amy says. "They're okay with me."

"Maybe because you're a girl," Matthew tells her. She looks at him as if to ask, "What difference does that make?"

"Those guys probably think they can get some action with you and your girlfriend. With me they're afraid I'm going to grab their asses."

"Don't worry," she says. "I'll stand up for you." And she does for a while. But when she finds she's spending most of her day telling people to back off, or stepping in between Matthew and someone who seems seconds away from punching him, she soon distances herself from him. At first there are a few missed lunches together, then fewer and fewer phone calls in the evening. Then he's on his own again.

Cyber Secrets Revealed!

One day I came home from school and my mother was waiting for me. Her face was as far from the greeting I expected as ice is from hell. I put down my backpack at the door, and, without a word, I followed her into my room. Her boyfriend was sitting at my desk.

"Chuck's found pictures of naked men on your computer," she said, and she asked me again if I was gay. I lied again and said no.

Her boyfriend said he checked the computer's history and it was all there. "All the web sites you've been to. Gay sites. Porn. The only way it could have got on the computer is if somebody went to those websites and looked at what's there."

I told them, "None of that's mine."

My mother said, "It's a new computer and you're the only one who uses it." She wanted to know why I went to those sites, but I didn't answer.

Chuck erased everything he could find and left my room. He wouldn't look at me. My mother left, too, and I could hear their voices in the kitchen—not their words, but their noise.

They were arguing.

Barriers to Making the Grade

Now they won't let him in the boys' locker room. Last week they stared at him as he undressed, and told him in all kinds of vulgar ways he shouldn't be in there with them. It's absurd—they watch him to see if he's looking at them. They fear Matthew as though he's a sexual predator. They think if you're gay you're attracted to everyone of the same sex. They fear he fantasizes about them or wants to go with them.

Today they barricade the door so he can't get in, holding it closed from the inside. From the other side of the door he hears them calling him "fag," and one of them repeatedly asks, "Do you like it up the bum?"

The gym teacher is in the gym setting up for class. Matthew goes to speak to him. He tells Matthew he can get changed in the storage room if he wants. Matthew finds this funny: every day in gym class he'd get to come out of the closet.

He goes to the principal again, and the secretary goes and tells him Matthew wants to speak to him. Again Matthew is made to wait a long time. It's more punishment, this time for needing help. After a while the gym teacher shows up and goes into the principal's office and shuts the door. Matthew waits some more. Finally they call him in and the principal tells him he shouldn't go into the locker room anymore. The gym teacher nods agreement.

"It's a safety issue," the principal says. "If you're in there we can't see or hear what's going on." Matthew wants to ask why the gym teacher doesn't go into the locker room if he wants to see and hear what's going on. "We don't want you to get hurt," the principal says with a sympathetic smile.

"And what about them?" Matthew asks. "Will you talk to them? Will you make them stop?"

"Well," the principal begins. "It's difficult to know who's said what and who's done what."

Matthew describes them to the principal again. He gives some of their names; he lists which of his classes they're in and repeats what they do to him. He says there are six boys, but only two cause the trouble. The others just stand around and laugh, or say stuff, or look around to see if teachers are coming.

"It's always the same ones," he says.

"What proof is there that it's them?" the principal asks. "You say there's a whole group. Are there witnesses?"

He waits for Matthew to answer—it's like he doesn't believe him. Matthew thinks it's a form of harassment in itself, a Chinese torture of his coming to the office to ask for help, the promises to do something, then nothing being done, repeated daily, over and over again. At what point does it become unbearable? Now he needs witnesses. He knows there are five or six boys in his gym class who don't harass him, who remain quiet, the ones who are shy in class, or are new and don't know anybody. When the trouble starts, they look away, hoping no one notices them. Would they come forward and tell what they saw? Matthew doubts it.

The principal clears his throat and says, "I have parents to meet with. Go back to class."

So Matthew changes in the boys' washroom, but they're not clean and he doesn't feel secure there—it's the one place in school a teacher seldom goes, and he worries what will happen if his harassers follow him in there. So he speaks to the guidance counselor and she lets him change in her office. Now he's either late for gym, or late getting to the class after gym, because he has to walk from the other side of the school over to the gym. Again he's the unique one, singled out as different, made to feel less than everyone else. He feels so down about gym that he no longer bothers to participate in class. Soon he stops getting changed at all, and the gym teacher starts deducting marks. Matthew knows he'll fail the course.

He thinks, "Whatever."

Quick-change Artist

He stops wearing baggy pants and untied shoes and trying to fool them into thinking he's tough. No one believed it anyway.

A Show of Support

Some girls in his grade come up to him at his locker and tell him they heard what's happening to him.

"They're so stupid," one says to him.

"It's so wrong what they're doing," another one says. "You should do something."

"My family knows their families," still another one says. "Their mothers should be slapping them so's their children's children are born with bruises."

"Just change in our locker room," the first one says. "It's not like you're going to look, and we won't care." They laugh. "You're just going to get changed."

They continue talking, it's loud and excited, and Matthew is both exhilarated by their energy and worn out trying to understand what they're saying as they talk on top of each other. Matthew knows they're making the effort to be nice to him, to be his friends even, but he also knows that like most people, words are as far as they can go without actually doing something about it.

Exploring Diversity

It's Black History Month. Teachers make them read articles about black heroes and they watch videos and write essays about major events in civil rights. It's the first and only time Matthew's heard teachers at that school talk about diversity. As he works on his essay about Harriet Tubman and the underground railroad to Canada, a wadded-up piece of paper hits the back of his head. He turns around and sees them staring at him menacingly. One asks, "What are you?" Matthew would never tell them he's Mohawk, it would just be another thing for them to mock him. He turns back to his work. "Just some whitey, huh?" he hears one of them say, and they all laugh.

A Crush of Convenience

A girl from math walks with him to his next class and tells him her name's Jessica. Before long she's calling him at home, and they quickly fall into the habit of spending hours on the phone talking about everything. Music. Movies. School. The usual. She tells Matthew about her messed-up family and how she's tried to commit suicide. There are many long nights when Matthew listens to her unhappiness. Eventually he tells her about "the court case" and how "he" pleaded guilty and was sentenced to seven years. She tells Matthew she wants to go out with him as boyfriend and girlfriend even though she knows he's gay.

"You're a great person," she tells him. "I love who you are."

He asks her about sex.

"Sex doesn't matter to me," she tells him. "You've done so much to help me out. I just want to be with you. I don't want sex."

"You'll find someone else," he tells her. "We can still be friends. You'll find a boyfriend. If you can ask me, you can ask anyone."

She seems to understand, but the next day at school he hears she's telling everybody they're a couple. People come up to him and ask him if he's *really* gay, angry he could be lying.

Matthew stops talking to her.

Like Father, Like Son

When I left the police interrogation room, I saw my mother waiting for me. She pulled me closer to her than I can ever remember her doing before. Through tears she kept saying over and over that everything would be all right.

On the ride home she told me she was proud of me, and no matter who I was or what I did in my life, she'd still care for me and would always love me. There was no use lying—it was all coming out anyway: the pictures on the computer; telling the police how I chatted with men on the Internet; how I even met a man.

What he did to me.

As we're driving home, I could see her tears, and for days after my mother's eyes were red from crying. I felt a bridge had been built between us then. I knew I could trust my mom with whatever was going on in my life. I wondered why I didn't know that before. Why was I so scared to tell her? The reasons no longer seemed important.

That night she phoned my father in Canada and told him what had happened. She was on the phone for a long time, and from my room I could hear what she was saying. That night she used "he" for the first time.

My father wanted me to come back to Montreal right away. I heard her tell him I'm gay, then she called me to the phone, and my father asked me for himself. For the first time I said, "Yes."

My father said, "It's alright. I know now. It's not going to be easy, though. I won't lie to you. There's a lot of stuff you're going to have to go through. But I guess you already found that out."

I passed the phone to my mother and went back to my room, but I could still hear enough to know they decided that once the preliminary hearing was over, I'd be going back to Montreal.

Later my mother came to my room to check on me and ask, "Why was it so difficult to tell me you're gay when your father's gay, too?" I didn't know how to answer that. My father being gay seemed so normal to me growing up—having my mom and her boyfriend, and my father and his boyfriend—it didn't seem at all like what I was going through. I knew the story: my father tried to be straight, tried various relationships with women, tried to be married, even tried having a child, me, as a way to break his homosexual feelings. It all seemed so long ago, a story about someone else. It wasn't my story.

My parents never mention what happened to me. You know, what "he" did. Now if they do talk about it, they just refer to it as "the court case."

An Ally

In English class he writes an essay about his life and how difficult it is dealing with the harassment. He writes how powerless he feels, unwanted and unsafe, and how he now knows nothing he does or could do will change his situation. His English teacher, Ms. Porter, keeps him after class and asks if he's okay—she's worried he's suicidal. She's young, late twenties, and Matthew sees her as open-minded and cool, so he tells her what's going on and she listens.

"I have a gay friend, you know," she says when he's through. "Sometimes we go shopping together in the gay village. He lives in the apartment at the end of the hallway on my floor. He's alone now. His boyfriend died from AIDS. I tried to get him to date again, but he doesn't want to find anyone else."

As Ms. Porter speaks, Matthew sees she's really moved by the man's life and his loss.

Matthew starts going to see her at lunch, and on breaks, and after school. He can tell her things he can't necessarily trust with his friends or even his family. He knows she won't go and tell other people.

"I'll speak to the principal about the bullying," she says. "I'll make sure the principal does something this time."

Project 10

As Matthew leaves the guidance counselor's office after changing from gym, having decided this would be the last time, she stops him and tells him about Project 10. She's looked into it, and she found they give information sessions in schools on homophobia, and she tells him it might be helpful if she invites them to one of his classes. She says she'll speak to his morals teacher about it. For the first time in a long time, Matthew allows himself to feel hope.

You Can Go Back

On weekends at his grandmother's he explores the reserve, going to the places he remembers playing when he was younger. The old fort. The church with Kateri Tekakwitha's tomb. The seaway bridge. The tunnel. It's too cold now, but he remembers swimming in the quarry, his mother sitting nearby watching his every move, worrying he'd disappear in the dark water.

Odd Man Out . . . Again

My father brought me to be tested for STDs. The police back in the States told me I should be tested, it's what they routinely say in cases like mine. When I told the doctor why I was there, she referred me to a social worker who told me about a support group where they would understand what I went through. It was weird. I was the only boy there.

I didn't go back.

Everyday Heroes

They're throwing papers at him again and calling him "batty man" and "sodomite" and "faggot." The math teacher is God-knows-where, having left the room after handing out the worksheet for the day. Matthew struggles with a page of binominals. More paper balls. More insults. Then a voice in the back of the class booms: "Hey! Shut the fuck up!"

Everybody looks over their shoulders at Delano—he sits in the back corner, away from them, and seldom talks. They see in his eyes he's serious—they know he's not someone to mess with. Quickly they turn around and go back to their work. The girls smile at Matthew in support.

At lunch he sees Delano walking towards the cafeteria. He's alone and there's no one else in the hallway.

"Why did you do that?" Matthew asks as the boy walks past him.

"I don't care if you're gay or not," Delano says, "but they should leave you alone. It's just when your family's from the Caribbean you can't be a gay no how. Nobody likes the gays back in the islands. If you think it's tough here, you should see what they'd do to you over there. I'm talking machetes and setting you on fire."

Matthew sees he's waiting to be thanked for standing up for him. But, instead, Matthew says, "Fuck you."

Delano laughs. "It's okay. Just don't start liking me or anything."

Down the hallway students are walking towards them, making their way outside for an after-meal smoke. Delano says, "Later," and walks away. He doesn't want anybody to see him talking to Matthew. Matthew understands. He knows if they're seen together and people make a big deal about it, then Delano will never stick up for him again.

It's in the Mail

Matthew's dying to know. He waits behind as the other students swarm out of English class. Ms. Porter tells him: "The principal asked me to write him a memo about the harassment. I left it on his desk last week, but I still haven't heard from him." She sees how easily his face melts to the bare bones of disappointment.

"Don't lose hope," she says. "He's probably busy."

Matthew doesn't ask her about it again.

New Kid on the Block

A new student starts in school and his locker is next to Matthew's. Matthew can tell he has no friends: he sees him walk to class alone; he never talks to anyone; he eats lunch alone, too. He's a bit of a nerd, but Matthew says "Hi" to him. The boy says his name's Adam, and he looks relieved that finally someone's talking to him. Matthew shows the new kid around school. They laugh together and tell each other stories about their old schools and how much they both miss them.

When they come to rough Matthew up again, to knock him into the wall, to take his backpack and empty its contents on the floor, they start pushing Adam around as well. He stops hanging around Matthew. When he sees Matthew he says, "Hi," but keeps on walking. Soon even the greetings stop. Adam makes new friends, and Matthew sees them laughing as they tell each other stories.

Matthew doesn't blame him—he's doing what he has to do. He's just protecting himself.

A Beautiful Day

I went by myself to get the results of my HIV test. My father wanted to go with me, but I felt it was something I had to do on my own. The doctor took me right in to his office as soon as I got there, which made me worry. Right away he got to the point—I was negative.

I walked most of the way home. I didn't want to take a bus or the métro or anything. It was a beautiful day, even though it was a bit cold, but it was sunny and that was good enough for me. I couldn't help smiling all day, I was so thankful.

When I got home my father was waiting at the door.

"Negative," I told him, and he hugged me. I think he even cried. I didn't have the heart to tell him the doctor had suggested I come back for another test in a few months "just to be sure."

The Ripple Effect

Matthew can't concentrate on what he's supposed to be doing—two people behind him are talking. He tries to hear what they're saying, if it's about him. He wonders if they're someone else he has to worry about. School is a minefield of subtext and innuendo and clues he has to read to know who he has to watch out for, where they'll be, and the areas and people he has to avoid.

He no longer passes his work in; he knows he's failing; he's nervous all the time.

His history teacher keeps Matthew after class and tells him he'll have to work harder if he wants to pass the year.

"Remember," he warns, "decisions you make now will affect you for the rest of your life."

Just Another Day

The school has a carnival day. There's a choice: you can go to the gym and learn acrobatics and weight training and other activities—they seem fun to Matthew, and they're things he'd like to try—or you can just stay in class and do normal school work.

He hears them talking about going, all excited to show how good they can be, challenging each other to competitions to find who's the best. Betting whose ass will be kicked.

Matthew chooses to stay in class.

An Intervention

Project 10 comes to Matthew's morals class. It's the first time he hears the words "sexual orientation" mentioned in that class. In any class. There's a man in his thirties with dark hair and glasses who stands at the board and asks everybody to tell him the names they've heard people call gays and lesbians. They start yelling those names all at once, laughing while doing it. They yell at the man, but Matthew knows who they are really yelling at. The man tries to quiet them down, but they just laugh and yell more.

Matthew doesn't feel comfortable. They know what's going on, they give him looks, they blame him for having to sit through this. Even schoolwork is better than hearing about fags. The teacher sits beside him, no doubt thinking that will protect him. He asks her if he can leave, but she tells him to stay for a bit and see how things go. The man from Project 10 tells them about Joe Rose and why he was killed. They argue with him saying being gay is a sin, and all "batty men" go to hell. Some girls and a few boys start arguing back, but when they're called names, too, they stop. They return to calling Matthew and the man from Project 10 "sodomites" and ask if they've fucked each other yet. It's almost a chant. The teacher yells at them again and again to be quiet. Finally she turns to Matthew and tells him he can leave the class. She can no longer protect him.

Later, Matthew hears from the morals teacher that when the class was over, the man from Project 10 asked to see the principal, but was told the principal wasn't available to meet with him.

Small Victories

For the next week Matthew notices the harassment lessens a bit. Instead of being confronted by them ten times a day, it's only nine—instead of being physical, it's mostly verbal. Sometimes they rough him up but they no longer outright attack him. They still say something every time they pass him in the halls, but his locker hasn't been damaged in a week.

Crocodile Tears

One of them walks towards Matthew as he waits in line to get on the bus home, and he braces himself to be hit or even worse, although he can no longer imagine what "worse" can be. This one has hit him before; he's called Matthew all those names; he's pushed Matthew into walls and lockers and down stairs every chance he got. Matthew prepares to run.

The boy looms over him, and just when the inevitable seems about to happen, he says he's sorry. Matthew wonders if this is a trick.

"I was a jerk," the boy says.

Matthew says nothing.

"Did you hear me?" he says to Matthew. "I'm saying I'm sorry."

Matthew pushes past him and gets on the bus.

He finds out later the boy no longer hangs around with them, there's been some falling out. Matthew sees him alone at his locker now, not far down the hallway from his. Matthew thinks maybe he should have said something back, but then it's not like they'll ever be friends, so what difference does it make?

A week later the boy's friends with them again. Matthew sees them all standing at the boy's locker before the first bell. They laugh. They grab hold of their prodigal friend and push him down the hall towards Matthew, telling him to "kiss his girlfriend," and to "kiss the faggot."

He playfully fights them off, but he's serious enough when he starts calling Matthew "batty man" and "fag" and "sodomite" again. He fits back in with them. Matthew thinks that at least when you're fitting in you don't get picked on the same way.

Dreams Never Die

They've stopped me again. It's in gym class, and I'm in the changing room with them. It's just them and me. The other students have gone on to the next class. The gym teacher is God knows where as usual.

"You love cock, eh?" one of them says to me. The tall one. The one who greases his hair so it'll shine, but it just looks matted and unwashed under the strong fluorescent lights. He grabs himself. "You gonna suck this?" His voice has an edge to it, a hard confidence that tells me he knows he has all the power. He can humiliate me at will.

I say, "Sure. Whip it out."

He plays at pulling down his shorts while his friends laugh.

I pull out a knife. The flash off the blade captures their attention and changes their attitudes real fast. His friends start backing away. He's on his own now.

"I'm ready for it," I say, and smile. I twist the knife in the air to emphasize its metallic gleam and so they can see it from every angle.

"Hey," he says, putting his hands up in the air, shoulder height, no longer touching himself when ironically he *should* have his hands down there if he wants to leave with them intact.

"It's just a joke," he tells me. His voice has dulled to a plea. "Come on, man."

One of the others starts to move towards the door. I wave the knife at them, gutting the air between us. It quickly puts an end to any thoughts of escaping.

"So you don't want me to suck that," I say and knife-jab the air towards his crotch.

"No. No." He looks unsure if he should keep his palms facing towards me, showing me he means no harm, or make that sudden move to cover up his dick. Both may have dire consequences.

"Then you can suck mine," I say. "On your knees." His friends look more scared than he does. "Now!" I command him.

He looks like he's about to cry, or lunge at me, both at the same time. But I don't need to tell him twice. He begins to kneel. Even though I wasn't talking to them, the others get on their knees, too, the cattle that they are.

I feel the electric thrill rush through me as his hands slowly lower to his sides, not to protect himself, but as a sign of his defeat.

That's when I wake up.

*O:nen**

His grandmother teaches Matthew some words in Mohawk. When he was growing up, he never learned any. He remembers asking his mother, but she knew very few words and didn't seem to want to know more. "When your mother was younger," his grandmother says, "there was a ban on learning our native language. At school your mother was punished if she spoke it, punished for who we are."

His mother won't talk about that time.

"Memories like that wound the spirit," his grandmother says.

He realizes he knows so little about himself as Native, but learning some Mohawk words is a start.

He now says *"O:nen"* whenever he leaves family or friends.

An Island Never Cries

Another girl starts hanging out with him. She just comes up to Matthew after class one day and asks him questions about being gay. At first the questions are about sex. He's wary of what she's getting at, then thinks it's funny to humour her. She listens attentively when he tells her that the feelings behind being gay and in love are just like the feelings she'd have for a guy.

One day Matthew asks her if she'd go to the gay village with him, he's never been. As they walk past the cafés and clothing stores and bars, he watches the people—men strolling along the sidewalk who look over their shoulders with a smile at other men walking by, same-sex couples hand-in-hand, a group of women laughing with each other as they go into a restaurant—and he feels exhilarated. He tells her he thinks the world would be better if gay people could just stay in the village by themselves.

"It'd kind of be like if society set up a curtain with gays on one side and straight people on the other. Personally I'd be a lot happier if I could spend my whole life only with gay people, only going to a gay supermarket or buying clothes at a gay store. It would be so much better than what you have to live with every day with straight people."

"You're being close-minded. Not all straight people are against gays. Look at me."

---

* Pronounced "oh-neh," meaning goodbye in Mohawk.

"I wish there was a school for gays only." Matthew imagines it being a bright, vibrant place, full of creativity, where he'd be able to make gay friends his own age. He's heard on the news about the "Alternative Grad" in Toronto for gay high school students and how they can bring their same-sex dates. "I'm jealous," he tells his friend. His graduation is next year. "If Montreal had one, I'd go for sure," he says. "My parents could be proud of me and they'd want to be there to support me. They could be with other parents who have gay children, and they could meet, and talk, and be proud together." He doesn't want to think how awful graduation at his school will be.

"Gays have been around for how long?" his voice rises. "Centuries? Millenniums? In the past there's been trouble and problems between Blacks and Whites and Asians, and yet today everybody's able to mix and be okay with each other. With gays and straights it's a constant problem that isn't getting any better. If it hasn't changed, and it isn't changing, then maybe it's better to just be separate."

"But—"she says, trying to tell Matthew the reasons why she disagrees. He cuts her off. Their voices get louder, each not giving ground on their point of view, each thinking the other wrong. Each of them thinks the other is ignorant for thinking the way they do.

That's the last time they talk. Now he doesn't remember her name.

Straight-bashing

It's time they have a taste of their own medicine, injected intravenously, stabbed into their arms with the biggest fucking needle there is. The ones they use on horses. Ones they must need to get through rhinoceros hide.

My friends and I will gather at Kilos in the gay village. I won't be able to stop them from ordering cappuccinos and smoothies and desserts, but if that's what it will take to get them pumped for what's about to happen, so be it.

We'll go over the plans. We'll have maps. Places circled in black Sharpies all across downtown Montreal. The hangouts of breeders. The locales where straights flaunt themselves and their sexuality and their all-too-public displays of affection. Parks. Movie cinemas. Restaurants. Bars and clubs. The street. On every fucking street.

I'll ask who brought something to fight back with. Knives or chains or baseball bats. They'll all nod, suddenly serious, suddenly knowing what has to be done and that it's about time.

Anyone who's gay will know that.

And Then . . .

Finally the school year ends.

My Gay Summer

Now that school's over, Matthew decides to go to one of the Project 10 discussion groups. They meet each Saturday afternoon to tell each other what's going on in their lives and what they've done for the past week. At first he sits and listens as other sixteen-year-olds tell of how they came out, problems with parents and friends, and rocky romances. Then Matthew begins to speak, and bit-by-bit he tells them about what's happened to him in his life: how he knew he was gay, how his mother found out, even "the court case." He finds he doesn't have to explain that much—they understand. They've been through what he has. They know.

After group, they hang out together for the rest of the afternoon in outdoor cafés, or go to movies together.

All summer Matthew hangs out with his friends from Project 10. He goes to the pride parade and rides on the Project 10 float. He has a great time and he can't believe how many people are there—the streets are filled with a million people. He tells everyone he's there to celebrate who he is and to express his pride about who he's becoming. Later that night he goes out clubbing with his friends, and that's where he meets a boy. His name's Nathan.

Another Beginning

He changes schools. His father tells him he's given up, but Matthew doesn't care. Now he goes to an alternative school where he's heard they're more accepting of gay students. The first day he notices the teachers are always around, walking the well-lit hallways, stopping to speak with students, standing outside their classroom doors greeting them as they arrive. He walks from class to class with a smile on his face, the first time he remembers being able to do that in a long while. He's studying math, English, French, and physical science, and history, the subject he failed last year. He vows not to get side-tracked this year, no matter what happens. He keeps telling himself as incentive, it's just this year and then he graduates. This summer he's seen there's a larger world outside of school—it won't be long before he can be out in it for good.

There are about eighty students in the school. He's already spoken with some of them in his class, and discovered them to be open-minded. They talk about their summers, and Matthew tells them that this past summer has been the best in his life. He doesn't tell them details. He thinks about coming out to them, but before he makes up his mind, another new student shows up. It's a student from Matthew's old school.

It doesn't take long before everybody finds out about Matthew. To help counteract this, Matthew comes out to people he's spoken with, people he feels he can trust. Without exception they're cool with it—they become his friends—while those who find out from word of mouth don't seem to like the idea of his being gay much.

The harassment begins again.

Three boys stand near the lockers, and when they see Matthew walk by, they say those all-too-familiar words. He ignores them because he doesn't want a conflict all over again. But soon it's too much.

And the dreams have started again. He thinks about how much he wants the knife with him at school. How easily *he* can show *them*.

With a long sigh, Matthew goes to the principal and tells her what's happening. The woman listens to Matthew, and when Matthew's finished reciting his story, she asks him how he wants it handled.

"Would you prefer me talking to them first, or do you want to have a sit-down with them where we can try to work this out?" The principal goes on to speak of zero tolerance and repercussions. "Harassment and intimidation won't happen in this school," she says. They're wonderful words, but Matthew doesn't allow himself to fall under their spell. Not this time.

The next day Matthew hears nothing from the principal. He knows he wasn't going to allow himself, but he finds himself still holding out hope, however faint, that this time it could be different. He gathers up his books and jams them into his backpack. As he walks out of the class, his English teacher stops him with an "Oh!" and hands him a note. He's to see the principal.

The principal tells Matthew she spoke to the three boys, and two of the boys apologized and promised not to bother him again. "I'll be monitoring them," she says. The third boy, the one from his old school, refuses to stop. When Matthew asks, "Why?" the principal says it's better she doesn't tell him the reasons. "Let's just say he has very strong opinions. They're not right, mind you, but I don't think he'll change them any time soon." The principal says she had no choice but to suspend the boy. "Opinions are one thing, but opinions that fuel actions are something else. I won't put up with intolerance of any kind," she tells Matthew.

If there's one thing Matthew's learned is that actions speak louder than words. It takes a couple of days before Matthew notices the two boys are avoiding him, which works out fine because Matthew avoids them as well. But when the third boy returns to school after his two-day suspension, nothing has changed. There are names again. More names. Always there are names. Then pushing. Tripping even. Then there is a threat to "put out your fucking lights." Many mornings before school, Matthew puts the knife in his backpack, only to take it out again at the last minute.

So Matthew takes it until the principal makes a point to seek him out and asks if things are better now.

The third boy is expelled from the school.

The Essay

Slowly Matthew starts enjoying himself. Students are talking to him, and soon he finds himself hanging out with them at lunch and recess. He tells some of his teachers he's gay. His French teacher tells him they've had gay students in the past and they had the same issues. "We know how to deal with it," she tells him and winks.

In English class he writes an essay about himself and his old school, and he's surprised when the teacher doesn't make a big deal about it—she just corrects it for grammar. It makes Matthew think there isn't an issue or anything big or spectacular about his being gay. It's just . . . normal. For the first time he writes that he's Mohawk. He writes how everything in his past has made him a stronger person, and how he's proud of the person he is.

For the first time he feels he has security at school and nothing's going to happen to him.

Sometimes, though, he still feels that fear, but he does what he can to push it away. He wonders if it will ever go away for good.

Love's Bumpy Road

Matthew tells his school friends about an argument he had with Nathan. Matthew and his boyfriend haven't spoken for three days, and he feels the need to talk to someone about it. His friends are sympathetic—they listen, and give him advice, and tell him stories about fights with their boyfriends and girlfriends. When Nathan calls Matthew, and they start talking again, Matthew tells his friends and they're happy for him. One says, "We knew it'd work out for you two. You're meant to be together."

Matthew never thought as long as he lived he'd hear someone say that to him. At least not at school.

C'est Montréal

I was walking hand-in-hand with Nathan downtown along St. Catherine Street last week. We always walk holding hands. I guess people notice, but if they do, we don't hear a word about it. Only this time we had a problem—on the métro going home Nathan went to get off at his stop and he gave me a good-bye hug and kiss. A guy in his thirties in the next section over kept staring at us and giving us dirty looks, and saying stuff under his breath. We just ignored him. I think he was drunk or something. There were five other people in the same car, and they just ignored him, too.

As Nathan was leaving, he told me to watch out. He said the guy could have a knife or something. He asked me if I wanted him to stay with me, but I said I'd be all right.

I could see Nathan standing on the platform with this worried expression on his face as the métro car pulled out. He told me on the phone later that he regretted not staying with me.

I stood up when the métro pulled into my station, and the man yelled at me, "Run away, you little fag." I just turned to him, gave him the finger, and got off the train and walked towards the exit holding my head high.

It was great. I was only a bit afraid.

Dreams Come True

The year ends and then there's graduation. His mother comes up from the States and meets Nathan for the first time—she takes to him like he's a second son. She invites them to visit her next month in Florida, and she hands them tickets as a graduation gift. And, yes, Matthew's parents beam with pride, just like he thought they would.

At the graduation dinner-dance, Matthew takes Nathan as his date. He introduces him to his teachers as his boyfriend, and they shake hands with him and smile and say, "It's a pleasure to meet you" and "We've heard a lot about you." The couple sits at a table with Matthew's school friends, some of whom have already met Nathan before from when he's come to pick Matthew up after school.

Matthew wears the ribbon shirt his grandmother made special for him for that occasion. He's never had one before. His teachers and friends ask him about it, and he explains its meaning to his Mohawk culture, as his grandmother has told him. They ask to touch it.

He's excited beyond belief. He had such anticipation for the evening—and now it's here. It flows over and around him with such intensity, he finds it impossible to focus on any one thing—it's all too wonderful. He can't stop smiling. He takes lots of photographs so he'll always have memories of that evening.

Matthew and Nathan hold hands while eating dinner, and, later, when the music starts, they dance. When Matthew finally has a moment to catch his breath and look around, really look around, he sees that nobody seems to mind. He can't get over how normal it is that he'd be sharing his life with his boyfriend, his family, and his friends and teachers. Just like everyone else. Such a simple thing. It's exactly how he wished it had been like all along.

It's a Small Gay World (and Other Open Wounds)

Last weekend Nathan and I went to a movie and I saw this kid there that used to go to my old school. He was with another boy, and they were being way more affectionate to each other than straight friends would be—lots of PDAs. I had no idea he was gay. After the movie I saw him again, and I went up to him to talk to him. When he saw me, he was all smiles, and he asked me how I've been. I said, "How have *you* been?" and I looked right at the hot boy he was with, so he knew what I meant. He just smiled, and shrugged, and blushed a lot.

I asked him, "How come you never came out at school? I was all by myself. It could have helped me out a lot just to talk to somebody." I think it came out more angry than I wanted. Nathan told me later my voice was pretty loud. But at school everybody had their cliques—that's what high school is. The black kids hung out together, and the Hispanics, the Chinese, the Asians, whatever, they hung out together, and I always thought they must feel safe. That at least they had someone like them to watch out for them, while I was always stuck on the sideline by myself.

He didn't say much—I guess he didn't know what to say. He looked nervous and he shrugged again, and then he said, "Well, you know how the school was. I didn't want people to know I'm gay. I didn't want to make the mistake you did. I saw what they did to you, and I didn't want that happening to me."

It pissed me off to hear him say my coming out at school was a mistake. I've asked myself so many times if that's true. By coming out I no longer had this huge pressure within myself. And that was good. But when he said that, it made me think it was wrong for me to have come out what with everything I had to go through.

If I could go back, I want to believe I still would come out. Even though it's been a difficult path for me, I know it's helped me grow into who I am today. A person I do like being. A person I actually like.

I was sure of that as much as a person can be sure of anything.

But as I stood there and watched him and his boyfriend walk away, it all came back to me in this intense flash. It didn't matter that time had passed or things had changed—the person I had become suddenly meant nothing.

In an instant I was at that school again, alone, and more afraid than ever.

For Principal Kinean
Pages from Joe Rose's Notebook

———————

LAST WEEK, I ran into the principal of my old high school while in line at a coffee shop downtown. Why he was there, I have no idea. I thought he lived closer to the school. Hell, I though he lived *in* the school. It's difficult to imagine principals and teachers having a life out in the real world.

He was impatient, stepping out of line to look at what was going on up front at the counter. There were five people ahead of me, and when he came up behind me in the line, I turned and smiled. I knew right away who he was, Principal Kinean. I'd never had any run-ins with him—I was the kind of student who kept to himself and just went along to get along, but when I came out, I had some problems at school, and it was Kinean who had to deal with them.

To be honest, he didn't do that much. Thankfully it was near the end of my final year, so I stayed home whenever I could. Avoidance was a solution that worked for me. I squeaked by with just enough credits to graduate.

When I said, "Hi," Kinean smiled, but his face showed he didn't have a clue who I was. He was looking at my hair, spiky and pink, and I could tell he didn't know what to make of it.

"It's me, Mr. Kinean," I said. "Joe Rose. I graduated a few years ago."

"Oh, Joseph," he said, finally remembering. "How have you been?"

I told him about university and how I was involved in the Queer Collective there. I have to admit I said it because I wanted to see his reaction. Past experience told me he wasn't all that comfortable with gays or anything not run-of-the-mill hetero and boring. I'm not sure what kind of reaction I expected, shock maybe. Maybe even a hint of disapproval. But as I spoke, he looked at me with a concern that stopped me from saying anything else.

After a long pause where I could see him struggling to find his words, he said, "Let me ask you this. I have some students this year at the school who are—" He spoke quieter suddenly, so quiet he might as well have whispered. "Well, gay. A couple of them are having a difficult time with other students. What should I do?"

That wasn't at all what I expected.

Before I could answer, it was my turn to order. I mechanically spoke to the server, all the while trying to come up with something to say to Kinean. In the time it took for a coffee and a chocolate chip muffin to appear on the counter before me, I came to the conclusion I couldn't respond to a question like that just off the top of my head.

I waited while Mr. Kinean ordered and the server scurried about filling it. He paid, and turned to me, clutching a large coffee in one hand and a balancing a box of doughnuts in the other.

"I don't know," I said to him, feeling obliged to answer. It was like I was back in high school again and had just been put on the spot by someone in authority. "I guess just do something."

He thanked me and we said goodbye. All the way home I kicked myself for such a weak, useless piece of advice. For all the help I was, I might as well have advised passengers on a plane plummeting to the ground to "think positively."

In the days that followed, I thought a lot about what Kinean had asked. It would've been easier for me, I have to tell you, to have forgotten it and go on with my life. In so many ways, high school was a long time ago. But I couldn't. It nagged at me. I kept coming back to it when I was thinking about something completely different. It wouldn't let me go.

So this is for you, Principal Kinean.

If a gay student comes to you with a problem, listen to them. Accept what they are telling you as important, because it is to them. If the student is being harassed, ask them how it should be handled. Then do it. Don't put the gay student on the spot with the harassing student by bringing them into a room together to "work it out." That almost never happens, and it leaves the gay student open to more harassment, often during that very meeting. Talk with the harassing student separately and make sure they understand what the consequence will be if they do it again. If it does happen again, suspend them and tell their parents what's going on and why. Make sure the parents get involved in coming up with solutions to make it stop. Educate them if you have to.

Reinforce zero tolerance for discrimination in your school. If there's zero tolerance, it means nothing flies, not one comment, and it applies to *everyone*. Staff as well as students. Everyone has a right to go to school without fear.

If there's a problem in a specific class, talk to the teacher and have them talk to the students about it. Students see teachers every day so it's better coming from a teacher. Get some popular students involved in coming up with ways to stop harassment. Students will listen to them, too.

Educate students early. Promote awareness of this and other human rights issues. Fight for the equality of all people. Tell students about sexual orientation and have articles and books in the library so they can learn more. Have more courses about human sexuality in general so students see it's a part of life.

Defend your gay students and don't be ashamed of them. There are gay students in your school—it's a fact, live with it. Be proud of it. Be proud your school has a safe and accepting enough environment where a student can come out. That's a good thing.

And next time I run into you, Principal Kinean . . . the coffee's on me.

E-mails to My Brother
Christopher's Story

———————

To: Jamie <sidthekid0087@hotmail.com>
From: Chris <snowflake92@hotmail.com>
Sent: Friday, September 4, 2009 4:23:34 PM
Subject: Hi!

I know you've been expecting me to call and say I'm sorry. It's just that if I phone, he might answer, and I really don't think that would be a good idea right now.

I hope you're OK. I've already seen you at school a few times walking to the bus. Yesterday I saw you waiting with your friends, and I was going to come up and say something, but I didn't want to get into everything with other people around. Did you see me wave? Too bad we don't have the same lunch 'cause we could talk then. Where do you hang out at morning break? I still go to the breezeway to watch Anna and her friends smoke their disgusting cigarettes. I know you hate smoking, too, so I don't think I'll be seeing you there second-hand smoking with me any time soon. ☺

How's school going? The work at high school is a lot more difficult, eh? Everything's going OK with me. You can tell Mom I'm doing OK in all my classes. She'll be happy about that even if there's only been 1 week of school so far. You know what she's like. Oh, I started working part-time at an after-school program. I take care of the devilish grade 4s, but for a job it's a lot of fun because all we do is play. The kids love to talk to me about themselves, and I remember what grade 4 was like, so I think I know what they're going through.

Write back and tell me if we can meet after school to talk. I want to explain. On the days I don't work, I just stay home and listen to my CDs, do some homework, hang out with Anna at the mall sometimes. Nothing too spectacular. There's not many people I can talk to about all this. Poor Anna, she's had to listen to me go on and on. But what are friends for? We can go to that café I like in the mall. They have cool things to eat there. I'll buy you something.

Love,
Chris ☺

P.S. I miss playing Final Fantasy together. It's not the same playing against myself. I'm still the king of high score though. ☺

P.P.S. He can't stop us from being brothers, you know.

———————

To: Jamie <sidthekid0087@hotmail.com>
From: Chris <snowflake92@hotmail.com>
Sent: Monday, September 7, 2009 7:41:26 PM
Subject: Hi again!

I'm sorry I left home like that. Mom told me that's why you're mad at me. I don't know if you know all the details about what happened, but at least give me a chance to tell you my side of things. I know they keep stuff from you because they think you're too young, but you're my brother and I think you should know. I'm not keeping quiet about who I am.

You have to understand I can't go back and be what he wants me to be. It's better living here at Nanny and Poppa's, at least I don't have to put up with his comments. I'm not sure how much I showed it, but it was so difficult for me living there. I was so much angrier on the inside because I knew who I was and I wanted people close to me to know. It felt good when I told Mom and I didn't have to keep it in anymore. You know how I was back then, lying around all the time listening to music and not doing much else. Nothing interested me. I didn't bother with anyone. I was too busy being sad.

The few teachers who noticed anything said they thought it was just a phase I was going through. I guess they figured I was trying to be cool like my friends who were all going through that depressive phase.

Coming out was like walking out and seeing a light. I kept saying to myself, "Oh, my God, it's not so cramped anymore."

Now I can talk about it, I'm not keeping everything in all the time. The weight just comes off your shoulders. It's freedom for sure. People know and I don't have to hide it. I don't have to worry about people finding out and the whole stupidity of it.

I hope you understand.

So are we meeting?

Love,
Chris ☺

———

To: Jamie <sidthekid0087@hotmail.com>
From: Chris <snowflake92@hotmail.com>
Sent: Thursday, September 10, 2009 6:51:01 PM
Subject: Wot up???

I don't know if you're reading this or if you've blocked my e-mails or what. Why are you keeping this silence up? I want you to be a part of my life. Please don't be like him.

I'm no different a person now than I was before I came out. Most everyone accepts me. Well, most of the people who are important to me. My friends. Mom. Nanny and Poppa. Well Poppa doesn't want to know about it. He's like, "I don't need to hear the details." He makes me laugh. Nanny is more like, "Oh, really?" And she asks me questions 'cause she's never really known a gay person before. "What's it like? Is it difficult for you? If you need to talk about it, you can always talk to me." You know how she's really open about things like that.

He can't accept me and I guess never will. I thought because he's my father and because I'm his son he should at least try to understand

and try to cope with it. Maybe even change his opinion a little. Everyone else I've told has been great. Remember what it was like before I came out? Always trying to hide it? I'd dress in those big baggy clothes and, you know, try to be more macho and all thugged out. I even went out with Anna in grade 9 so no one would suspect anything. Oh, God! That was really trying too hard. That didn't last very long. You must have been laughing at me. Finally I decided to hell with that! Everyone was telling me, "That's so not you." Even Mom said, "You're trying too hard to fit in. Just be yourself. Screw what people say!" I wish I'd realized that before.

My friends have been great. Nothing has changed there. Like Anna, she's so happy for me. I told her in English class because I was like, "OK. To hell with it. I'm going to tell you 'cause I have to tell someone, and I know I can trust you because you trust me with everything." I knew she wouldn't feel weird around me and it wouldn't change anything. I knew right away I'd tell Anna because she'd just take it like it's a grain of salt. No big thing.

I wrote a letter. She read it and ripped it up because she respected me and didn't want anybody else to find it. Then she just gave me a hug and said, "It's OK. I love you."

It did cross my mind Anna could have been angry at first since we'd gone out, but when I told her that she just laughed and said she'd always known I was gay. "I thought it was weird when you asked me out back then. Anyway, you can't say we were real boyfriend and girlfriend, if you know what I mean?" I guess not. We never even kissed. TMI?

But I should have known how he'd take it 'cause of the way he is. How many times have we heard him say shit like, "In this house you bring women home, you don't bring men home"? And the way he treats Mom sometimes? Anyone who still has a problem with women for sure has a problem with gays. He's so predictable. I knew he wouldn't accept me. I don't know what I was thinking.

If you're reading this I want you to know I can't lose you, too. Can we still be brothers?

Love,
Chris ☺

––––––––––

To: Jamie <sidthekid0087@hotmail.com>
From: Chris <snowflake92@hotmail.com>
Sent: Monday, September 14, 2009 9:22:29 PM
Subject: Not giving up!

I had a cool day today. My French teacher was talking to me about how things are changing in schools and everything. I suppose by now all the teachers have heard about me. She said, "It's good to see diversity in the school. It's good to see that students are more aware because of brave people like you." I was like, "Wow! That's cool."

None of the teachers look at me different. They're all adults about it. A lot of people in my grade have said positive things, too. Sure there's a few who like talk and gawk with each other about me, but who cares? I don't have to hear what they say because it doesn't really get back to me. But a lot of people said they respected me even more because I was able to come out with it and tell people. A lot of people said to me, "I'd be too scared, you know, to say anything." Me being out has actually opened a few doors for other people who've stopped me and said, "I was scared to say anything, but now I'm not." Like three or four people already this year. I'm like, "Oh, cool." It feels good to show people it's OK. I think more people are starting to realize, "OK. That's more common than I thought."

Is it too much to want him to say something nice about me and be proud of me?

Love,
Chris ☺

P.S. I waited after school to see if I could catch you before you got on the bus, but I didn't see you.

P.P.S. Are you there?

––––––––––

To: Jamie <sidthekid0087@hotmail.com>

From: Chris <snowflake92@hotmail.com>
Sent: Tuesday, September 15, 2009 4:15:03 PM
Subject: Re: hey

What's the point in telling me Dad always mentions me and he thinks it's weird me not being there? Are you trying to say he's lightening up? After what's happened, I don't believe that for a nanosecond. I don't think he'll change just like that.

You didn't answer any of my e-mails and now that's what you write me?

To: Jamie <sidthekid0087@hotmail.com>
From: Chris <snowflake92@hotmail.com>
Sent: Wednesday, September 16, 2009 7:11:08 AM
Subject: Re: hey

I'm sorry for that e-mail yesterday. I'm not mad at you. It just makes me angry to hear he's saying stuff like that. And why is he telling you that? He hasn't spoken to me since I've left. Mom won't even talk to me about him anymore.

I mean, come on! You were there when he started in on me. Just another quiet evening watching TV. What a joke! At the part when the gay character on Six Feet Under was coming out to his brother, Dad had to go and ask you, "Would you still respect Chris if he was gay?" I still can't believe he said that. Did you see Mom trying to stop him?

That's when I was with my summer fling and I figured I couldn't keep something like that from my own family. I already told Mom. I thought I should be able to tell Dad and you as well, so I was like, "You know I'm gay." You weren't around the house much after that, but he didn't talk to me for the next 3 days.

I guess I kind of felt he must have known anyway. Well go figure, I never had a girlfriend. You can't really count Anna in grade 9. Come on, give me a break.

Your brother forever,
Chris ☺

____

To: Jamie <sidthekid0087@hotmail.com>
From: Chris <snowflake92@hotmail.com>
Sent: Thursday, September 17, 2009 4:04:57 PM
Subject: Re: Hello

I'm glad you answered. I was worried you're mad at me. I do want to tell you my side of things. You weren't there when he was like, "Get out," and he was screaming at me that he'd probably do something to hurt me. I thought not talking to me was bad enough.

I think you were at your friend's that day or at that summer day camp you went to. Everything was happening at once. First Dad was giving me the silent treatment, then suddenly he started yelling at me all the time. For real stupid things, too. The garbage. Coming home late. Talking on the phone too long. Anything. Everything. But what really pissed him off was when I broke up with my boyfriend and he heard me call Anna to tell her about it.

He lost it. Mom had to stand in between us. I never saw her stand up to him like that before. When she came to my room to see how I was, she said she'd always care and she'd always love me, but she told me, "Go. Here's your chance to get away from him. Go to your grandparents' house and maybe you can be happy there." What choice did I have? So I packed my bags and left. That's why I wasn't there when you got home.

You know, with everything that's happened, it's music that gives me the strength to keep going. If I didn't have that, I don't know where I'd be. When he first kicked me out of the house I kept listening to Jewel songs over and over.

You know I've never been close to him. Even when I was small, he never wanted to be with me like he did with you. You 2 were always playing hockey in the driveway or throwing a ball. I've always been closer to Mom. And with you, too, of course. I'd always want to take care of you, bring you on walks and to the park swings and stuff. We used to be together so much. I don't want to lose that.

Peace,
Chris ☺

———————

To: Jamie <sidthekid0087@hotmail.com>
From: Chris <snowflake92@hotmail.com>
Sent: Friday, September 18, 2009 8:45:33 PM
Subject: Re: hey

Just to let you know, I'm not working at the after-school program anymore. I only lasted 3 weeks. I got into a fight with the boss, so I just figured enough is enough. It was too much stress. Anyway, it's OK because I found a job at a restaurant on the weekends. Steamies and poutine. Me! Imagine!

Love,
Chris ☺

P.S. Write back and tell me how things are. Mom calls me every few days, probably when he's not there. She doesn't really have much to say though. You can call me, too, if you want.

———————

To: Jamie <sidthekid0087@hotmail.com>
From: Chris <snowflake92@hotmail.com>
Sent: Sunday, September 20, 2009 1:51:24 PM
Subject: Re: hey

Wow! A question! ☺

We don't really talk about much when she calls. Just the usual. School. Friends. You, too, of course. The last time she called I finally asked her if she spoke to him about what happened and, maybe, I could come home now. It's been two months already. But she didn't answer. Before she had to go, I asked her to try to talk to him.

Chris

———————

To: Jamie <sidthekid0087@hotmail.com>
From: Chris <snowflake92@hotmail.com>
Sent: Saturday, September 26, 2009 11:53:09 AM
Subject: Where r u?

I haven't heard from you for over a week. Is something wrong? The last few days I've been waiting for you after school, but I never see you. Do you take the late bus now? Are you doing sports? I even phoned last night, but he answered so I hung up. Thank God I blocked my number first.

Are you involved in anything after school? You love basketball. Did you try out for the team? I started working on the newspaper this week. I love writing, it's my new thing. With all the shit that's happened to me, everyone's telling me I should be keeping a journal. English has always been my favourite subject.

Too bad there's not going to be a talent show because of "the incident" last year. The school frowns on nudity. ☺ But I heard we might still have a play. Remember last year when I was Kenicky? In Grease? We actually put a lot of effort into it. Maybe we can try out together.

Write back, OK? Or phone me. I'll be waiting Monday after school near the bike racks.

Chris ☺

P.S. It must be difficult for you having a brother who's queer. But that shouldn't change things between us. Why should it? I hope no one's been giving you shit because of me. You'd tell me, right?

––––––––––

To: Jamie <sidthekid0087@hotmail.com>
From: Chris <snowflake92@hotmail.com>
Sent: Sunday, September 27, 2009 6:21:41 PM
Subject: Re: Where r u?

NO I didn't get fired. The boss just didn't like me. She didn't like any of the younger workers there. I know I was doing a good job and the kids liked me because they were pretty mean to some of my coworkers, but with me they were always fine. Every time I replaced one of the workers the kids were like, "Yay! We get Christopher."

It really is stupid why I had to quit. A few of the parents were like, "There's something about him we just don't enjoy." And I was like, "OK. Obviously we know what kind of person you are."

I guess the boss knew what the parents meant. She was like, "Is there any way you can tone it down? Just don't be so energetic. Don't be so, like, Ahhh! You know?" Funny, I didn't really notice it. I didn't think it was so bad.

I even spoke to one of my co-workers, but she said, "Let it go" because they complained about her, too, stuff that wasn't even true, and she almost quit. But I said, "To hell with it. I don't have to put up with that shit. I'm not changing for work or anyone." I quit and got another job. I went to my boss and told her I was leaving, and she had no objections. She was happy to see me go.

I was pretty upset because it just showed how people can be so intolerant. I guess they wanted to "protect" their children, or whatever. The whole thing's pretty pathetic.

But don't tell everyone about it, especially you-know-who. They'll just make a big deal out of it. I'm telling you because I want you to know you're a part of my life and that's not going to change no matter what. OK? I hope you'll always believe that.

C ☺

P.S. See you tomorrow.

———————

To: Jamie <sidthekid0087@hotmail.com>
From: Chris <snowflake92@hotmail.com>
Sent: Tuesday, September 29, 2009 7:33:40 PM
Subject: Sorry!

Sorry I wasn't there after school yesterday. I hope you didn't end up waiting for me. I had some trouble with these macho types. I won't go into all the gory details, but I had to wait around the principal's office for him to see me. He's an idiot. I have no respect for the man. Everyone says, "Tell the principal," but no matter what you tell him he's like, "What do you expect me to do?" Every time I speak to him he makes me real angry, so I figure I won't waste my time anymore going to him for help.

––––––––

To: Jamie <sidthekid0087@hotmail.com>
From: Chris <snowflake92@hotmail.com>
Sent: Wednesday, September 30, 2009 8:50:18 PM
Subject: Re: r u ok

There's nothing to worry about. You didn't tell, did you? Mom called last night, but I was out with Anna at a movie. She spoke with Nanny, and Nanny told me now Mom's got the idea I'm out partying, doing drugs, and going to clubs 24/7. She probably got that from Dad.

I'm gay, not stupid. I'm only sixteen and I don't even have a fake ID, so how can I be at bars and clubs? I've only been to the gay village a few times, only to like restaurants and cafés. And I was with Anna. So he doesn't know what he's talking about.

Stop worrying. What happened wasn't anything big. It started with these jocks screaming comments like, "faggot," and stuff like that. I'd be sitting in class and I guess they'd just feel like looking cool in front of their friends. But I can handle it. Like if I'm talking with some of my friends and we hear it I'm like, "Meh. Anyway. Back to what we were saying." My math teacher does nothing about it. Well, sometimes he screams really loud, "Shut the hell up!" As if that solves anything.

Miss McIntyre is one of the few teachers that does something. She actually tells people to lay off the comments and not to be so homophobic. She made me laugh the other day when she told them, "Calm down. It's not like he's going to jump you and have his way with you. Get over yourselves." That shut them up for the rest of the period. I can tell she thinks they're idiots, too. It's getting better. They don't do it as much as they did at the start of the year because I think after spending almost 2 months with me in the same class they've realized I'm not as bad as they thought.

They think calling me names can hurt me, but I won't show it. "Queer" has been used as an insult to me for so long. Like people have always called me "the queer." Or "faggot." Even when Dad didn't know about me, he'd call me that. I never want to hear that word again as long as I live.

Don't get the wrong idea. It's not like that all the time in every class. Well, I do get it in gym class. You know how much I hate gym. We usually have to play a team sport and some of the guys don't want me on their team. So I don't really try hard. The bigger ones, like the know-it-all hockey players, look at me and go, "OK. This is like playing with one of the girls. He doesn't know anything about sports. He's just a fag." But some guys in my class will still be like, "Keep trying. Don't let it get to you. Ignore them."

Sometimes I don't even bother doing gym. I'll just sit on the bench and talk with friends. The gym teacher knows about me, so when she sees I'm stressing she asks me what I feel comfortable doing. She asks me if I'd rather play with the girls because they're more open. Sometimes I do it if it's something I feel comfortable with, or I just stick with the guys and keep on trying.

Chris ☺

––––––––––

To: Jamie <sidthekid0087@hotmail.com>
From: Chris <snowflake92@hotmail.com>
Sent: Friday, October 2, 2009 3:35:47 PM
Subject: Re: r u ok

If you really want to know, I was just walking down the hallway at lunch towards the library. You know, by the door to the breezeway? They just don't like me. Some of them are these macho hockey jocks in grade 11 and are probably gay themselves and just too scared to admit it. One of them punched me in the back, and I turned around and went, "What the fuck was that for? I never did anything to you?" I think it was Tommy Desjardins, the wannabe king of the school. He's all like, "Fag," and started pushing me around, and all of them were laughing at me and stuff. Really immature for grade 11, eh? I just walked away 'cause I figured why bother, but I went to speak to the principal and he was like, "We'll solve it. We'll figure out what to do." But he never did anything. I think he doesn't believe me and that I made it up or I'm just some drama queen.

I'm sure he didn't talk to them because, if he had, they'd have confronted me the minute he said anything to them. All last week I kept going to him and I gave him their names and everything, but nothing happened.

I try not to take it personally. I'm not the only one they're against. They don't respect anybody, girls too. Anna was with me and she screamed at them to stop, so they told her, "Shut up bitch." But when they were like, "Fucking fag. Why don't you die?" to me, I was like, "OK. Thanks for telling me that." I just grabbed Anna by the arm and we walked away and they didn't come after us. I think they gave up because I didn't cry or show any emotion. My attitude was like, "Yeah. Sure. That's how you feel about me. Too bad. If you want me to disappear, that's not going to happen."

Now it's quiet. I know you want to help me but this is something I have to handle on my own.

Love,
Chris ☺

P.S. Don't let anyone push you around.

———————

To: Jamie <sidthekid0087@hotmail.com>
From: Chris <snowflake92@hotmail.com>
Sent: Sunday, October 4, 2009 4:07:52 PM
Subject: Re: r u ok

No, they aren't bothering me anymore. I don't know why they stopped, probably because they got tired or they wanted to see a reaction, you know, like, "I hate you," but I was just like, "OK. Bye."

I told my history teacher Miss McIntyre, but she said, "If the principal's not going to do anything about it, there's nothing I can do." That kind of surprised me. But then she told me she spoke to them anyway and she told them, "Listen. This nonsense has got to stop. Everybody should go to school in peace. High school's difficult enough, don't make it worse." So maybe that's why they've given it a rest.

When I first got kicked out of the house, everybody around me was like, "Why aren't you upset? Why aren't you crying?" I wanted to, but I didn't. I was listening to Jewel's "Hands" the whole, time and that song made me realize, in a way, I didn't have a reason to be upset because I knew this had to happen. It's only another life experience for me to go through, and I'll be stronger because of it. Hopefully. ☺

Love,
Chris

P.S. We still haven't met after school. This week for sure. OK?

———————

To: Jamie <sidthekid0087@hotmail.com>
From: Chris <snowflake92@hotmail.com>
Sent: Tuesday, October 6, 2009 4:05:28 PM
Subject: Latest news

I wanted to tell you something funny that happened today. You know the macho hockey players? Well two of them, count them, two of them, were put in my project group in history class. Actually it's all very ironic. So my group is me, one of the more accepting jocks, Brent, who thinks I'm OK, and the real macho one who doesn't like me at all. Never has. Never will. His name is something like Skip. Or Trip. Or Fall. He's a Neanderthal.

So today he told Brent, "I don't want to work with that fag. I'm not going to try hard." It's like, "Ooooooh! Screw you! You failing, yeah, that will teach me a lesson." I hope he hates me enough to repeat the whole year.

Brent told me because he thought what the caveman-with-a-puck said was mean and he doesn't find anything wrong with me. I don't really care. I mean, if that asshole doesn't like me and he's like, "I'm not going to try," well that's his problem. I wish Brent hadn't told me anything, though, because I'd rather not know.

So how about I wait for you Friday after school? OK?

Love,
Chris ☺

P.S. Anna says "Hi."

To: Jamie <sidthekid0087@hotmail.com>
From: Chris <snowflake92@hotmail.com>
Sent: Thursday, October 8, 2009 7:09:21 PM
Subject: Hanging out

I'm really happy we're meeting tomorrow. I'll be waiting for you near your bus after the final bell. Did you tell Mom? She'll wonder if you don't come home right after school.

I spoke to her again last night and she said I can't come home just yet because he's "not ready." Like what does that mean??? She'd only tell me, "He needs more time," and he loves me, but I'm not sure he said that part or if she's only saying that to make me feel better. Whatever.

Something weird happened today. At lunch I was walking down the hallway near the science labs and I saw this kid in your grade, or maybe a grade higher, being pushed around by these big kids and calling him, "Faggot!" I was like, "Yo! Leave him alone. If you think pushing people around makes you some sort of a hero, you're pathetic." One of them was like, "Oh. The faggot sticks up for the faggot," but I was like, "Go to hell." You know? And they walked away. The kid who was being pushed around even said "thank you" to me.

Well I guess it's not weird, really. Actually it made me kind of proud.

So 3:15. Be there!

Love,
Your brother,
Chris ☺

P.S. I miss you.

The Last Coming Out Story
A Novella

Chapter 1

THE BIGGEST QUEER at our school was Jean-François Giroux, the president of *Coalition arc-en-ciel*—the Rainbow Coalition—or "the gay club" as everyone calls it.

Now that the graduation ceremony is over, J.F. walks with his parents to their car, his father's hand placed protectively on his son's shoulder. As he leaves the school for the last time, I can't help but think he must have broken a speed record for going from the most popular student to the most hated. Though not for being gay.

And I wonder if I'll ever see him again.

I first noticed J.F. last September—the start of *secondaire IV* for me, and *secondaire V*, the graduating year, for him. One day during morning *récréation* he was standing near my locker at the students' bulletin board looking at the announcements for clubs, sports, and lost cats. He caught my attention because he looked hot. At our *école secondaire*, hot boys are as rare as Canadian flags, even though there are over eighteen hundred students, one of the biggest Francophone schools in Québec.

He had to be at least six-foot-one. My motto then was *Tall boys are worth the climb*, although I had yet to kiss a boy, let alone scale one. I'm well aware I'm an unimpressive five-nine. Well, almost.

Thinking I wasn't being all that obvious, I watched him as he stapled a big fluorescent pink poster to the bulletin board. His dark brown hair was buzzed short with a small Tintin patch sticking up in front, just above his forehead. He wore blue shorts with an ironed line down each leg, and a coordinated blue short-sleeved polo shirt. I wondered where the matching pail and shovel were. His clothes were definitely off drumming to their own beat. I'd learnt long ago how you dressed was Step One to fitting in at high school. It's simple enough— look at other students and wear what the majority's wearing. Usually I had on some loose jeans, a fitted cap, and either some obscure band's T-shirt or one with a random word on it. That day it was "ponder." And, yes, I wear my jeans so low you can see my boxers. That drives my parents mad. Sometimes before I step back into the house after a day at school, I tuck in my shirt and pull up my pants to make them happy.

What a strange mix! The softness of an oval face, the subtle curve of his nose in profile, his long eyelashes, but also the rugged strength implied by a natural tan and muscles that fill out clothes in a way mine never will. He stretched to staple the top of the poster, and his shirt rode up. I couldn't help but notice what had to be some rock hard abs. It was a change from the stick boys and doughy flesh forced on me during gym class. I quickly looked away. It's kind of pervy to stare like that.

It took some maneuvering—I had to fake-drop a book and "accidentally" kick it a couple of feet away—but when I moved closer to him to pick it up, I could see the eyes behind those lashes. Dark blue. Damn he was hot! It was love at first ogle.

J.F. glanced over at me and chuckled. Obviously he'd caught me looking at him, so I slammed the locker shut and speed-walked down the hall. Now that I think about it, I must have been quite a sight.

During lunch I went back to put away some books, but that was just an excuse. I wanted to see what he'd put up on the bulletin board. The poster wasn't hard to miss—it almost made my eyes water, it was that bright and cheerful. There were rainbows, hand-drawn and cut out of magazines, upside-down triangles, and a collage of hot models, girls and boys, that he probably found in fashion magazines. The biggest words were "*Coalition arc-en-ciel*," and underneath text described a new club forming "*pour combattre l'homophobie*" along with the date and time for the first meeting, a week away. *Straights welcome* was underlined.

"Is he gay?" I said out loud. Luckily no one else was in the hallway by then. Everyone was either in the cafeteria eating or outside racing across the playing fields to the nearest *dépanneur* to buy chips and chocolate bars and Coke and cigarettes. "The National Lunch of Québec," my father jokingly calls it. Eating junk food and destroying their lungs are all kids can do since they no longer can buy scratch lottery cards—the Québec government was trying to look like it was enforcing the legal age limit.

All of a sudden I felt weak. I sat on the cold floor under the bulletin board. I wasn't out at school yet. I didn't have a good reason *not* to tell everyone—I'd told my parents and sister and they were fine with it. But school might be another story. Not because I'd be beaten up or harassed in some horrible way. I didn't think my school was like that. Sure there's the everyday dose of ignorant homophobia—"*C'est gai*" is thrown around way too often for anyone's liking—but Québec, after all, is pretty damn progressive. It was one of the first places to put protection against discrimination on the basis of sexual orientation in the *Chartre des droits et libertés de la personne* way back in the 1970s. There's even a section in our history book about it.

My father loves to go on and on about how liberal Québec is. He sees himself as a keen observer of all things Québécois, an "outsider" well placed to note "foibles and quirks," even though he's been living here for thirty-five years.

My parents are British immigrants and only became Canadians after I was born. They would've done it sooner, but they were still test-driving the country. Since neither of my parents was educated in English in Québec, I'm not eligible to attend an English school. *La loi 101*—the Language Law. A way around it would've been for my parents to have sent me to private school, but they don't go for posh elitist nonsense. So that's how I ended up pretty much one-hundred-percent bilingual—living in an English home and going to school all my life in French. The best of both worlds, I suppose. When I speak French, no one would guess I'm English—my accent's spot on. Well, my father insists I have a mid-Atlantic accent sometimes, like when I meet someone new. Francophones only know I'm English when I tell them my name, Spencer Roache, although I avoid saying my last name to Anglos so I don't have to hear the exterminator jokes. It's not even pronounced that way. Last year my English teacher made a dumb Kafka remark to me, although I didn't know what he was talking about until I looked it up on Wikipedia.

Had I wanted to come out to the world and his dog, Québec was certainly the place to do it. I had no real reason not to other than I didn't want to draw attention to myself. I was already the token Anglo at school. I didn't need *gay* added to that shepherd's pie.

I saw J.F. again a few days later, putting up another one of those posters outside the *bibliothèque*. He was wearing a multi-coloured tie-dyed T-shirt and frayed jeans that went wide at the bottoms. And a headband. Seriously.

I'd like to say he was re-inventing the style, making it trendy again with a few new twists thrown in, but his clothes merely looked old like they were found in a second-hand store. Maybe someone was unfairly tear-gassed at a riot in 1969 wearing that outfit, but how wrong would it be to gas someone who'd wear that today?

Like usual, I had on jeans and one of my one-word T-shirts. "Whimsy."

J.F. chewed on his lip as he positioned and re-positioned the poster on the wall until it was just right. The meeting was the next day, and I don't know why, but it worried me. I half-expected someone would stop him or something, even though that didn't make sense. Surely he must have permission from the administration. Now I know I'd only been worried about the inevitability of my own coming out at school.

I had to walk by him to go to the library, and when I pulled open the library door, he nodded at me.

"Ça va?"

I nodded back, though it just as easily could've looked to him like a nervous tic or a mild stroke. A just-saw-a-hot-boy brain aneurism. I tried entering the library before I had fully opened the door, so I had to squeeze in like toothpaste in reverse. I'm sure he found that amusing as well.

That night I lay in bed and argued with myself whether I would go to the meeting. The poster said straights were welcome, too. If someone wondered why I was there, couldn't I say I was doing my part for human rights? By morning I'd convinced myself I could go to the meeting and be assumed to be as straight as the next guy, without having to say anything that would betray who I really was. *The gay me,* I called it. Cowardice I could live with. Hypocrisy, not so much.

Self-delusion was something else altogether.

Chapter 2

I PUT ON MY BACKPACK, overfilled with books I'd never take out later, and walked towards *la chapelle*, the school's common room where the first meeting was being held. It wouldn't hurt to pass by and see what's going on.

All day I'd kept changing my mind about going, finally deciding to take my regular bus home when the last bell rang. But when school was over, I'd lingered at my locker debating which books to bring with me, distractedly putting book after book in my backpack although studying was the last thing on my mind. I even organized the top shelf—where I found in its farthest reaches a one-bite-missing sandwich of some dirty dark brown paste-like substance I was positive had never been mine—until the buses left. I'd have to take the late bus home.

Approaching the room, I didn't hear the expected sound of people, and I figured the meeting had been cancelled. For some reason I'd anticipated the place would be filled—an oasis of gay boys and lesbians, with a sprinkling of straights for good measure. This picture fed my fantasy that a real cute guy I'd never seen before would be waiting for me. I was such a sucker for a happy ending back then.

I walked past the open door with the air of someone who had a completely different destination in mind—someone straight who was most likely off to do sports or have sex with his girlfriend. I only wanted the chance to glance casually into the room to see who was there, but as I walked past I saw J.F. in front, in full view of the door, sitting alone. He seemed so lonely I couldn't help but slow down to take a good look. Naturally he saw me. He smiled, and I looked away. I quickened my pace. Sometimes I'm such a pussy.

Five steps past the door, I stopped. This is stupid, I told myself. On pure impulse I turned around and walked into the room. My big chance to be brave. Anyway, it didn't take much guts since I thought J.F. was alone.

He wasn't.

"*Bonjour! Bienvenue!*" J.F. motioned for me to take a seat.

"*Salut,*" I replied and beelined it to a chair in the back. From where I sat I could see what J.F. had on—tight black pants and a white dress shirt buttoned to his throat. He'd have looked like a waiter, except he had on a thin tie with a piano keys pattern. His fashion choices were a mystery to me.

There were two other people there: a girl with a long, droopy face and stringy brown hair stood in the middle of the room, dressed overly *bohème*, and a *secondaire II* or *secondaire III* boy with a red cap who sat in the back opposite me, intent on reading a poster on the wall beside him about *Journée internationale de l'alphabétisation*—International Literacy Day.

The mousy girl was talking about animals. I began to make sense of what she was saying—she was telling J.F. how little our school did to ensure the dignity of animals. She spoke about animal testing and fur and leather. She made frequent references to the cafeteria. We sat there for what seemed like forever while she pleaded for a world where animals, apparently, could roam free and people would eat weeds. Or one another. What did she care? It wasn't her issue.

It was amazing how patient J.F. was with her. I couldn't do it. He listened like someone who was interested. He nodded his head as though he understood her point and might even agree; he made direct eye-contact; and he shook his head with appropriate disgust at the gory parts, like when she described in detail how chickens are killed to make McNuggets or a barrel of *Poulet Frit Kentucky*. She only stopped talking when the boy with the red cap stood up and walked out without a word.

She looked startled that someone had the nerve to leave in the middle of what she was saying, as if the gravity of the topic should glue someone there. For a second J.F. also looked concerned that a third of his audience had just deserted him, but he did nothing to stop the red cap boy from leaving. I doubted we'd see the kid again.

The room was a former chapel, transformed into a meeting room now that the school's no longer religious. Stained glass windows remained along one wall and there was a raised platform in the front where the altar must have been. On the platform there were a small round table and two wooden chairs, one placed upside down on the seat of the other one. Above was some track lighting, and all three spotlights were aimed at the chairs, illuminating them like they were important. The back of the platform was a wall of red brick, and exactly where I imagined the cross had been now hung a framed picture of children's hands, one on top of the other, with the word *"Diversité"* underneath in bold black letters. It was like the room was trying too hard.

My father would love to see what became of the school's chapel. "Despite decades of domination by The Church, the Québécois are now decidedly anti-Catholic," he tells people, especially visitors from outside the province. Last summer he went on about that to my mother's cousin from England who came to visit us for a week. I think it's a strange thing for him to rabbit on about, as he likes to say other people do about politics, when he's not religious at all and never talks about religion at any other time or in any other situation. My mom's cousin is excessively religious, and I'm sure she went back to Manchester vowing never to come back to such a heathen place.

He's always on about how Québec's "the epitome of social liberalism gone mad." He used to give the legalization of same-sex marriage as an example, but I notice he doesn't do that now that he knows I'm gay, except to tell people that in Québec seventy-six percent of the people support it. I can detect some pride in his voice when he says that. All these years in Canada have made him into a Socialist, even if he's in the closet about it.

"I want to know," the girl said, finally getting to the point. "What is your club's position on animals?"

The question echoed in the near-empty room and it was answered by a long silence. J.F. blinked three times most likely choosing which of many possible answers he should go with. I'm not sure how much consideration he gave to the more serious responses, but given the way his mouth turned up ever so slightly at the corners, I knew he had picked something less reverential than she might have liked.

"Well, we won't date any, if that's what you're worried about."

The rabid PETA-girl went through a handful of tortured expressions as she took in J.F.'s reply. Her face relaxed as she settled on her understanding of J.F.'s words, classifying them, and him, in whatever box she has for meat eaters, fur and leather wearers, and other such butchers.

She turned on her sandaled-heels and walked out the door, too.

"Okay," J.F. said more to himself than me, "this is going well."

He walked to where I sat, dragging a chair along with him. It scraped along the floor until he could sit down in front of me. He put out his hand.

"Jean-François."

"Spencer."

I shook his hand. I have to admit, I was a bit shy to touch him. When I did, tiny ribbons of charged sensation goose-bumped my arm, and I had to fight against giving him this goofy grin that would've easily betrayed my thrill. He leaned in closer, and for a second I thought he was trying to smell me. My cheeks warmed and I pulled back slightly, then I realized he hadn't understood my name. Spencer isn't one Francophones hear that often, so I said it again. He smiled and leaned back on the chair, his leg momentarily rubbing against mine as he did. Another thrill.

"Guess there's only the two of us, Spencer." In his mouth my name broke into two distinct parts: spen-sair. I should've corrected him, but the way he said it was kind of cute.

Just then one of the *adjoints*, the male one, stomped into the room and looked around as if scouring for drug caches. I never liked that vice-principal. He rushes around and marches into classrooms and barks at people. He hunts for problems that don't exist and accuses people of things that haven't happened. What creeps me out the most about him are his eyes—they're forever moving, searching, seeking out anomalies that might be warning signs. He's like a truffle-pig on a sugar-high. He makes students nervous, but I guess that's the idea. The female *adjointe*, on the other hand, smiles all the time, and whenever there's a problem she hides in her office with the door closed. We like her more.

"*Ça va?*" Monsieur Courtois said, and tugged on the reins of his tie that everyone said the *directrice* held at the other end. His clothes never fitted—they were too small, or more likely he was too big for them. He seemed ready to pop out of his suit, like a tube of refrigerated dinner rolls, should he bump into the edge of a counter.

"*Pas pire,*" J.F. swatted at his bare arm, then scratched it like a mosquito had bitten him. He left white lines on his tanned skin that I watched fade away.

"Is there a teacher here?" His Buddha belly pointed straight at J.F.

"Why?"

In a vice-principal's world, being asked a question is a direct challenge.

"This is an after-school activity, right?" he said with a controlled tone, clearly willing himself not to show anger. Still, his thick eyebrows shrunk together to form a single line above his eyes. They'd been left to grow freely as if to compensate for his receding hairline. One morning he must have woken and decided to shave off what was left of his hair, but you could still see the stubble where hair ended and scalp began—the line between youthful hair and a head like peeled garlic.

Perhaps it was just me, but he made the word "activity" sound highly suspect, like we were up to something sordid and diabolical. Sex came right to mind, but that could've been my hormones.

"You need a teacher advisor if you're starting a club." Monsieur Courtois spoke slowly as though addressing five-year-olds. "Don't you know that?"

"We'll look into it." J.F. gave the man a reassuring smile. As quickly as he stormed into the room, the *adjoint* was gone.

"*Bizarre!*" J.F. said.

"*Farfelu!*" I said, and it made J.F. laugh. I have to admit I was pleased with myself about that. It either impresses or pisses off Francophones that I have a bigger vocabulary in French than a lot of them do. Not to mention how I get in trouble in English class because of my vocabulary there. I mean, come on! The English teacher, Monsieur Félix, barely speaks it. He tried to tell us the English word for "*pantalons*" is "pantaloons" instead of "pants." He kicked me out of class when I tried to explain to him what pirates wear. It would've been better all around if he'd stuck to letting us silently read *The Great Gatsby* like we usually did.

Language is a hot-button issue here in Québec. Both my parents speak French more or less—my mom more, my dad less. He speaks it like a real *vache espagnole*—like a Spanish cow. It makes me cringe to hear his accent, but I have to give him credit because he still tries given he started so late in life, even if he speaks more *Franglais* than French proper. I know some Francophones see him as *un tête carrée*—some English "blockhead." In return he calls them "separatists" and not the more politically correct "*souverainistes*" like my mother does, which my father says is just "separatist lite." He likes to think he's more controversial than he is.

In the vice-principal's vacuum, J.F. and I sat there. In the hallway I could hear a janitor walk up and down with a push broom rounding up the day's litter of loose-leaf paper balls and snack wrappers. When I was sure J.F. and I were doomed to remain trapped in an uncomfortable silence, he said, "So, I guess you want to know what this is all about."

I nodded, a bit too eager, a bit too grateful.

"I'm hoping *Coalition arc-en-ciel* will make the school aware of homophobia. You know, try to stop gay insults and bullying. Things like that. Maybe more students will join when it gets going. And by *more*, I mean a few more people than only us two." J.F. laughed again.

As he spoke, not once did his dark blue eyes move away from me. *I* wanted to turn away. Looking unwaveringly into someone's eyes makes me uncomfortable. What teenage boy doesn't feel that way? But I didn't look away, though I have to admit I didn't take in much of what he said. He was so close now, leaning towards me so he could speak to me as though he was about to reveal some deep dark secret. I wasn't really listening as I was too busy asking myself if he was coming on to me, and at the same time doing my best not to give the impression that worried me.

He said something about letter-writing campaigns, and how he'd been involved in the Amnesty International Club last year, and how that's where he came up with the idea to start *Coalition arc-en-ciel*. I got that much. His hands moved as he spoke, direct and forceful one moment as they poked the air to make a point, light and musical the next as they arced through the air when he explained something.

I won't even go into his ever-so-slight hint of a "wisp" when he spoke, as a relative from England calls it, the daughter of the born-again who'd visited us last summer. The girl has one, too, although my mother, ever the optimist, says she'll outgrow it. She's twenty-two now.

It isn't right for me to say—it makes me sound shallow and ignorant and fooled into giving stereotypes more power than they deserve—but J.F. had an obvious gay vibe. Yes, I know. I've read online all about self-loathing gays who have contempt for anyone who's not straight acting. Surely noticing this about him didn't make me *that* bad. It's a good thing, I told myself. If I had the slightest doubt, if there was ever a second or two when I couldn't believe there existed another gay guy at school, I watched J.F. and the way he spoke or moved, and I could pick out my evidence one-by-one. As stereotypical and sad as that was.

"We can do some good here," I heard him say as I tuned in again. "Maybe we can make this place a bit more . . . open." He smiled some more. "Out and open," he added, then laughed some more.

"What about him?" I jerked a thumb towards the door and wherever in the building the *adjoint* was ferreting out evil. "Is he trying to stop us?"

J.F. grinned. I could tell he liked that I used "us," although I hadn't meant to. I hoped he didn't think I meant "us" as more than us working together. I had to have been blushing.

"Leave him to me," he said. I admired his confidence. I was still waiting for mine to be delivered.

J.F. continued looking right at me though he'd stopped talking.

Could he tell I think he's hot? And now that I'd listened to him speak with such passion, even hotter? I turned away and squinted as if I'd just discovered the literacy poster myself and was intent on learning more about the festivities that went along with such international theme days.

"Are you with me on this?" He tapped me on the knee to get my attention. It worked. But I didn't need any distractions right then. This was my chance to dodge being drawn into what had all the omens of an impending high school disaster. A big *gay* high school disaster at that. I looked back into his eyes and mumbled, "Yes. Of course I am."

Straight up, I was crushing on him big time and would've agreed to anything he'd have asked me. Gutting a puppy to the wailing of that PETA girl wouldn't have been off the table.

Chapter 3

A WEEK LATER in the cafeteria, J.F. bounced over to my table, sat down, and listed all the things *we* needed to do once the coalition was up and running. I was sitting at one of the long tables near the salad bar with Rachelle Monchamps and her boyfriend Étienne Leblanc who was brave enough, or fool-hardy enough, to be eating the daily special, coagulated red sauce ladled onto soggy spiral pasta. Even from the other side of the table it smelled like it was well on its way to compost. Rachelle's a year ahead of me, in *secondaire V*, J.F.'s grade. Étienne's in mine.

"We still have to find a staff advisor. Any ideas?" He pulled out an apple from his pocket and presented it to me like it was the ending of a magician's trick. I shook my head. Then he held it out to Rachelle and Étienne. They looked shocked like offering someone fresh fruit was comparable to pushing heroin.

J.F. shrugged and took a bite.

"Not a clue," I said. "I don't really know teachers well enough to say." Maybe that would shut him down.

Despite my telling J.F. I'd be involved, I'd rethought the whole thing and had decided that as much as I wanted to see him again, I didn't necessarily have to be a part of his gay club to do that. I was working on sly ways to run into him in the hallways, near his locker, and outside at morning *récréation* or after school. *Par hasard.* I'd thought up a few good ones, but minimal scrutiny told me they were all very obvious, and I knew I'd appear desperate if I actually did any of them.

It's a bit pathetic strategizing like that. I know it's a little sad. But I couldn't help myself.

"Everything's a go for Tuesday's meeting," J.F. said, and made some of his hand gestures.

I watched Rachelle and Étienne to see if they were picking up on his gay-vibe, and instantly felt guilty that I cared about something like that. I thought Rachelle would be taken aback by how . . . well . . . *energetic* J.F. was being. I knew she wouldn't be best pleased that he interrupted her mid-story about her new cell phone and how many text messages she'd already received. Étienne even stopped wood-chipping through a double-decker ham sandwich, having already devoured the daily special, to look J.F. over. He tried giving him a "gangsta" glare, but it came across as slightly peeved and mostly constipated.

Rachelle and I had lunch every Thursday so she could brag about what's been happening to her and update me on her plans for the weekend, and Étienne could nod while power-eating.

I've known Rachelle since I was seven years old. Our parents used to have dinner parties and go to the cinema, though they don't do much together anymore. Rachelle's mother's a bit of a drunk and likes to "be real" when she's inebriated. I heard my mom say to someone on the phone, "How often can that woman point out other people's weight problems and not think she's offensive?"

Rachelle and I used to be baby-sat together by the mother of a French teacher at my mom's school, a large woman my mother's size from Haïti who'd make us pick dandelions from neighbours' yards so she could make wine. It was fun actually. For a long time I thought dandelion wine was a Haitian thing until my mother told me Anacaona, or Ana as we called her, had worked for a German family when she first arrived in Québec. Rachelle and I would laugh while we were picking because in French dandelion is *"pissenlit." Piss*-en-lit. *En-lit* means *in bed.* It was at par with giggling at the French word for seal, *"phoque,"* the little animal prone to being clubbed to death. No matter what language you speak, that word never needs translating. Ana must have said *pissenlit* a thousand times, and we'd laugh each time, until I went too far and teased Rachelle that her hair was the same colour as the flowers. She didn't speak to me for a week.

Rachelle was cool when I came out to her. When I'd told her last year, waiting for the week before summer vacation, I thought it would've spread through the school like mono, but Rachelle reassured me no one was talking about it. I wasn't that important.

"Don't forget to remind me to put up more posters." J.F.'s "wisp" made *posters* sound mushy.

He stood, ready to rush off. He wore another shovel-and-pail outfit, this time it was beige, and instead of shorts he now had on pants. The harsh cafeteria lights practically gleamed off the razor-sharp creases. For some reason he had a plastic protector in his shirt pocket with one old-school, cheap, clear plastic Bic pen. He probably had the matching lighter, too.

My T-shirt word was "sophism" that everyone, including the art teacher, mistook for a girl's name.

"I'm sure we can get at least three members by this time next week," J.F. joked. He waved goodbye by making his fingers dance in the air. Then he was gone again.

My emotions were ramped up *au maximum*—an intoxicating mixture of lust and embarrassment. I was worried what Rachelle, and to a lesser degree Étienne, thought of J.F., as if it reflected on me, which of course it didn't. I still felt I should apologize to them, but I couldn't figure out what for. His interruption? His energy? His clothes? I wasn't so disconnected from healthy self-doubt to know the bottom line was I was worried what they would think about me by association.

Before I could think up something to say that didn't make me seem like the superficial jerk I was, Rachelle leaned towards me from her side of the table and said in English, "He's hot!" Then she gave her head a slight tilt and added, "In a pretty boy way."

Étienne snapped up from his rapidly disappearing sandwich as though it was morning and his dream of owning some motorized vehicle, like a scooter, had just been interrupted by the alarm clock.

"Yes, I said it," she warned him in French. "I'm allowed to look. Anyway, he's gay."

"How do *you* know?" Étienne said. Or at least that's what I heard him say with his mouth full.

"When he came out, everyone was talking about it. Back in *secondaire III. Tabarnouche!*" Rachelle loves to swear, although she's not that good at it—it never quite rings true. It's not only the way she says swearwords, pronouncing each syllable clear and elegant like she's at high tea, it's also her choice of them. "*Tabarnouche*" is a watered-down version of "*tabernacle*," much like "shoot" for "shit" and "fudge" instead of "fuck." As my father has pointed out more times than I care to remember, "English profanities are about sex while in French they're all about religion." The Church can't get a break with my dad. Given the choice, Rachelle inevitably chooses the lesser of two curse words. Still, she's convinced her feeble attempts at swearing make her edgy.

She turned to Étienne, one eye squinting with disbelief. "It was a major news flash. He was like the first to come out in my grade. Where've you been hiding?" As it usually does when Rachelle states what she thinks is obvious, her nose wrinkled in a way that some people might think cute but for the annoyed tone of voice that accompanied it.

Étienne shrugged and went back to chewing. Before he swallowed, he began licking butterscotch pudding off a spoon with a pained expression like it was offensive to the core of his being.

It was a big deal when he showed up at school with a tattoo on his neck, but it's so small it can easily be mistaken for a love bite Rachelle became disinterested in halfway through. I still don't know what it's supposed to be. A skull? A Japanese symbol? A panda? Rachelle says it makes him appear dangerous, but for someone so dangerous, I've never seen him do anything she hasn't told him to.

Rachelle could very well ask where Étienne's been hiding, but the real question was, *Where had I been?* How did everyone in the school know J.F. was gay except me? I spent *secondaire II* and *secondaire III* wondering if I was the only one. I'd heard of a gay guy in the grade ahead of me, but it always seemed more a high school urban legend than fact—the elusive queer everyone's sure is sitting right in the next class. I could've put down a foothold trap to find him, but I'd be lost to come up with anything to bait it with that isn't a tired gay cliché. My first instinct was to go with old boy band CDs.

"So," Rachelle said to me. "Interested?" She was speaking English again. She usually spoke to me in English—while her father was Francophone, her mother was an Anglo, too. Whenever we spoke English at school, especially if we might be overheard, Rachelle did it quietly, as quietly as she could and still be heard above hundreds of kids eating and talking all at once. If that wasn't enough ambiance, it was fashionable about then to drop a tray of plates and cutlery when you were through eating so it made a loud clatter. Everyone would laugh and clap and stomp their feet. Trust me, there was no shortage of assholes who were willing to do it.

We had to speak so no one could hear us—we'd already been caught once by the *adjoint*. "You aren't allowed to speak English except in English class," Monsieur Courtois had told us. He squinted repeatedly so his unruly eyebrows came alive, struggling to escape his face. I could tell Rachelle was gagging to take tweezers to them.

He'd threatened to give us detentions or tell our parents if he caught us again. What a joke! While I didn't give a damn about the detention, I didn't want my father finding out.

Not that he'd do something to me, like ground me or something. I just knew if he heard the school had a rule against speaking English, he'd threaten to speak to the *directrice*, and I'd have to listen again to his backpacking-across-the-continent stories until he calmed down and forgot about showing up at school.

As though our silly school rule was at the same level of Cold War totalitarianism, my father, no doubt, would tell the story of how he was followed and *almost* kidnapped by the Stasi in Communist East Germany. He makes it sound very MI6, but combined with his hatred for how the Québec government thinks promoting one language has to mean denigrating another, it wouldn't be a fun tale to hear one more time.

"The insecurity of being a French fish in an ocean of English," he'd say to the principal if he found out, shaking his head in disbelief and a finger of disapproval at the woman. "What a load of codswallop!" It'd be the start of a full-blown language war, and knowing my father, he'd try to recruit me to the cause. "Can you believe it, Spencer my boy?" He'd wait for me to add my two cents to the *directrice*, and I'd be forced to fake Ebola or something, running out of the office to spend the next half hour hiding in the disgusting boys' toilets trying not to breathe in or touch anything. Yes, Mélodie St-Onge *does* have gigantic boobs. Even I noticed. The cubicle wall doesn't lie.

"So?" Rachelle repeated and fluttered her eyelashes at me, then said with a slow, breathy emphasis, "Do you want him?" She leaned over to me so her face was close and I could smell the perfume on her, a mix of cotton candy and lilies that made me throw up a little in my mouth. It was like pigtails at a funeral. I was sure she secretly knew it smelled awful, too, and only wore it because it was popular and expensive. Étienne looked up again with a worried expression like it actually limped through his mind that she might cheat on him with *me* of all people. That was when I decided their relationship was at a frequency only dogs could hear.

I'm sure I blushed at Rachelle's question, and her physical proximity, desperately trying to think up a witty comeback that didn't involve comparing her to a *pissenlit* again.

Thankfully the bell rang. Lunch was over. I'd successfully dodged more embarrassing questions.

Chapter 4

THE NEXT MEETING of *Coalition arc-en-ciel* had already begun when I arrived. J.F.'s voice echoed in the hallway as I neared the room.

"Our purpose is to create a safer, more respectful learning environment for all students, gay or straight."

When he saw me walk in, I swear his face lit up.

Imagine, I almost wasn't there to see that. First I'd struggled with showing up at all. Then I'd tried until the last minute to convince myself that even if I did go to the meeting, I didn't have to become involved. I suppose that kind of reasoning is like wanting to go swimming without having to get wet. I believed I could be an observer, not do anything, and still win J.F.'s heart, somehow, though I'd yet to come up with a feasible plan to achieve that.

"We also want to inform students and teachers of issues that effect the lives of lesbian, gay, bisexual, transgender, and straight ally youth." He went to the whiteboard and drew one of those upside-down triangles and coloured it in with a red dry erase marker. The marker made noises that sounded like he was torturing mice. Well, relentlessly *teasing* them at least. It was J.F. after all.

"This is the pink triangle. The Nazis made homosexuals wear it in concentration camps during the Second World War. Lots of LGBT organizations use it today as a reminder. If anyone's good at art, maybe you can design a logo for our group." J.F. looked around the room.

Madame Maria, the Spanish teacher, sat at her desk. J.F. had asked her to be the staff advisor, and now we met in her classroom. She'd been the staff advisor for the Amnesty International Club when I was in *secondaire II*. She wouldn't have been my first choice—she's Mexican-American and a Catholic, so I was unsure what she'd think about the whole gay thing. But J.F. assured me she was "on our team," although I hadn't an idea what team he was talking about. Sports analogies escape me.

"Give her a chance," he'd told me earlier in the day, having stopped me on my way to gym to deliver the news. I tried to look pleased. "She said she'd deal with the vice-principal so we won't have problems." I was surprised to hear him say that—J.F. gave the impression he was well able to deal with Monsieur Courtois himself.

Rachelle loves her, though. Well, she loves the woman's "Texas hair." Once when all those curls and big volume walked by, Rachelle gushed, "It's so late seventies, y'all," imitating the accent as though half-pronouncing words was sexy. Don't ask me. I thought the style was more suggestive of early drag queen. Tomato, potato.

While J.F. spoke, every so often Madame Maria picked up some random piece of paper off her desk and then put it back down, like she wanted us to think she wasn't listening. She wore the black camisole that Rachelle loves her in, and I call underwear, and a mustard jacket that made the woman look like she was desperate to talk mortgages and closing dates.

J.F. had been right that the ranks of the coalition would swell, that's if you counted the four new members at that meeting, all girls, three of whom sat in desks in the first row and looked up lovingly at J.F. and giggled a lot. He leaned against the teacher's desk right in front of them, which caused more giggling and a few stifled shrieks of delight. They were the type of girls who stayed home on Friday and Saturday nights to write fan fiction about *Lord of the Rings* characters—Aragorn and Legolas in sweaty embrace. That is, in between instant messaging each other about all the cute things and cuddly boys they "♥" for life.

And the red cap boy was back, sitting next to a wall again, looking with great interest at the poster Madame Maria liked to call our attention to when reminding us how to conjugate Spanish verbs: *yo quiero, tú quieres, él quiere.* Some things never change.

I still don't know if the girls were gay, straight, or bi, but I seriously suspected they were straight since they seemed attracted to the club more by J.F.'s hotness than any real commitment to social justice. What bothered me the most was they were so blatant about it. They were at the age where they melted over nonthreatening, non-sexual boys. If that's how they saw J.F., it made no sense to me at all. But as far as I was concerned, they could go right on thinking J.F. as non-sexual, since to them that's what he might as well be. As if he'd be interested in them! Looking around at the options, I was the only one in the room whom J.F. could possibly have sex with. I mean, that's *if* he was going to have sex with anyone. Not that he was about to or anything. And, no, I'm not saying I'm hot or anything.

Near the windows, a girl with glasses and iPod earbuds that hung around her neck like jewelry since they were never in her ears the times I'd seen her around school, put up her hand like J.F. was a teacher.

"I'll make the logo."

J.F. thanked her and continued explaining about the coalition. The three girls seemed to be holding back squeals of glee whenever he said *"arc-en-ciel."* God they were annoying! Just because you like some Katy Perry song about kissing a girl doesn't make you an advocate for gay rights. Far from it!

I tried to keep focused on what J.F. was saying, but I have to admit I was distracted by and a little pissed off at the girls in the front row. They kept nodding their heads, agreeing with everything he said, though I'm sure they didn't understand a word of it, especially when he brought up heterosexism and heteronormativity. I was even lost for a minute. Their eyelids weakened with adoration. He might as well have been talking about unicorns. Having to witness that, I felt like I'd been gored by one.

Madame Maria cleared her throat and said a few words of welcome, then the meeting was over. I wanted to hang around so I could speak with J.F., but the girls ran up to him, and it was all uncontrolled screeching from then on. So I left.

As I walked out of the room I heard one of them say, "I love your idea for the club. I want you to know I'll do anything I can to help you."

I felt sick and angry and light-headed all together. I don't remember ever experiencing that before.

I went to get my things and catch the late bus. By the time I slammed my locker shut, J.F. was there leaning against the locker next to mine.

"What do you think?"

I shrugged. I was pretty down. If car accidents seem like they're happening in slow motion, why don't people do something to avoid them? Here was my opportunity to steer clear of the impending ten-car pile-up of the coalition. I only had to turn the wheel.

"Hey!" J.F. said with his usual hyper level of energy. "Wanna get a coffee? There's so much I have to tell you."

Naturally I said, "*Bien sûr,*" trying not to sound *too* enthusiastic. I'm sure I failed. From doom to the moon in one second flat. I felt like a banana on the day it's ripe. This was so much better than any plan I could've come up with. Ha! Spencer, one. Giggling fan club girls, zero.

At a restaurant near school, a deli where natural lighting went to die, I followed J.F. to a booth near the back next to the kitchen doors. I'd been there a few times before to wait for my parents when I missed the bus. The place smelled of smoked meat sandwiches and French fry oil.

"My usual place," J.F. said. Not that I was a regular, but I'd never seen him there. I made a mental note that that had to change.

"Slowly but surely we'll get there," he said after we'd ordered from a waitress who took a long time to write down the two simple things we asked for—a cappuccino for him and an Earl Grey for me. She walked away without a word.

J.F. chuckled.

"You're laughing at me." Suddenly I was self-conscious and acting pathetic *au bout.*

"Not at all. It's the waitress. I don't think she's heard silent movies are dead?" He paused. "Well, it's a bit you, too. I don't know many English." As if that explained it all. Maybe I *was* being insulted and it was time to leave, but J.F. was looking at me, again straight in the eye, so I felt I couldn't get up and walk out. It would've been rude, right? And then he put his hand on mine. What chance did I have?

"It's okay," he said. "I'm not laughing *at* you. You're cute—I mean, the things you do." He must have seen the immediate sting of those words on my face, as much as I tried to hide it. "Cute looking, too," he added reassuringly. Nothing about me seemed to slip past him. We both smiled, him wide and happy, me shy and inwardly ecstatic.

The waitress returned, placed our order on the table and stood there. Only when J.F. said, "*Merci,*" did she walk away. Still not a word.

"This place's not unlike mime hell." J.F. emptied two packets of sugar into his coffee.

We sipped our drinks, then broke out laughing at how hot they were. We left them to cool down, and sat in silence.

I tried appearing like I was intent on the contents of my cup, knowing very well his eyes were probably still looking at me. I didn't know what to say to break the quiet—I mentally rehearsed things I hoped would make me sound funny and smart, but they were all lame.

"So," he began. I looked up. I was right. His blue eyes were fixed on me, filled with the usual joy. Dancing even. "English, eh? Where are your parents from?"

Francophones are always asking me where my parents are "from," like my mom and dad climbed out of the bowels of a ship last week to find themselves blinking in the sunlight as they walk down a gangway, steamer trunks in tow. I hoped for more from J.F.

"Oh, sorry." His brow wrinkled with concern. "I'm not trying to make some *pure laine* statement, like you're family's not welcome here."

Not to argue, I recited my parents' bios, hoping they were dry enough to cause him to change the subject.

"They're British. My dad was born in London and grew up near Hampstead Heath. He came to Montréal as a young mechanical engineer, like many from the U.K. before him, to work for a Canadian engineering company on a natural gas pipeline. He met my mom at a club on rue Montagne downtown, an old funeral home converted into a disco."

Here I paused for air. Whenever my father tells the story—and he does it more often than you'd think—he likes to say he made a point of dancing right where the coffins stood during services. But I don't say *that*. He showed up the whole family last summer when he repeated it to my mother's born-again cousin. The poor woman. The Rapture won't happen soon enough for her.

"My mother came from Manchester to be an au pair for some Richie-Rich Westmount family. She went on to become a teacher, and she still teaches at an English elementary school near our house. Grade one. Every year she builds a bear cave with her students in the corner of her classroom, and they have teddy bear picnics inside."

J.F. laughed. As boring as I tried to make it, what I was saying amused him. I'm not one for talking up a storm, but it was cool that I had his attention. Even if I had to talk about my parents to get it.

"My dad loves telling the story of how they met, making it sound so exotic." My voice went low and mysterious for him. "Two expatriate Brits venture into the darkness of the New World, finding each other and love in the Canadian wilderness. The way he describes it, you'd think he was Henry Hudson sailing here on HMS Discovery in the seventeenth century, with a similar fate, rather than having flown here on a British Airways jet in 1974."

My mother usually adds to the story that the "stewardesses" (and she still calls them that) were "sweet" and gave her ginger ale to help calm her stomach since it was her first time on a plane. She thinks everyone's sweet. She's the kind of mom who hugs a lot and doesn't let go. That's the one thing that bugs me about her.

Story time over, J.F. gave me a big, content smile that could melt ice on a February morning. At least he found me entertaining. It was a start.

"And *your* parents?" Turnabout is fair play. I wondered if anything made him uncomfortable.

"My family's only my parents." His voice went quieter like he'd walked into a library or a church. He told me his mother and father never married but they've been living *en union de fait*, common-law *con-joints* for almost twenty years now.

Don't get my father started on that subject either. "Did you know," he says at the slightest mention of someone's relationship, a lecture *prêt a l'emploi*, "that Québec is the world's leader when it comes to common law marriage? Thirty percent of couples here are living together and *aren't* married. That's more than Sweden and Finland!" His voice goes higher when he lists facts.

"Not married, huh? How's that?" Sometimes my parents seem so boring with their twenty-five years of off-the-shelf wedlock, stamped and approved by the Anglican Church and everything, despite my father's atheism. It's probably too late for them to consider giving polygamy a go just to give me a more interesting back story.

"If they got married now it would sketch me out," J.F. said. "It's a bit late to change my name to Jean-François Archambault-Giroux."

"Hmm," I agreed. "A bit of a mouthful. I doubt it would fit on the back of an iPhone."

"They love each other so much, though. I see it every day. I catch them holding hands all the time. It's so cute. They're two of the most loving people I know."

I could tell he respected his parents a lot. I love my parents, too, but I'm not above teasing them a bit. I mean, that's what kids do.

J.F. tried to make it sound like his parents not being married was unimportant, but I couldn't help pick up on how when he asked me about the marital status of my parents, it was like he was ticking off points in his life against mine. Comparing. Measuring. I'd found his Achilles' heel. Not that I was proud of that. It just seemed something too intimate to know so soon.

The waitress returned and placed paper napkins on our table, as if an afterthought, then walked away. J.F. and I exchanged grins and fell back into silence. We tried our drinks again, but they were still too hot. My tea seemed more the product of nuclear fission than a proper steep. The cook hadn't run the water, though, as my mother gets me to do. It tasted like pipe.

"I saw that kid was back," I said suddenly. When did I become so chatty?

"Great, no? I tracked him down and talked him into coming back. *Secondaire III.*" He stirred his cappuccino with a spoon more suitable for eating breakfast cereal, the only one the waitress left between the two of us. "He didn't like that girl much. The one who supports PETA. I think he's afraid of her. I can't say I blame him."

"What's his deal?"

"Confused. He doesn't know if he should come out or not. Parents and all that. But that's what the coalition's for. We can help him."

"What can we do?" I asked. Perhaps it came out more uncaring than I'd have liked, but instead of being about hot guys, I feared this gay club would turn out to be all about rescuing wide-eyed kittens in trees.

"For some people, coming out isn't an easy thing to do." Suddenly J.F.'s eyes were no longer playful.

"I'm not saying we should out him or anything." I backpedaled something awful. I had to remind myself to watch what I said if I didn't want him to get the wrong impression of me.

"It's for him to decide," he shrugged.

"Well, you've managed it alright." I tried giving him a big smile, hoping to re-ignite his eyes. For a second that sunshine peeked out, but just as quickly it was gone again.

"The most difficult decision I ever had to make. I mean, it worked out great for me, but at the time I was going through hell."

"When was that?" I carefully sipped at the tea feeling older and more mature, like the couples I saw when I went downtown with my parents and who sit in cafés and decide what they're going to do that evening. The theatre. Museums. The symphony. My imagination was more boring and posh than I was.

"I was fourteen. The start of *secondaire III.*" As he spoke, he played with the paper napkin. He folded and unfolded a corner with one hand. His other hand was clenched tightly into a fist that surprised me—his knuckles were so white. "I was being bullied a lot. Everyone was calling me '*tapette*,' and 'homo,' and '*fifi*.' I just took it all."

I couldn't imagine a defenseless Jean-François. Not given the person sitting before me. Tall. Confident. Muscular. It didn't make sense.

My disbelief must have shown.

"Seriously, I was in a pretty dark place. I hadn't had my growth spurt yet, so I was a lot smaller back then. And the way I looked, the way I acted, everyone was giving me a hard time."

I took a quick sip of tea, mindful that my pinky didn't fly off to parts unknown. I knew I was no better than the assholes who'd harassed him, having made a big deal of his "vibe" like it was something important instead of just an idiosyncrasy. I'd be terrified to know all the peculiarities J.F. could find about me.

He looked down and was now using both hands to tear tiny pieces off the napkin. A small paper snow bank formed on the table next to the spoon.

"I was totally into sports back then. Swimming. Wrestling. Hockey. Though hockey was a bit of a joke for me because of my size. But I was pretty good at wrestling, what with weight classes to even things out. And I started working out a lot, though it didn't show much back then. Some of the guys on my wrestling team didn't like having me on the team. This one guy always made homophobic remarks about me, so one day I told him to put up or shut up and challenged him to a match. I pinned him in about 30 seconds. He quit the team after that. But I was still being harassed. In the halls. The locker room. On my way home after school. Not as much as before, at least, but it still was happening. It was kind of like, one down, eighteen hundred more to go."

He looked at me again.

"But when I told people I was gay, everything changed. It was as though when I hadn't come out yet, people thought it was okay to harass me. Like they thought I had a dirty secret and they could get away with treating me like shit because they thought it would reveal too much about me if I told someone or did something about it. When I came out, it was no longer cool to fuck with me. It was the strangest thing. Suddenly everything was so much better. It even changed the way I felt about myself. I could come to school without worrying about having the shit kicked out of me."

"Didn't you tell your parents what was going on?"

"They wanted me to report it, but I knew it'd only make it worse. They told me they were going to the police. That's when I decided to come out."

"And they're cool with it?"

"My parents just want me to be happy. If it took coming out to change what was happening to me, they understand."

J.F. must have realized what he was doing to the napkin—he shook his head ever so slightly, balled up the paper snowdrift in what was left of the napkin, and softly said, "Sorry," as if apologizing to the napkin itself.

"And suddenly I was taller." J.F. gave one of his laughs I was coming to know and love. His eyes hopped, skipped, and jumped again. "And I started doing weights more seriously than ever. One growth spurt and a few muscles and no one messes with me." He gave out another burst of pure joy.

It was close to suppertime. I had to call my parents to tell them where I was or I knew my cell phone would be vibrating like crazy. J.F. only lived a few streets over and he said he could run home and be there before his parents could sit down to eat. While I waited for my parents to pick me up, we continued talking. He asked me about my family again, so I threw him a bone. I told J.F. how it was a big thing a couple of weeks ago when my sister moved out to a flat downtown to be closer to her university. It was difficult for my parents to see her go.

"Parents worry," he said. "You know, I felt so weak when I was being bullied, like I was disappointing them. I spent a lot of time in my room crying. More weakness. Later I realized it wasn't true—my parents could never be disappointed in me. And I know now it's because of my parents' strength and all they've given me that I can cry."

He looked down at one of his hands rubbing something from the palm of the other, like he was trying to remove a ghostly stain.

How could any of that fail to win my heart?

Chapter 5

OVER THE NEXT FEW MONTHS, the coalition went into action. Every week J.F. brought us another LGBT cause to champion in the school, issues he'd heard about on the news or read in newspapers and magazines. We had our work cut out for us. Two teenage boys in Iran were publicly executed because they were gay. There were brutal machete killings of gay activists in Jamaica, incited by homophobic dancehall songs. The president of Gambia gave gays twenty-four hours to leave the country or they'd be beheaded. Not to mention the dire situation in the over eighty countries where being gay was illegal, punishable by death or long prison sentences. Kenya. Nigeria. Barbados. Pakistan. Saudi Arabia. I never told anyone, but I'd always wanted to travel until I heard that.

Even with the Americans as occupiers in Iraq, or maybe because of it, death squads now roamed there killing gays.

"I wouldn't say the U.S. is complicit," J.F. addressed us at one of our meetings, "but I don't think stopping the killing of gays is one of their concerns. The Americans' own back yard proves how homophobic they are. Look at their hard-ons for laws stopping same sex marriage."

At times he was both passionate and outspoken. I won't go into half the things he said. I imagine somewhere he's the youngest person on a No Fly list.

We wrote letters and started petitions demanding justice. One week we worked every day after school making a condolence card the size of a desk's top for the family of a fourteen-year-old boy in California. While sitting in class, he'd been shot twice in the head by another student for being openly gay. Almost everyone in our school signed it. J.F. asked me to take the card to the post office, and I had to figure out how to send it "without folding it a hundred times," as J.F. cautioned me. He knew me so well—that was my first impulse.

We also pushed for more gay books in the library. "And by *more*," J.F. said, "I mean at least one." It was his favourite of his running jokes. He had two. When things were deathly serious or boring, he'd flex a muscle in one arm like he was a mindless body builder. That never failed to make me laugh, especially when he did it from across a room when he caught me looking at him.

Before I could object, J.F. put me in charge of letter writing and petitions—"The political side," he told me. I guess he was trying to make it sound important so I couldn't say no. Trying to impress him, I came up with the idea of selling rainbow wristbands at lunch that said "*Tolérance*" or "*Fierté*." They sold out in two days, though I'm sure half the kids who bought them had no idea what they were being tolerant or proud of. We sent the money to human rights organizations that help LGBT people around the world.

J.F. was busy, too, taking care of the dramas that erupted in the club—and there were plenty. Lesbians fighting, breaking up, then reconciling. Kids in tears because they were being called names or threatened. Unrequited crushes. Coming out sagas. One boy in *secondaire III* was kicked out of his house, but a couple of days later his parents let him back home. I found out from one of the kid's friends that J.F. had gone to speak to the parents. I can't imagine what you say to a mother and a father to make them regret turning their backs on their child because he's gay. Appealing to the decency of people who were capable of acting that way seemed to me like too much wasted effort. But somehow J.F. did it, as incredible as that seems. He had secret powers I could only guess at.

We had elections. J.F. was voted president, naturally, and I was elected vice-president. I'd prayed one of his fan club girls would've run instead, but they were content to drool over him. J.F. made a big thing about my being V.P. He acted like I had the position because I deserved it and was being recognized by my peers, not because no one else wanted it. "The team," he called us and high-fived me. That was awkward. He still had that sports mentality. Once a jock, I guess.

I'm not sure how much good we did in the grand scheme of things. I'm not sure we changed the world, but I like to think our efforts at school did make a difference, no matter how small.

J.F. and Madame Marie spoke to the administration, and we were able to show *The Laramie Project*. J.F. had me organize his fan club girls making posters, and it was as painful as it sounds. They argued nonstop about what colour of glitter to make everything—I didn't stand a chance. Madame Marie asked the *secondaire IV* and *secondaire V* teachers to bring their classes to the auditorium to watch the film. When it was over, I heard lots of kids say how sad it was—some girls even cried—and that what happened to Matthew Shepard was *"vraiment dégueulasse."* Really disgusting.

"At least they're seeing what hate's like," J.F. said to me during the movie, leaning against me in the dark auditorium. I lived for the times he'd be that close to me. He smelled clean and fresh and warm like he was taken out of the clothes dryer moments before.

The coalition had fun, too. You'd think with everyone calling us "the gay club," that's all we'd be, frivolous and glib twenty-four-seven. All slumber parties and makeovers. We were much too serious for that. But we sponsored a best costume contest on Halloween, and J.F.'s old wrestling team walked around school all day in drag. I wasn't sure if that was a show of support or mockery. Were they taking the mick? But J.F. saw it as a good laugh, jokingly making "phone me" signals to them with his hand.

I had no idea why J.F. was even speaking to them. How could he forgive them for what they'd done to him? As they walked away, laughing and fondling their own fake boobs, which wasn't that amusing—it was so straight—I asked J.F. that question.

"Some things you just have to let go."

"And some things require the surgical precision of a machete."

As a joke I dressed as Lance Bass from 'N Sync, but no one knew who he was. They were never big in Québec. More infuriating than that, at least a dozen people asked me why I hadn't dressed up as Harry Potter because of my glasses.

I was anxious to see what J.F. would be dressed as. For some reason a Roman gladiator came to mind, but I would've settled for anything shirtless. Tarzan. A surfer dude. Michael Phelps. But when I saw J.F., he had on beige cargo pants and a Canadiens hockey shirt. He looked like half the school on any given day. When I asked him why he wasn't wearing a costume, he said, "I am." Sometimes the only thing I could manage was to shake my head at him.

Of all the things J.F. had us do, I was the most impressed with the Day of Silence—a day where students who are against LGBT bullying, name calling, and harassment stopped talking and handed out speaking cards to explain why. It was incredible! We walked through the halls and sat in class without saying a word. Some of the coalition tied bandanas and scarves over their mouths to make the point. When we handed over the cards I heard "Super!" and *"C'est cool!"* As J.F. said, "Too often people don't think of social issues like that."

There was this one asshole in *secondaire IV* who asked me, "Why do gays always need a day? Gay Pride. Day of Silence. Why don't straights have a day?" I almost broke my silence and said something, but thought better of it, although I'm not sure what exactly I'd have said.

J.F. spoke up, though, looking pretty pissed off. "Because straights have the other three hundred and sixty-four days of the year."

That shut the kid up.

The next day J.F. spoke at an assembly for the students in our grades. He came across so sure of himself and calm standing in front of everyone as he spoke. I'd have been a wobbly mess. Madame Maria had spoken to him about being too passionate—he tended to become emotional when he spoke of injustice—but he had just the right tone. When he finished there was loud applause. Of course I couldn't help but notice his "vibe" when he talked—his "wisp" a bit more pronounced, his hand movements freer. But if J.F. was aware of it, he didn't seem to do anything to rein them in. *Bien dans sa peau.* Comfortable in his own skin. One more reason I admired him.

By then *Coalition arc-en-ciel* had grown to thirty members. Besides the fan club girls, the next members to join were five lesbians who sat by themselves at meetings until J.F. coaxed them over to the front of Madame Maria's classroom so they'd become more involved. After that it was difficult to shut them up. Then six gay boys showed up, one-by-one to meetings over the space of a month, mostly from *secondaire V*, but also two guys from my year as well. One was Maxime something-or-other, whom I'd noticed in my math class. Kind of cute, but very shy. His light brown hair was gelled into a small shark fin running down the middle of his head, and he had dark grey eyes that looked into you.

Something about him nags at me even now, like I know him from somewhere but can't place where. He sat next to me at meetings. I assumed he was going to be clingy, but he never was. With Maxime you had to start the conversation or you'd be waiting a long time for him to say something. The other kid in my year, Olivier Jutras, stared at Maxime during meetings, so I could tell he thought he was hot. I suppose I could've played matchmaker or something, but that was more a J.F. kind-of-thing. I'd never met anyone more socially uncomfortable than Olivier. He had bad skin, a nasal voice, and a staccato laugh that he used too much. Everything was funny to him. Except he had the saddest eyes I'd ever seen, even when he was laughing.

The rest of our crew were straight girls, some who showed up for the same reason as the original fan club—because of J.F.'s looks. Others came because they thought it was cool to have gay friends or they honestly believed in social equality and human rights. Sometimes I didn't know which of them were bigger pains.

I'd like to say tons of straight boys joined as well, but our school's not *that* progressive. Occasionally some of the straight girls dragged their boyfriends to meetings to wait around for them. Those boys shifted in the desks or looked intently at their cell phones or MP3 players. Some even pulled out a book to read. They were that uncomfortable.

And the red cap boy was a regular, though I never saw him speak to anyone except J.F. The kid's name turned out to be Jérémie, and J.F. told me his story: problems at home and bullying at school because he's gay. Often I'd have to start the meetings because J.F. would be sitting with Jérémie off to one side talking with him. Sometimes the kid was crying.

One day during one of our meetings Monsieur Courtois twisted his way into Madame Maria's classroom and demanded to speak to J.F. I carried on with the agenda, trying to make out J.F.'s writing on the paper he shoved at me as he went to see what the *adjoint* wanted. I was sure that was the end of the coalition, especially when the meeting ended and J.F. hadn't come back.

The next day J.F. didn't show up at school either, which was unusual since he was never sick. When half the school was absent with the *grippe* right after Thanksgiving, J.F. never missed a day, even with the remaining kids coughing their germs all over everyone else. "It's like an eighteenth-century consumption ward in here," my father said as he walked into the office to sign me out of school when I came down with the flu, too. Like most things, he said it loudly and in English. Everyone looked at us, and I couldn't have rushed him out of there faster if I'd have strapped a jet pack to him and pressed *ignite*.

Sometimes I think he does things like that to wind me up. He already stirs it enough at parent-teacher interviews. He puts on a thicker British accent if he thinks one of my teachers is anti-English. He comes all Cockney with everything "apples and pears" and "china plate" this and that. I dread parent-teacher interviews. Sometimes I think my father sits in front of the TV on Christmas Day with mince pies and a pot of tea watching the Queen's message just to drive me insane.

I was worried about J.F. I went to the restaurant and waited on the off chance he'd turn up. I sat by myself with an extra curd cheese, gravy-soaked *poutine* wondering what had happened to him. I picked at my fries and debated about calling his house. I pressed "1" on my cell phone, but before the first ring I flipped the phone closed. I was afraid to hear the bad news. Okay, I still didn't love the gay club, but it *did* give me a reason to be with J.F. That was pretty sweet. And now it would end just like that.

I finished off my gooey French fry mess with a face on me that must have looked like "a bulldog chewing on a wasp." For *les bons mots*, I never have to look farther than my dad.

The same waitress was working. I paid the bill at the cash, handed her three toonies and told her to *"Gardez la monnaie."* I couldn't wait any longer—I was already late for supper. As I pulled open the door to leave, I swear I heard her say, *"Bonsoir."* She must've felt sorry for me.

At school the next day J.F. still wasn't there. I asked Madame Maria and some of the other coalition members if they'd heard from him, but no one had, so I went to the office before the first bell to ask one of the secretaries if he was ill or something. Maybe his parents had phoned in. Before I could ask, Monsieur Courtois boomed at me, "Can I help you?" Even from where I stood I could smell the bubbling cauldron of coffee and cigarettes on his breath.

"It's Jean-François Giroux. He's not at school and I haven't heard from him. I was just—"

He leaned towards me across the counter and lowered his voice. "What business is it of yours?"

"None," I said. "Well . . . It's just that—"

"Go to class." He turned and went into his office.

For the first two periods the worse possible scenarios ran through my head. Car crashes. Serious illnesses. Leaving town for unfathomable reasons. For a brief moment, I even imagined one of his fan club girls had gone stalker and J.F. was trapped in his bedroom suffering all manner of romantic, possibly even sexual, humiliations. I worked myself up so much I was about to scream when the bell for morning *récréation* rang.

This was ridiculous! I ran outside to use my cell phone to call his house. No answer. I must have tried his number another ten times during the day, once in the middle of Monsieur Felix's class when his back was turned to the board explaining the difference between borrow and lend. Which he had wrong. In his world, banks were *borrowing* money to people left and right.

Still no one picked up. And a family without a computer certainly didn't have voice mail. J.F.'s the most unplugged person I know. Not that he's some Luddite like my father claims to be. If anything, I was more a Luddite than anybody else, forced to be only because my father doesn't think much of technology, or "fads" as he calls them. We only got the Internet last summer, but it doesn't work properly on the old computer my father brought home from his work for me. Surfing's more like wading. I only have a cell phone because I paid for it myself by cutting lawns and shoveling snow.

That evening I went back to the restaurant and waited, but no J.F. Instead of going home, I started walking to his house, but realized I didn't know where he lived exactly. There wasn't anything left to do. Anyway, at what point had I officially become the stalker? I went home and hid in my room, listening to music, more depressed than I had a right to be.

After two days of hell, J.F. reappeared at school. I saw him waiting for me as I moped off the bus. We walked into school together.

"So where've you been?"

He shrugged and puckered his mouth like it wasn't important. I asked again, but he shook his head ever so slightly.

"What have you been up to?" he asked like nothing was wrong. But he looked shaken. His eyes looked beyond me as we spoke.

I was relieved he was okay, no matter what had happened. We were standing at my locker, and before I knew what I was doing, I reached out and rested the palm of my hand on the side of his neck. It stayed there no more than three seconds, both the longest and shortest time span I'd ever experienced. Then J.F. reached up and gently removed it.

"It's nothing. Don't worry." He wiped his upper lip as though he was sweating. It was early winter and our school wasn't known for its heating.

I asked again where he was, but he shook his head so I didn't push the issue.

The school day inched on and I went over and over what had happened. I told myself off for being such an idiot—what must it have looked like touching him that way in the middle of the hallway? Worse still, I'd come to the horrible conclusion the feelings I had for him weren't going to be reciprocated.

As bad as I felt about the whole thing, I couldn't stop thinking how his neck had felt. Smooth and hot to my touch, the muscles tensing slightly then relaxing again. I thought about that for weeks.

That evening I arrived at the restaurant at the usual time, fully expecting J.F. not to show. I almost hadn't gone, but I had to know. At the darkest point that day, I'd convinced myself I'd seen disgust in his eyes when I'd touched him. I needed to know if we still were friends.

But J.F. bounded in and gave me a smile. As hard as I searched, I couldn't find any sign that things were now different between us. Despite my boldness and my shame, nothing had changed.

I asked J.F. again where he'd been those two days. It took some doing, but slowly I got it out of him. It involved the red cap boy.

"He tried something stupid." J.F.'s voice cracked, then looked angry for having given that much away. But I could see he had to tell someone. "Jérémie asked for me, that's why Courtois showed up during the meeting." He ripped at a napkin again. I grabbed it from him, and he looked at me with surprise. It shocked me, too, that I had the nerve to do something like that. What was going on with me? I motioned for J.F. to continue, impatient to know what happened.

"I went straight to the hospital and stayed there until one, two a.m. Until the nurse told me to go home."

Without something to fidget with, he didn't know what to do with his hands. He drummed his fingers on the table, then cracked his knuckles. Finally he crossed his arms and hid his hands in his armpits. I felt bad that I'd taken the napkin away from him.

"They kept telling me that not just anyone can see Jérémie, even if he'd asked for me. So I went back the next day and sat there until they let me in."

I could see him doing that. Sitting there in the hospital waiting room, arms folded and with a face that defied anyone to move him. A one-person protest.

"I think he'll be okay now." He looked off midway between our table and the front door. "At least I hope so." I could tell it scared him—he was much less . . . energetic than usual. Less himself. And his "wisp" was more noticeable.

I wanted to tell him he did the right thing , but I was only able to say, "He's lucky to have you." I hated that I said that. It could be taken the wrong way.

After a long silence, out of nowhere J.F. said, "I'm no superhero, you know." I didn't know why he said it. I wasn't thinking that. I was just happy I still had him as a friend.

Jérémie wasn't at school for the next week. J.F. swore me to secrecy about what he told me, so I certainly didn't say anything. But I saw how J.F. was with the kid from that point on, all nervous and watchful and a little too cheerful when he was around. No, I've thought more than once since then, he isn't a superhero. But that made me like him even more, if possible.

It's funny. Until *Coalition arc-en-ciel*, I was a nobody. I'm not good at sports despite all those summers playing soccer. I have no musical abilities to speak of, though I took both piano and guitar lessons. My marks are okay. Just okay. I have to work at doing even that well in school. I think not being good at anything disappoints my parents more than me. They used to try to get me involved in every activity imaginable, hoping, I suppose, something would click with me. Some hidden talent would miraculously reveal itself. I don't know what the obsession is with having to be good at something. It doesn't only come from my parents. Teachers say it all the time: "Everyone is special at something." They're always looking for "gifts." Can't you just be yourself? A regular person? Nothing too special, nothing too great. Isn't that enough?

But with the coalition, I was suddenly somebody. The other members asked me questions, especially when J.F. wasn't there because he was off involved in someone else's soap opera. It was as if they thought J.F. and I shared one mind. Madame Maria began calling me "my little activist," in a good way, even if I heard "gay" in there, too. I mean, I don't think she was implying I was constantly going around poking people in the eye with a rainbow or anything.

Suddenly the rest of the school saw me—how could they miss us? J.F. and I walked through the halls together, tall and short, muscular and skinny. But all gay, I thought with a chuckle. Everyone greeted J.F., and I suppose I caught some of the shrapnel. At first people said, "*Salut!*" to me *because* of J.F. But soon just as many people said "*Ça va?*" and stopped to talk to me when J.F. wasn't there. It was a long way from being the token Anglo, all but invisible except for my mother tongue as my claim to fame.

My involvement with the coalition was how I came out at school, I guess. It wasn't some big announcement over the intercom or some big drama where everyone spreads rumours, and looks shocked, and takes sides for and against you. As the school year went on, people saw me with J.F. and assumed I was gay, too. Some people even asked if we were going out together. I kind of liked that assumption. Still, when they asked, I made a show of being annoyed. "Come on!" I'd say with indignation like the suggestion of us as a couple was unthinkable. Laughable almost. When he was asked, J.F. gave one of his smiles.

When I think of how worried I'd been about drawing attention to myself. Wasted energy. Now I was front and centre, and being noticed didn't bother me as much as I'd thought it would. But there's a difference being one of a kind—the only Anglo or the only gay—and being one of many. It meant everything to know there were others beside me, and that J.F. was there, too, of course.

The day it became clear to me that I was out to everyone, I'd been sitting at a table outside the cafeteria collecting signatures for a petition in support of some students in Florida who'd met with lots of opposition trying to form a gay-straight alliance at their school. This guy in *secondaire V* with blond hair and a T-shirt that said, "I broke the first rule of Fight Club," looked up at me as he signed and said, "It's cool you're doing this." Then in the next breath said, "But I'm super straight though."

What did that mean? Was he *that* worried someone would think he was gay for putting his name on a piece of paper? Or was he afraid I'd hit on him? Maybe it came across less as a joke than I meant it to be, but when I said, "Oh, does that give you any super powers?" he shot back all bitchy, "Well, you're super gay. What can *you* do?" I had no comeback, and I let him walk away. I don't suppose he'd have been impressed with the ability to leap tall boys in a single bound.

So, there I was—out and proud. No turning back now. And that was okay. I wasn't alone.

J.F. and I met up at the restaurant most evenings after supper. It became our thing. It took a lot to convince my parents to let me out on school nights, but they could see how much it meant to me to have someone to hang out with and talk to. I can't say I've had a lot of friends, or many at all, to tell the truth. There's Rachelle, obviously, and, I guess, her boyfriend can be called a friend though I never call him up or go out and do things with him. I used to hang around with this kid back in *secondaire II*, Philippe Beaulieu-Gagnon, but he moved to Laval in the summer before *secondaire III*. Anyway, I only hung out with him once or twice a month when the kids he was usually with weren't around. We played video games and he'd always win. See, I'm not good at that, either.

Sometimes some of the other members of *Coalition arc-en-ciel* joined J.F. and me at the restaurant. We laughed and gossiped and told funny stories about crushes and love gone wrong. Maxime and Olivier were often there, and J.F. liked to ambush Maxime with random questions to get him to speak. "What's the capital of Mongolia?" "Who's the all-time NHL goal scorer?" In return there'd be a shrug. Naturally Olivier would machine-gun laugh at that, sounding like a Mafia hit gone wrong.

Mostly it was only J.F. and me. I liked those times the best. He'd call me when I got home and we'd talk for the rest of the night, sometimes until the next morning or until my mother picked up the other phone and simply said, "Spencer." That was the cue to say goodnight.

I was stupid enough or giddy enough in a schoolgirl sort-of-way that I told Rachelle about our late night calls.

"Are they dirty?" she asked right away. My saying no with a pinch of disgust didn't disappoint her as much as when I told her J.F. doesn't have a cell phone, or MSN, or Facebook and MySpace pages. Given how Rachelle's face lost its shape at that news, I might as well have told her I'd discovered a dodo egg under my bed that morning. She wanted to check up on him. She worried he'd break my heart.

"All men do," she told me with a world-weary sigh. She was going through a bad patch with Étienne that week.

I'd like to tell you the coalition had loads of opposition that we fought to overcome, of course, struggling to win everyone over and finally triumphing to the swell of a catchy song, but it wasn't like that. The school supported us from the start. Only Monsieur Courtois slimed into our meetings every so often to check up on us, although J.F. tried to convince me he was "just taking an interest."

Even if it was J.F. doing the persuading, I didn't buy it. I didn't like Courtois, although I had nothing solid on which to base my dislike for him.

At last he shed his skin and showed his true scaly self.

At one meeting, J.F. stood at the board giving us tips how to write a protest letter that had impact. It was late afternoon in November, and everything in Madame Maria's classroom reflected in the dark windows. Only the core of the club remained: J.F. and me, Maxime something-or-other and Olivier, and Lily and Sophie, Lily's new girlfriend and the newest member to the club. For once Lily's iPod earbuds no longer hung around her neck. One sat in her ear while the other was in Sophie's. Maxime nudged me—clearly he thought it was cute—but I acted like it was stupid, turning up my nose at them as though they weren't sharing music but rather the same toothbrush. Publicly. Secretly I thought it was cute, too.

Madame Maria sat correcting at her desk. We heard the leakage from Lily's iPod, and despite Madame Maria warning about hearing loss, her shoulders moved along with the music while she hummed to herself.

I looked up from the notes I was taking and saw the *adjoint* standing at the door. Madame Maria didn't see him until Olivier said, "*Madame*," and nodded his head towards the man.

The two adults went out into the hallway, and a moment later Madame Maria returned and asked J.F. to join them. He handed me the dry erase marker and I had to take over at the board. I tried explaining how we wouldn't be taken seriously if our letters contained insults. It was an uphill battle. Lily was all for referring to penis size.

We could hear their voices from the hallway. Monsieur Courtois especially. Clearly agitated, his voice grew louder as he spoke.

"It's been two months and I still don't have clue what your club *does*."

"What do you think we do?" J.F. said in a soothing voice.

"Have there been complaints or something?" Madame Maria asked. "Can we speak about this later?"

"What are you worried about?" J.F. said. "We aren't making bombs."

"I just want an answer to my question." The man's voice grew louder still.

"Gérard," I heard Madame Maria say, "be calm."

That did it. They might as well have lobbed a grenade at him. Monsieur Courtois shouted at Madame Maria to stop telling him what to do.

I looked at the others. I'd been making feeble attempts at continuing what J.F. wanted to say about letter writing, but all eyes were on the drama in the hallway. Even I couldn't help but look. As I turned back to the others, I saw they relished Madame Maria and J.F. getting their own back at the *adjoint*. Like I said before, none of the students liked him. They smiled in a way that was just this side of gleeful. Except Olivier. His face was pale. His eyes wide. He still held a pen in his hand, poised to write, but it was shaking.

I went to the door and closed it. As I did, J.F. looked at me and shrugged, helpless to do anything as the teacher and vice-principal argued. When the door shut, Lily groaned and complained I was stopping them from seeing *le spectacle*. Maxime leaned over to Olivier and whispered something to him.

"You're such a teacher," Lily said. I grimaced at the insult. Those were serious words. I'd have preferred she'd said something about my penis.

I carried on like nothing had happened, but there wasn't much more to explain about protest letters. I pointedly explained again how insults were not helpful, but that made me sound *exactly* like a teacher, so I quickly added, "Don't make threats in your letters. Thank you."

Everyone gathered their things and rushed to the door. Lily was the first there—her girlfriend was right behind her trying to keep up. She opened the door, but by the way her head arced from left to right, I knew there was no one in the hallway.

We went our separate ways, but I knew we'd all meet at the restaurant later.

Supper for me was a blur of cutlery.

"Have a hot date?" I looked up and saw my father looking back at me with awe. I knew I wasn't doing my mom's meat-and-two-veg meal any justice, but I was anxious to tell J.F., "I don't want to say I told you so, but . . ." If I was right about Courtois, maybe J.F. would see I was right about a lot of things. Maybe he'd see I was right for him. It's that kind of twisted logic that gets countries involved in wars.

"You could always invite round your friend," my mother said. Her face was full of hope and good will. Sat there eating supper, I couldn't imagine J.F. coming over for tea and scones like my mother obviously could. What would he make of our place with its décor so reminiscent of a British theme restaurant. Every morning when I go downstairs, I'm surprised there aren't tourists patiently waiting to be served bangers and mash. My parents' friends and coworkers think giving them souvenirs from trips to the UK will lessen any homesickness. I don't see how some old, made-in-China tat is able to do that. True to form, that morning my mom had rotated her Coronation Street tea towels. That week it was Bet Lynch.

My parents drove me to the restaurant, and I hurried in only to find Maxime and Lily sitting at our usual table. Olivier hadn't wanted to come out that evening, and Sophie wasn't allowed out on school nights. A moment later, J.F. came through the front door, all smiles as usual.

"What a day. What a day." He plopped down in the booth and motioned to the mute waitress. She brought us our usual orders. We all drank cappuccinos now. Even me. I told myself Earl Grey seemed too much like my parents' drink.

"Did you punch Courtois?" Lily's eyes were wide with anticipation of a good fight story. "Because I'd have punched him."

J.F. laughed. "No, it wasn't that bad." He took the time to stir his cappuccino so the foam on top disappeared into the coffee below.

When he looked up, he saw us staring back at him, each of us waiting with the same expectancy and dumb expression that I've seen on my sister at the toaster just before it pops up. She isn't a morning person.

"What?" He shook his head. "You have it all wrong. Monsieur Courtois is only worried for us. He doesn't understand the gay thing. It's new to him. He doesn't know any gay people."

"How could he be alive that long and *not* know any?" It seemed a feeble excuse to me. A variation on *Some of my best friends are . . .*

"Madame Maria and I spoke with him in his office—"

"Is that where you punched him?" Lily asked.

"No. He calmed down a lot. We explained about the club. He was very nice actually. I think he gets it."

"Right," I said. "Next he'll be showing up at meetings handing out rainbow stickers."

"Or condoms," Maxime said. I looked at him, surprised as much that he was speaking up as I was at his words. They were a bit much, but funny, and it did nicely support what I was trying to say. I thought he was speaking to J.F., but he looked right at me and gave me a goofy grin. What was *that* all about?

"Anyway, how would he know any gay kids?" J.F. said. "It's not like they'd come out to a vice principal."

The others nodded in agreement. Did they really believe Courtois transformed so easily? From homophobe to gay supporter in one easy step. Instantly. Just add water. They'd all fallen for the typical TV movie ending. As I said before, I didn't buy it.

We talked for a while longer. Mostly about nonsense. J.F. asked Maxime "How fast can a dog run?" and Lily looked bored now that tales of fisticuffs were no longer a possibility. She left to go home and call Sophie. Maxime hung around a bit longer, but soon he left, too.

J.F. tapped his spoon against the lip of his cappuccino cup and smiled. "He likes you."

"Who?" For the sickest second I thought he was still talking about

Courtois. There's falling through the rabbit hole and then there's being launched into it by a cannon.

"Maxime. He likes you."

I shook my head at the insanity of that thought. Then J.F. said the cruelest thing he's ever said to me.

"You should ask him out."

I sat silent. I couldn't even bring myself to think of a response. Everything was pure emotion churning inside me. I restrained myself from blurting out, "What the hell does *that* mean?" I felt so stupid. I didn't see it coming that he would try to match-make *me*. The others, sure. Why not? He'd become good at that. Engineering opportunities for one coalition member to work with another. Or inviting them separately to the restaurant in the evening, with the real intention of them getting to know each other better. Or having them sit with him at lunch, then rushing off somewhere so they'd be left alone together. Had he done that with me and Maxime that evening? Was this what was happening? It sickened me I'd think like that. Then the anger really hit me. J.F. was trying to palm me off on someone else. Anyone else.

I reached into my pocket for money to pay the bill so I could leave, but I stopped myself. I counted to twenty, then thirty, just to make sure I remained there long enough to make it look like my going would be for any reason other than what it was. I even managed a smile as I told J.F. that I'd better be heading home.

"But you haven't called your parents yet."

"I think I'm going to walk," I said as calmly as if I'd ordered another drink. Hell, a round of cappuccinos for everyone. And keep them coming.

I stood up and J.F. put his hand on my arm to stop me. I waited to breathe again, expecting my happy TV ending as well.

"Thank you," he said. Then when he saw I didn't understand: "For looking out for Olivier today." Clearly I was still not getting it, so he added, "For shutting the door. It was good of you." I forgot about that. How did he even know?

"His parents are divorcing and he spends all his time at home having to hear them arguing. He doesn't need that at school, too. Maxime called me to tell me what you did." God! Now those two were talking on the phone together.

"Ya, well I have to go."

I walked to the door and out into the cold evening air.

Chapter 6

THE SCHOOL YEAR continued much the same way: fighting injustice where we saw it during the day, and meeting at the restaurant for coffee in the evening. It should have been a great time in my life, and in many ways it was, but I couldn't see past my own issues with justice right then. The ongoing exposure to the day-to-day wrongs LGBT people experienced wasn't the only reason—that was a given. I'd started obsessing on not having made any progress with J.F. romantically.

We'd settled so easily into being best friends—that was cool—but for the life of me I couldn't scale that friendship wall that kept us from being something more. After the knock-backs I'd received for my feeble attempts to woo J.F., I'd resolved to keep everything between us strictly business. There'd be the coalition and nothing else. Once bitch-slapped, twice shy. But whom was I fooling? I was still crushing on him like you wouldn't believe. I can't begin to count how many nights I couldn't fall asleep because of him. When I did, he appeared in my dreams no matter how random and unrelated the circumstance. Often he popped into the one where I'm on the roof of my house and the only way I can get down is by inching hand-over-hand along the electric wires to a telephone pole. Or he'd appear in the dream where I'm being chased by some evil force I never see, and the only way I can escape is by flapping my arms to fly away, but only ever rising ten feet off the ground. He'd be there watching me. I'd wake up sweaty and anxious, and I'd dread falling asleep again.

He was always on my mind and that made me feel helpless, unable to do something about it or shake him for good. Where was the justice there? It was all very Emo.

One evening at the restaurant I gave him my standard spiel about how I'm not good at anything. "Except now," I said, putting an upbeat spin on it for him so he wouldn't think of me as totally pathetic, "with the coalition, I'm kind of good at being gay."

"You're also pretty good at being my best friend."

Previous humiliation aside, those words should have made me as happy as though all my Christmases had come at once, but I could only think: Friend! Friend! All Transformer stickers and hockey cards and traded lunches. I needed the bucket and pail that came with his clothes so I could dig a hole and bury myself in it.

Rachelle counseled me to "make the first move." This caused more sleepless nights trying to figure out what that first move should be. All of Rachelle's advice involved variations on throwing J.F. down and having my way with him. Whatever I came up with, regardless of how great an idea it was, turning into a burning pile of shit when it was lit with my fear, the kindling that fueled my inaction. When it came down to it, I liked the idea he *might* still be in love with me more than ending up knowing *proof positive* we'd remain platonic friends. Despite how many times Rachelle prodded me, I still did nothing. It was hopeless. *I* was hopeless.

The school year was almost over by then—it was already May. Like every spring, my mother wouldn't stop talking about the buds on the lilac trees. I spent most of my days rolling my eyes at her, and pining after J.F. with nothing to show for it.

Then on the Saturday before my birthday, he rang up and asked if I wanted to go downtown to Unity, a dance club in the gay village. There were some house parties that weekend, and though J.F. was invited to all of them, he told me he just wasn't into the high school party scene anymore. I suppose in his mind he had already graduated and moved on to college and another world.

I told my parents J.F. and I were going to a movie downtown—my parents wouldn't be amused if they knew their under-eighteen son was going to a club for the first time. They still saw me as a kid—they wanted to throw me a birthday party until I finally convinced them I was too old for one. I'd rather spend my seventeenth birthday with J.F. I saw their faces register the implications of my words, but they did their best to hide it. It's never easy to disappoint your parents, especially when they're trying so hard.

After the club, J.F. and I missed the last métro, so we had to take a late bus home. My parents caught me trying to sneak in through my bedroom window, which I'd left unlocked, just in case. I told them everything. They grounded me for two weeks, though we hadn't been drinking or anything. But that wasn't it. To them it was the whole lying thing. I felt bad about that part.

Not being allowed out for two weeks wasn't a terrible price to pay for the night I had, even if it meant I couldn't meet up with J.F. at the restaurant for a while. At the club, J.F. and I danced together, lights whirling above us, squeezed into the middle of the floor with hundreds of other gay boys, the music booming rhythm that echoed inside our bodies. At one point J.F. took off his white T-shirt while we danced—as a condition of my going clubbing with him I told him I had veto power over his choice of clothes—and it hung out of the back pocket of his jeans as he pulled me to him, smiling that smile of his. Everyone must have thought we were a couple. All of it thrilled me to no end.

J.F.'s hair was longer by then. Dancing made him sweat, and he ran his fingers through his hair to move it out of his eyes. It slicked back off his forehead showing his eyes more, making them appear even bluer. More beautiful. And as we danced together, those eyes looked only at me.

"The world's your oyster," my father likes to tell me when things appear to be going swimmingly well.

Sadly I'm allergic to seafood.

When J.F. and I walked to the late bus in silence, both of us too exhausted to talk, I thought back over what had happened since that time I first spotted him putting up the poster near my locker. Getting to know J.F., spending so much time together, becoming close to him, when he touched me on the arm, or on the shoulder, or took my hand to reassure me, it was all so wonderful.

But wonderful *friends*, I reminded myself. Nothing more. And I wanted more. I wanted him. I wanted him so much that it hurt.

Chapter 7

TWO WEEKS BEFORE GRADUATION, Madame Maria came outside during lunch looking for J.F. We were sitting at the benches where kids are caught smoking and making out, next to where the "sküter boyz" park their Viaggios and Vespas and Japanese blenders.

It was a beautiful spring day, and Jérémie, Maxime something-or-other, and Olivier were with us. I had on new Nikes, crisply white, and Maxime jokingly tried to step on them to scuff them up. I ducked and dived away from him in mock horror and to everyone else's amusement. Who knew someone so quiet could be so playful?

J.F. wore tennis whites with rainbow sweatbands on his head and wrists. He didn't play tennis. I long ago gave up rolling my eyes at his clothes. If only there existed some time machine you could use to go back and warn people of fashion mistakes.

The word on my T-shirt that day was "penultimate."

"I have special news." Madame Maria paused, I suppose, for

effect—the woman's so dramatic. My heart skipped a beat. For a second I thought she was going to come out to us. "Jean-François, the teachers have nominated you for the *Prix du Courage.*"

We all wished him *felicitations!* and slapped him on the back. Jérémie looked at J.F. with admiration and pride. He patted J.F.'s shoulder with a tenderness that for a second made me envy the kid. I should have done something more to show J.F. I was proud of him, too. Madame Maria hugged J.F. All the attention, but mostly the hug, made his cheeks redden. I never saw him blush before. Could he be any cuter?

"But don't get your hopes up," she added with this too-serious-for-life tone of voice that pissed me off. Was she saying J.F. didn't have a chance? In her opinion was there no way someone gay could win the award? That evening at the restaurant, I went off on one, wondering aloud to J.F. about whose side she was on. When the foam around my mouth from my cappuccino must've made me look crazed and feral, he reached across the table and put his hand on mine. My breathing slowed. My heart returned to beating normally. Next he'd be removing a thorn from my paw.

"I'm sure she didn't mean it like that, Spencer," he said when I was ready to listen. "She's doing her best. Like we all are."

I had a right to be upset. The *Prix du Courage* is a big thing at our school. The biggest. The winning student takes home a plaque, and there's a bigger plaque that's put up right outside the main office. Everyone has an opinion on whom should win, and students and teachers debate the merits of the nominees. Besides J.F., this year there was a girl in *secondaire III* who circulated a petition against lenient sentences for drunk drivers—her little sister was hit by one and almost died—and a boy in my grade who went through an intervention to stop smoking weed, although he almost never came to school, and the few recent times he did show up he looked more stoned than ever.

The last month of school meant the coalition had stopped meeting—we were supposed to study for end-of-year provincial exams, and the *secondaire V* students also had to prepare for graduation and life after high school. It hadn't sunk in yet that J.F. would be gone next year. I tried not to think how awful it was going to be without him.

The night before graduation while everyone partied, J.F. and I went to the candlelight vigil for Joe Rose. Madame Maria had shown us a flyer about it. We all knew what had happened; it had been on all the news. J.F. told me he was going, as I knew he would, "Alone if I have to." Ever the loyal sidekick, I said I'd go, too.

When we arrived at Parc de l'Espoir, hundreds of people had already gathered. At a makeshift table, we bought candles for the price of a donation to help pay for Joe's funeral. At the front of the crowd I could make out someone speaking, a woman's voice, but we were too far away to hear what she was saying.

The park was a strange space, wedged in the corner made by two adjacent buildings. More of an afterthought meant to fill an empty lot than a real park.

"It's the city's memorial to AIDS." J.F. pointed to poles with long strips of cloth ribbon hanging from them, ribbons of all colours, weathered to stringy rags. Not much of a memorial, I thought, then wondered why I had to be a bitch right then.

The park made me feel uncomfortable, the actual physical place, even if I couldn't figure out why. Then I saw the benches, or what I first assumed to be benches since people were sitting on them. When everyone stood to bow their heads in silence, I could see they were long slabs, low to the ground, made of shiny black granite. It took me aback. They looked like coffins and tombstones. Were they meant that way? Where's the *espoir*—the hope—in that?

We stood in silent tribute until the woman at the front spoke again. Then the crowd turned and walked east along rue Ste-Catherine to where Joe Rose was murdered.

J.F. and I didn't speak as we fell in with the others, easing into our place amongst them, adjusting to their flow as we moved forward as one, hearing only the sounds of shoes and boots padding and clicking and thumping on the asphalt. We walked down the centre of the street. People ran up ahead to the intersections to stop cars, their hands up, waving wildly, pleading to be seen in the dim light. We passed cafés and clothes stores and fast food restaurants where the smell of ninety-nine-cent-a-slice pizza reached us, and saunas with their blackened windows and blatant posters of naked men.

I narrowed my eyes until I saw only the glow of the candles people around us held—tiny beacons, stars out to be with us for the night. Block after block we walked as one. Every so often J.F.'s arm brushed against mine as the swell of the crowd gently pushed us together. When I looked at him to acknowledge our contact, J.F. made a muscle that strained the sleeve of his T-shirt. He smiled at me, no doubt hoping to get a smile out of me in return like it had the many times before.

I looked away. I was uneasy with his attempt at humour at a time like that. He tapped me gently on the arm, and in his face I saw an apology. I'd been quick to judge. I should've known that if anything, J.F. had meant to bring a touch of reality back into a surreal experience. A few months before I never would've imagined I'd be sharing with my gay and lesbian brothers and sisters, sadness and anger at the loss of another human being.

Without a word, J.F. put his arm around me. I looked at him again, ready to forgive if needed, but he continued to look straight ahead as we moved forward. Some things you just have to let go.

Outside the Frontenac métro where Joe Rose died, we all stopped. Someone up front spoke again, and one sentence rose above everything: "He died because we hate."

J.F. squeezed my shoulder and pulled me in tighter. He touched his lips against my ear and whispered, "I don't know what I'd do if anything happened to you."

I pulled my head away and looked at him. Even in the feeble illumination of candles and streetlights, I could see his tears.

When the vigil ended, we took a late bus back closer to home, then walked the rest of the way to J.F.'s house. We didn't talk much. There were a hundred things I could've said, hundreds more I wanted to ask him. But I didn't know how to bring them up, although I'd had plenty of time on the bus to rehearse various openings over and over in my head. At the basement door to his house, J.F. said, "It's pretty late," and smiled, simple and sincere.

That morning when I had told my mother I'd be staying over at J.F.'s, one of her eyebrows arched ever so slightly, but with true British restraint she didn't ask what I knew was on her mind. I was ready to tell her, "No, we're *just friends*," in no uncertain terms, but that admission was in itself pretty incriminating. Better to suffer one of my mother's looks than to put up with what my father would have said if he had found out. He would have teased me within an inch of my life. The possibilities were endless, although knowing him it would be some variation on me being "the full English breakfast on offer."

As J.F. opened the door, my heart stopped. Then raced ahead. Then stopped again. This was the first time I'd be sleeping over at another boy's house. But then again there's sleep and then there's *sleep*. I fully expected J.F. to show me to the guest room, say good night, and I'd be left alone to toss and turn, wondering what signals I did or didn't see.

I followed J.F. through the basement, past a family room with a big screen TV and too many chesterfields, to his room. He didn't open the lights, but I could make him out in the moonlight from a small window, standing in front of me, facing me, undressing to his boxer briefs. Was this happening? I wanted to believe it so very much. I undressed too, shaking all the while, hoping he wouldn't look at me—thin and pale, with no muscles to speak of.

J.F. pulled back the duvet on the neatly made bed and lay down. I waited for some indication, something clear and telling, but he just looked at me. That was enough. I slid in beside him, and he gathered the oversized feathery duvet around us.

We lay facing each other in his bed, a small single not big enough for the two of us, me nervously perched as near to the edge as possible, J.F. with his arms around me to rescue me from falling off. He pulled me in close to him. His body emitted heat that, combined with his firm hold on me, stopped my shaking. Our arms were around each other, our legs entwined, our bare chests and stomachs pressed together, skin touching skin. Our faces were so close I could feel his breath and mine flow between us and back again. Our breathing synchronized.

As close as our faces were to one another, as close as our lips were, only a breath away, it still didn't seem possible that something more could happen. When our bodies touched, my thoughts slowed until all I felt was the sensation of it all. At that moment there was nothing I could think or say or do, other than to lie in his arms and feel happiness and excitement coursing through me.

And that's when he kissed me. J.F. moved ever so slightly forward, and when his lips touched mine, they were soft and warm and moist. He kissed me with tenderness and care as though what we were sharing might break.

We remained that way for a long time, our lips touching, our bodies pressed against each other, holding one another tightly as if not willing to ever let go. When it seemed we'd fall asleep like that, I felt his lips tremble as they began to form words I could barely hear, he said them so softly.

"There's something about tomorrow I need to tell you."

Chapter 8

LIKE ALL GRADUATIONS, the ceremony at our school includes boring speeches, awards for sports and academics, and family members who cough and fidget in the stifling heat and the stench of too many people on a Saturday afternoon in late June. The graduating students, decked out in academic gowns and mortarboards with blue trim, our school colour—"separatist blue" my father would probably call it had he been there—sat in rows in the front of the gymnasium, on a stage put up for the occasion, facing the audience. The teachers were seated off to one side. Madame Maria was all smiles as she adjusted her ceremonial robes.

I ran most of the way and arrived late. Showing up at J.F.'s graduation was against all reason, but I needed to see if he'd receive the *Prix du Courage* and if he'd go through with his speech, the details of which he told me as we lay in each other's arms not so many hours ago. I don't know why I thought it might not happen—I guess because I didn't want it to.

After we woke up, I sat on his bed and watched him as he smoothed the collar of his suit jacket and asked me whether he should press the trousers again. His clothes for grad were conservative. I looked around for a funny hat or colourful suspenders to go with them, but didn't see any. The costume party was over.

Last night I'd wanted to leave after what he told me, but he'd insisted I stay. He didn't want me to be angry with him. So I stayed, but only because I didn't want to be a drama queen and rush out into the night. I really didn't want to be there.

His father called down the stairs to him that there were things still to do and he was going to be late. His parents wanted to take pictures, and some relative or another wanted him to phone them. I took that as my chance to escape.

"Well . . ." I stood and looked around for my jacket or something I'd brought with me and didn't want to leave behind and have to come back for. His bedroom was spartan. A bed. A desk. An Ikea bureau for clothes. A closet door. The walls had nothing on them except a rainbow flag over his bed. On the desk there was a lamp and a framed photo of the coalition. It had been taken on one of the days we sold wristbands. We were huddled together around a table outside the cafeteria doors, smiling and excited. What fools we were.

There was no jacket. I realized I hadn't brought anything with me except myself. Nothing else.

"Do you want to stay for breakfast?" J.F. stood there in his boxer briefs, a white dress shirt hanging from his index finger. I knew his question was asked more as a test than as an invitation. But who knows? Maybe he was on to something. All the answers to the mysteries of the universe at the bottom of a bowl of Shreddies.

I didn't have to answer. My cell phone chirped so I made a production of flipping it open and reading the text. It was from Rachelle. One word: "Well?"

Along with my mom, I'd told Rachelle I was sleeping over. She raised more of an eyebrow than my mother had.

I phoned my parents to pick me up. J.F. put on some sweats and walked me to the basement door. We stood waiting, watching his neighbour across the street ride his mower back and forth across a patch of lawn the size of a small swimming pool.

When my parents' car pulled up, J.F. hugged me and held on to me, my arms flattened to my sides by his embrace—I couldn't have pulled away if I'd wanted to. Only when his father yelled down again that there were graduation cards and gifts to open did he release me.

On the ride home my father didn't try to joke with me. At first I chalked it up to the early hour or that he was a bit put out he had to come and get me, but then I saw myself in the rearview mirror, a quick glimpse as I adjusted my position in the back seat. "A face like thunder," my father calls it when he sees me like that. But not today. He knew the mood I was in—sitting in the back seat instead of up front with him gave it away. He hates when I do that. "Not a cabbie," he usually says. This time he drove in silence.

Back home, I stayed secluded in my room, thinking and trying to nap. It was no use. As tired as I was, my mind wouldn't let me sleep. I wanted to cry, not giving a damn whether that made me weak or tough, but tears wouldn't come either. Only anger. Sadness and self-pity would have to wait.

When I'd vowed never to leave that room again, there was a quiet knock at my bedroom door. I didn't answer. As dramatic as that makes me, I decided never to speak again as well.

"Spencer?" My mom knocked again, a bit louder this time. "It's gone two. Are you going to the graduation? We'll drive you if you need a lift."

I barked at the door, "No!" Silence. But I knew she was still standing there, her hand about to turn the door knob, wanting to rush in and give me a cuddle, but thinking better of it.

"Are you okay? Don't you want to see your friend graduate?"

"He has a name," I shouted. Even though I didn't want to hear it right then. "Leave me alone."

She padded away leaving me by myself again. I felt bad that my anger was so disproportionate to her act.

I lay on my bed staring at the ceiling where once as a little kid I begged my parents to put in glass so I could look at the night sky before falling asleep. Instead they stuck up glow-in-the-dark stars. The glue had left faint star-shaped outlines.

No doubt the grad had begun. But what does that have to do with me? I rolled over, my face pressed against the wall. The coolness of the baby blue gyproc felt good. I could've stayed like that forever.

I sat up. That's not good enough! I jumped up and pulled on some jeans and a T-shirt that said "bedlam." I supposed I should've dressed better than that, but, as it was, I'd have to pull my finger out if I was going to make it in time. There was something I had to do.

Arriving late, I'd found an empty seat off to one side of the gym, near the doors that were wide open to the outside, hoping a breeze would lessen the already heavy air and heat inside. The woman next to me held to her shoulder a blotchy-faced toddler who either stared at me or squirmed to reach for me.

One by one the graduating students received their diplomas and had their pictures taken with the *directrice* or one of the *adjoints*, whoever had handed them the rolled up piece of paper. I clapped for J.F. with everyone else as he paused, diploma in hand, for his photo with Monsieur Courtois. And Rachelle, too, when it was her turn. She looked beautiful with her hair in an "updo," as she called it when she tried it out the week before. Some of her *pissenlit* hair fell in soft curls framing her face. Rachelle glowed, powered by her happiness at finally being finished with high school. Étienne ran up to the stage to take pictures of her with the digital camera she'd bought for the big day. She posed like a fashion model. Well, her version of one at least, suddenly all miserable and pouty. Despite everything, I chuckled.

The ceremony meandered on, and I thought about whether I'd see J.F. again. Next year he'd go to CEGEP, one of Québec's academic and technical colleges before university or work. J.F. had been accepted at one downtown, and though he hadn't told me, I expected he'd move there when commuting began to wear on him like it had my sister. It followed that at some point he'd meet new friends. I'd still be a high school kid. Then *just* some high school kid. That would suck.

It suddenly occurred to me he might meet someone there and fall in love. Thinking that made me nauseous. J.F. stood on a boat the tide was slowly taking out to sea and I'd be left alone on the shore. What could I do?

A sudden burst of applause focused my attention on Monsieur Courtois standing at the podium describing the qualities that made a student eligible for the *Prix du Courage*. Bravery. Dedication. Selfishness. Compassion. Hard work. Courtois in robes—for the first time something fit him. Yet he still looked constricted like underneath he had on a straitjacket. Pun intended.

"As you know," he said, "this award is decided upon by administrators, teachers, staff, and students. It's an honour for me to present this award to a student who was brave in ways that taught us all, myself included, about equality and social justice. Over fifty years ago, Ralph Sockman, an American minister, said, 'The test of courage comes when we are in the minority. The test of tolerance comes when we are in the majority.' That's as true today. This year's recipient of the *Prix du Courage* is . . ." He paused, trying to make it Oscar-night exciting, "Jean-François Giroux."

The applause exploded. Most of the parents, and all of the students and teachers, as far as I could tell, jumped up. Some of the graduating students stomped their feet, and the wooden stage thundered throughout the gym. Other classmates whistled, fingers to lips.

I didn't stand and I didn't clap. The woman beside me gave me a dirty look, and I stood up, not because of the look, but to see what was going on. I saw the top of J.F.'s head and most of his forehead as he made his way from the last row to the front of the stage. His hair was cut short, back to the way it was the first day I'd watched him put up the poster, without the Tintin tuft in front, though. He must've had it cut after I left. As he emerged from the end of the row, a ginger-haired boy grabbed J.F.'s hand and shook it with all the conviction of someone parched by thirst pumping well water.

J.F. escaped and stood at the podium. The applause intensified. J.F. was as serious as I'd ever seen him. As serious as when he told me about the red cap boy's suicide attempt. Or at the candlelight vigil. Or when lying together last night and he told me what he was going to say.

He took his speech from his shirt pocket, unfolded it, and placed it on the podium. He ran his hand over it twice to smooth it, then made three attempts to speak into the microphone before the clapping finally stopped and everyone sat down again.

"*Madame la directrice, adjoints, professeurs, invités, chers amis,*" J.F. began.

Then he told everyone, the teachers, his classmates, the parents and brothers and sisters and grandparents, what he had told me.

It was almost word-for-word as if he'd rehearsed it with me as we lay together in his bed. It was difficult for me to listen to again. It's tough to accept the truth that as amazing as that kiss was, and the wonder of our closeness this last year, both physical and emotional, it had only been between friends. J.F. and I would never be in love. Whether I liked it or not, I had to accept that no plans or schemes I could devise as I lay awake at night wanting him so much my whole body ached, would change that. I felt a sadness I'd never known before. I couldn't imagine when it would lessen. Or if it ever would. He was my first kiss after all.

At one point in his speech, J.F. stopped mid-sentence. With one hand he clutched the side of the podium, and with the other he picked up the piece of paper and brought it closer as though he no longer could read the words. My heart leapt—I grasped at the faint possibility he reconsidered going through with it. Leaning forward, I slowly whispered "please" three times, and felt the woman beside me move her child to her other side. But that word had no magic. J.F. put the paper back down on the podium and continued.

Jean-François Giroux told everyone he wasn't gay.

Chapter 9

I LEAVE THE GYM as soon as J.F. finishes his speech. I've heard enough. I stand alone outside the school, out front, where a few weeks before J.F. had waited to give me a birthday card of a cartoon rabbit holding a yellow balloon.

I need air, but there's no relief here either. I face the direction of what little breeze there is, but it's as humid and foul smelling as the air inside.

The graduation ceremony ends, and people spill out through the front doors and swarm from around the building. Some of them head towards their cars, off to parties and dinners and family celebrations. Most people stand around whispering. Gossiping. Three guesses whom they're talking about.

I never understood what people meant when they described a crowd as having a mood. Three years ago when my sister graduated, a happy group stood outside after the ceremony: my sister's friends hugged each other, parents shook hands, wishes of *felicitations* fell like apple blossom petals on a breezy day. But this crowd stands and looks around with suspicion. A mood you can taste, chewy and sour. They're restless like they're waiting for something to happen. Waiting for something more.

J.F. and his parents appear from the front doors, walking with purpose, trying to make it to the parking lot as fast as possible. None of his classmates stop him to congratulate him. There are no hugs. No one waits to shake his parents' hands. Instead some people turn and stare while others turn their backs.

Monsieur Courtois pushes through a side door, no longer in robes, and stands in J.F.'s path, forcing him and his family to stop. J.F. takes a small step back, almost falling over. He offers a weak smile, but it quickly evaporates.

Constricted by a beige suit jacket that's sizes too small, the *adjoint's* arms struggle to wave about, looking both laughable and menacing at the same time. He's saying something, but I can't make out his words from where I'm standing. He jabs a finger at J.F.'s chest. J.F.'s father steps between them, then adeptly navigates J.F. and his mother around the man. His father's determination shows through his narrowed eyes and thinned lips. As they walk away, Courtois wipes his forehead then flicks the sweat from his hand onto the pavement.

Now as I watch J.F. leave school for the last time, I know what I have to do.

I make my way through the crowd, overhearing people saying J.F.'s name with all manner of sharp tone and pitch. Before I can reach him and his parents, Madame Maria grabs my arm.

"Spencer. Are you okay?"

I nod. I feel her looking at me while I remain focused on J.F. so I won't lose him.

"Don't tell me you're *not* gay, too," she says with a laugh. My face must be telling her I'm in no mood for jokes, because she says, "Sorry," and clears her throat.

"I guess we can forget about *Coalition arc-en-ciel* next year," she says.

I look at random faces as people step back to make room for J.F. and his parents to leave. Expressions haven't changed from back in the gym where they visibly hardened from shock to anger as he spoke. The faces I see now haven't softened at all. Not one grain of sand.

"Why?" I say. "There's still a lot to do."

I turn to look at her to show her I'm serious.

"Okay," she says slowly, unsure. She sighs. "The disciple John to the end, huh? Then we'll do it again. Do you see yourself taking over from Jean-François?"

"Of course," I snap like I think her question's too silly to deserve an answer. Madame Maria's eyes register the force of my words.

"I'm sorry," I say. "It's just . . ." Just what? Just my misplaced anger? I can't tell her that, though her expression shows me she probably already knows.

"Big shoes to fill," she says. "There are some angry people you'll have to deal with."

I know she means the other members of the coalition. I don't know what I'll say to them, how to explain everything that happened. How do you explain J.F.? I'm still trying to work that out myself.

"He did help people," I say, but it comes out more of a question than I like.

"Restitution." She gives her head a shake like she's walked into a cobweb. In English she says, "He'll be all right, Spencer. You've done all a friend can do." I'm not sure what I've done exactly, but for some reason it feels good hearing that.

Suddenly her arms are around me, holding on tightly like my mother does. And the strange thing is I hold on, too. When we finally let go, I give her my best effort at a smile and walk away to find J.F. She's not half bad, our Maria.

I make my way through the crowd, following the wake J.F.'s made, now closing in on itself. I can no longer see him, not even the top of his head. I break out of the crowd in time to see J.F. and his parents over in the parking lot. I could still run like a madman and reach them, but I don't move. They get in their car and drive away. As the car moves down the school's long driveway, I stand there and let my chance to say goodbye slip away. The car's brake lights flash, and the car turns onto the road. Out of nowhere I hear crisp, clear words. "It's over."

In my head I play what would've happened had I reached J.F. It's so vivid that for a moment it seems like a memory of something that's actually taken place. As I approach, his father and mother look at me with sad defeat, asking themselves, "What now?" Even J.F. gives a subdued smile that questions me. His open, joy-filled eyes now contract with concern.

But they're worried for nothing. I simply put out my hand and say, "*Merci mille fois.*" Without hesitation, J.F. takes my hand, pulls me to him, and hugs me goodbye.

Forgiveness is a funny thing. Sometimes it's better to give it even before you find it inside yourself to offer. Or before it's deserved.

When I can no longer see the car, I turn back to the people still standing around, loudly talking again. I scan the crowd for Rachelle—she's expecting me at her post-grad party. Then I change my mind. I start down the driveway to the road and the bus that will take me away from here. I need time on my own.

At the bus stop, I decide to walk home instead. I don't make it far down the road when my parents' car pulls up alongside me and my mother powers down the passenger-side window.

"Going our way?" I hear my father say from inside. I crouch down next to the car. Both my parents have that look, the one that says I might make a mess out of my life if not for their watchful eyes . . . and that look.

"We're feeling a little peckish," my mother says gently. She looks like she desperately wants to hug me.

My father booms: "Speak for yourself, Margaret. I'm starved. I could eat a scabby horse between two pissy mattresses. Care to join us, mate, or are you going to catch us up?"

I shrug, but reach for the car door anyway.

As I'm about to get in, Maxime something-or-other walks by with two adults, his parents, I figure, trekking back to their car. I hadn't seen him at the ceremony. What does he think of this whole mess? But he isn't graduating; he's in my grade. Why's he even here? For J.F.?

"*Salut!*" he says to me. He's wearing a dark suit and tie, his hair-fin at attention, and I have to admit he looks pretty good. Kind of hot, even. "Are you going to Rachelle's later?" he asks.

I nod like an idiot, shocked speechless he spoke without having the words strip-mined from him. That's it! I realize what it is about him that nags at me—he's Étienne Leblanc's brother, his fraternal twin of all things. I don't know why I didn't twig that before. Maybe because I've never seen them together. They're not at all similar in personality, even if they do look a bit alike now that I think about it.

Maxime waves goodbye to me. I nod back to him again, hoping I'm still coming across cool and casual—yes, it's ironic that now I'm the one at a loss for words. I chuckle as I get in the car and shut the door. It was time to change my "tall boys" motto, anyway. Maybe something like, *A twin in the hand . . .*

"You're in with a promise there, mate," my father says as we drive away.

"James!" my mother play-scolds him, feigning shock. "The vapours," my dad calls it. But she laughs when he says, "What? Can't a father give his support when his son's about to get a leg over?"

They carry on like that, talking about me and what they think is my love life as though I'm not there. Normally stuff like that drives me crazy. Right now, I have to admit, it cheers me up—it's almost funny. As we drive away, I massage my temples with my fingers at the madness of it all.

While they natter on, I look out the window as the car moves along this all-too-familiar road. Soon we pass the restaurant where J.F. and I did more than enough talking to make up for the silent waitress.

I think about J.F.'s speech. I understand everyone's anger. I know people are upset—some more than upset. J.F. wasn't honest with them. He deceived them. He led them on the whole time. Yes, there is that. I know that more than anyone. No one would judge me if I never spoke to him again. But no matter how angry I want to be, I can't help thinking about what he did for the school, how he helped people who needed someone when they thought no one was there for them. How he helped me.

When J.F. made his big announcement, the gym went quiet. No one coughed. No one cleared their throats or fidgeted. Even the babies were silent. The audience stared with puzzled faces and shock. Then someone in the back actually booed. That's all it took for everyone to start talking at once.

J.F. carried on, giving the impression he was oblivious to the uproar. When he finished, he carefully folded his speech, put it back in his pocket, and went back to his seat, disappearing among all the other graduating heads.

After he spoke those words, I don't think anyone heard the rest of his speech above the noise. I couldn't. But I knew what he said from when we lay in his bed last night. It surprises me how I can summon what he said so readily, when I really don't want to at all. I'd go so far as to say I'd feel better if I could forget it had happened at all. But it's right there—J.F.'s lips moving, saying how people judged him and labeled him until the only peace he could find was to become what they wanted him to be.

"I don't regret it," J.F. says, or, rather, his mouth continues forming words and I hear his voice from hours before in his bedroom. "Don't get me wrong. I've made some wonderful friends and stood up for what I believe is right, but it is those friends who are truly brave." His face twists as if he's hearing his own voice for the first time, detecting the "wisp" that's under the surface lying in wait to ambush him in times of stress.

"They fight every day to be out. For acceptance and all that's owed in human decency. Let's hope they don't have to keep fighting for the rest of their lives. I'm sad I couldn't be myself until I was what you wanted me to be—until I fit your label, your box, your stereotype. I'm sorry I was so weak. Maybe what I've tried to achieve with the coalition helps to make up for that."

Words only I heard. Words I continue hearing. Like echoes from a room with only a solitary chair.

As much as I hate to admit it, J.F. was right about one thing. It takes courage to come out—telling your family and your friends and not knowing for sure how they'll react, hoping for the best, sometimes experiencing the worse. I heard it all with the coalition as each member's story was placed at J.F.'s feet.

It takes strength to be honest with yourself and to lay yourself so open to others. Coming out is a never-ending process—for the rest of my life if I want anyone to know who I am, I'll tell them I'm gay. When I meet new friends. At a new school. A new job. At every turn in my life, if I'm going to be honest about who I am, that's one of the things I'll want to say. I imagine my life from now on will be a series of small, incremental coming-outs.

But there's only one time when you tell the world who you are, when you take away any chance to turn back, when you'll be known as "queer" from that point on. Own it or lose it! For everyone in *Coalition arc-en-ciel*, myself included, our telling the world meant coming out at school.

Despite everything, J.F. deserves that award. He *is* courageous. How many other people have had to come out to the world twice?

I look at my parents, talking away in the front seat, full of good humour. They carry on, well into planning future weddings for my sister and me. Beaches and sunsets. Heart-felt vows and lingering kisses. For some inexplicable reason they have my sister paired with a podiatrist and me with a lawyer who has two adopted children, a girl and a boy, whom he's named Chloe and Ethan. I can't help but smile. My dad catches it in the rearview mirror and winks.

In a few days I'll call J.F. to see how he is. Maybe we'll go for coffee, talk over what's happened, maybe even laugh again. When it doesn't hurt as much. Who knows, I might show up with eighties hair, a red and black leather jacket, and a single sequined glove. He'd get a kick out of that.

At some point, whether Jean-François's at college or university or work, even years from now when he's out in the world trying to make it a better place—as I know he will—surely he'll need an old high school friend.

If My School Asked Me Not to Be Out
Pages from Joe Rose's Notebook

IF MY SCHOOL ASKED ME not to be out, I'd be pretty upset. To be honest, I'd tell them to *Fuck off!* I wouldn't even entertain such a comment. I'd probably yell at them.

I'd tell them it's not fair because you can't tell someone to not act like himself. I've always been this way. I'm not going to change just for them. They have no right to tell me who I can or can't be.

I'd probably complain. I'd report them to the school board, because it's in violation of pretty much all of the school board's rules about acceptance. I'm sure all my friends would stand behind me. If the school said that, they'd all go, "What the hell's their problem? Where do they get off telling you that?" My family would support me, too. I'm sure the teachers would because they know me. They'd stand beside me. Some have already told me that.

No. I'm sorry, but I would not tolerate that. If they asked me not to be out, I wouldn't want to go to that school.

Who would?

**"In case you haven't noticed, I'm gay.
Pass the salt."
Tristan's Story**

The first time . . .

I wouldn't know where to begin telling you about what's been happening. It's no greeting card, that's for sure. You said I can talk about anything I want, so I'll start with school since I spend most of my day there. It's boring. It's deadly boring. I waste most of my time waiting with like baited breath for the bell to ring so I can finally, you know, leave and go home. Like I keep telling myself, "One more month." I mean, not that this is new or anything—the other ten years were just as boring. I go to school and I never really fit in and I have to listen to these immature conversations around me, and I just can't be into it. Then the curriculum is dull and repetitive and not challenging. Like the whole concept of how high school's set up is just such bull.

As far as suburban neo-conservative schools go, I'd say my school is a reasonably good one. I think I sort of found a niche with friends and whatnot. It has your standard contingency of assholes and jocks, but, you know, every place does, and I think the assholes-to-decent-person ratio is pretty reasonable. It doesn't have any gangs and it doesn't have many drugs—at least I've never been offered any. I saw on the news that at my old school they had this whole big thing with a drug raid, which was sort of fun because I got to see everyone who was mean to me being taken out in handcuffs crying. It was so perfect. It was like a Kodak moment.

I guess I've always been more mature than my peers, even in kindergarten through grade six. I always looked at people sort of oddly when they would do things that, I guess in retrospect, were normal for someone that age. Like laughing at the word "poop" or—oh, oh, oh!—giggling like schoolgirls through sex education. I remember in elementary school we had two sciences: science *naturelle* and science *humaine*. And science *naturelle* was like a French introduction to physics in grade four. We learned about pushing and pulling, except it was like *tirer* et *pousser*, and, you know, people would giggle at *pousser* because it sounds like "pussy" in English. I was totally horrified by that so I told off the entire class. "This is science! Snap out of it." I think it was just a maturity gap.

Things aren't much different now.

Like in French this year they randomly put me in the class with, you know, the assholes and the people who throw snowballs in class and do tiresome stuff like that. I know people in the other French class and it's like a hot bed of intellectual activity. I always lean back in my chair and look out the classroom door and see the other group in their classroom, and they're all focused and taking notes, and I'm like, "Sigh," while I'm being hit in the back of the head with a snowball. Actually that was a big problem at the start of the year—basically I was persecuted for being randomly assigned to the asshole group and ending up with a bunch of pretty immature people. But I didn't care as much as they probably would've liked me to care, trying as hard as they did to make my life unpleasant. But I have to admit it was stressful and tiring and I'd often say to myself, "I just don't know how I'm going to do this."

I started adopting various coping mechanisms, but, I mean, Gandhi was a great guy and all, but the only real way to quell pre-adolescent behaviour in, you know, late adolescents is sort of "an eye for an eye." Like once they threw their dictionary at the back of my head, right? At first I was sort of shocked and asked myself, "Is this actually happening? Did someone just throw a book at me? Aren't we like sixteen-year-olds?" And, so, the first time I actually gave it back. And then the second time, no. I turfed it out the window and they were like, "Hey," and I was like, "Well, I'm sorry, but what exactly did you expect?" Then they threw a more expensive book they needed for the course, which I tore in half and threw out the window. That actually worked. They didn't throw books at me anymore.

Yeah, I know it might be borderline maladaptive, but basically that's what you have to do to get through the day. That and reassuring myself how much better I am and that it doesn't matter. I shouldn't even be in that class—I take all the advanced math and physics and chemistry and bio courses. My marks are in the first quintile—my average is like eighty-eight-ish. I know there's always a few little bastards that run around saying, "My average is ninety-four point six," but, I mean, I'd much rather be me because I actually have some personality to speak of rather than, you know, doing good in math and then going home to watch TV and eat Cheezies.

Anyway, I don't give two shits if some people don't like me. If you ask my friends about me, they'd tell you I'm really funny, smart, charming—pretty much everything I guess James Bond would be, but with a twist of rainbow. And the people who don't like me, they'd probably describe me as, oh, let's see, "fucking faggot" type deal. You're sort of complimented with the slander.

Oh, oh, oh, oh! Get this! Today someone called me a loser and I was like, "Well you're pretty smug for someone who takes auto. Like geez, are you going to hit me with a wrench?"

The benefit of being in grade eleven this year is I won't ever have to see these people again. I was accepted in the first round to the best English college in the province in Health Science. I doubt any of them are even going to graduate. I want to pursue a career in clinical psychiatry—they just want to get laid and drink beer for a living.

My teachers pretty much think I'm what every other student should strive to become. Well my math teacher calls me lazy, but he calls everyone lazy. So I don't take what the assholes say or do too personally. I'd say I have a reasonable self-image with maybe a little chip on my shoulder.

Sure school can be hard sometimes, but you know, it can also be fun. It's the assholes that make school hard. But it's not the most difficult thing I've had to go through in my life. That's for sure. I can deal with it. I can find creative ways to cope with people who don't accept me and, I mean, I can pretty much solve creatively any problem that comes up. I'm not going to sit back and take it. Not any more. I used to. Like when they threw that dictionary at me, they were all like Mr. Man-like and furrowed their brows and, you know, threw out their chests and all that macho stuff. But I didn't back down. They were like, "We'll kick your ass," and I was like, "Well bring it, bitch." And, yeah, they didn't bring it. I was like, Whoa! Endorphin rush!

At the very least I'll have something appropriately witty to say, and, before you say anything, I know the whole-humour-is-a-defense thing. That's what I count on.

Some of my teachers are funny. They don't care I'm gay—they don't treat me any differently. Pretty much the only difference is they refrain from saying things like, "When you meet a nice girl and settle down . . ." For example, my physics teacher who I really like—he's funny, about your age, and you can really engage him in conversation even if it's not about the subject at hand—one day I was talking to him about how I'm going to college next year. He said, "Well, my son went there and that's where he met the girl who's now his wife." And then he was like, "You're going to meet a gir . . . person there who you're going to really love." And I was like, "Aww."

It's not like every teacher knows. Actually, in the back of my agenda I have this little anal-retentive list of people I've told. I think I've told twenty or so people at school, mostly friends and three teachers that I know of, plus I think some resource woman, plus a few teachers who I'm pretty sure are wise to me. I think I sort of hinted at it to the chemistry teacher, who isn't really a good teacher, but he's sort of slow, so I'm not sure if he picked up on it. It was something . . . subtle. I think it was like an "I'm on the other bus" sort of comment. He didn't really acknowledge it. I'm not a fan of his anyway. He's basically a nice guy and all, but he just lacks that skill to be a good teacher. He's not an emotional kind of guy, and he's fifty-something, so I don't want to scar him talking about boyfriends or things like that.

I like the teachers in general. They aren't as old as the teachers in many other schools, and they're more—well I judge aloofness by the probability a teacher will like bring cookies or something to class or like invite me to their house for tea. Not that they've ever done that, but, I mean, they're much more likely to do it here than at my old school. That's one of the reasons I changed schools two years ago—this one's much better than that cesspool.

It was funny how I told my English teacher I'm gay. Some guy dumped me and I was upset. I actually missed two days of school because . . . well that's a whole other story. When I came back she was like, "What's wrong? Are you feeling better?" because she assumed I was sick or something. I was so in, you know, poor humour, and I explained to her it was about a boy and I gave her like the whole background story. She was like, "Oh, yeah," and I could see her go into a corner with gears turning in the back of her head. I think she . . . well she caught on pretty quickly. She was completely understanding. She told me it's like mourning a loss. She was really cool about it.

Last week we were silent reading for the research project we have to do for her class, so I went up to her desk and asked her something or other and she said something about . . . I don't know . . . something about deadlines. So I said, "Well, you know, life is entirely too important to be taken seriously. Oscar Wilde." She was like, " Oh, well, speaking of which, I'm doing a unit about Oscar Wilde with my grade nines," and I was like, "Oh! Really? That's interesting. He was a great fellow."

She showed me this big biography of Oscar Wilde and it had pictures in it of him and his lover. We spoke about how his boyfriend's father had him put in jail and all that good stuff, and I commented on the boyfriend's cuteness, because he really was—I mean for the 1850's or whatever. They had these whole double portraits done—it was sort of sweet—and I pointed to the boyfriend and said, "He's kind of cute," and she was like, "Ha, ha, ha. Oh, Tristan, you slay me."

That was a lot better than when my economics teacher found out. I came to class one Monday after a pretty special weekend and she was like, "Well, you have an awfully big smile on your face?" And I was like, "Yes I do." And she was like, "So you have a girlfriend?" And I was like, "Well, it's hardly a girl." And she was like, "Oh!" Well, she's Greek Orthodox, right? So she was sort of like, "Don't talk about it. Keep it on the down low. You don't want people to find out." I asked her, "Why's that?" and she said, "I don't want you picked on any more than you already are." I told her, "I don't get picked on," and she said, "It's okay, Tristan." So I was like, Yeah. Whatever! Talk to the hand, listen to the finger.

I think she thinks I'm just trying to maintain my pride and I'm this doormat who's picked on, when I'm not picked on at all. Well, no more than anyone else is in that place. She wasn't being very supportive. I think she should have said something like what my French teacher said when she commended my bravery, instead of saying, you know, "Avoid all confrontation because confrontation is bad and standing up for what you believe in is bad."

Oh. My last year's English teacher was preaching to us about how he was unsure of the ethics of homosexuality, and he made me angry, so I yelled at him. He was telling this story about how he danced with a transvestite who he didn't know was a transvestite. I don't even remember how it came up in class—it wasn't as though we were doing Shakespeare or something. He was saying that after he found out that, you know, that the women or man was a transvestite, he got sort of freaked out and I guess was now spoiled on the idea of transvestitism. People in the class went "Eww" and I rolled my eyes.

He went on to say that because of his traumatic experience he was unsure about having gays in the school because he wasn't sure of the ethics or if it would corrupt the rest of the students. So, anyway, he went on about, "I'm a true Christian so I don't know how I'm going to take homosexuality and if I want homosexuals in my school?" He'd always bring up God, but until then he seemed more preoccupied with persecuting other groups. This was the first time he mentioned gays.

I told him after class he was offensive and what he said was unacceptable. I said, "You know, it's *public* education for a reason. We don't have to talk about God every day and you don't have to make us read your holy books. We're not the Taliban." That didn't go over well.

I stood up for something. Yay! I stood up for, I guess, *the cause.* I don't remember everything I said to him, but I'm sure I was biting and cynical like only I can be.

Anyway, that Oscar Wilde book my English teacher showed me was about the only thing about gays I've ever seen in the school. I went to the library once and there was this one book that was dedicated to homosexuality but it was written in like 1975. It was sort of funny because it said things like, "Can I still jive with my friend even if he's gay?" I like leafed through it for a while but, I don't know, it wasn't really interesting to me probably because I knew it already. There are like four books in all about sexual orientation in the sexuality section of our library, which is like in a corner so the prude librarian doesn't have to talk about it.

Oh, yeah, yeah. Okay. So one day in class the French teacher was like, "Tristan I want to talk to you for a minute when the bell rings." And I was like, "Oh, oh!" And she was like, "No, it's nothing bad." So I was like, "Oh. Okay." So I stuck around after class and she said, "I'm going to start a unit on homosexuality, and I wanted to make sure that was okay with you and you won't feel uncomfortable in any way." At first I was like, Wait a minute. Check the back of the agenda. She doesn't know! So I asked her how she knew, but she was like, "I have my sources. Don't worry." I thought to myself, The economics teacher! It had to be the economics' teacher because they're like best friends, right? These teachers gossip a lot, so I figured either she talked to the French teacher about this, or the French teacher mentioned to the economics teacher she's going to do this unit in her class and the economics teacher said to the French teacher, "Well, Tristan's gay. Maybe you should talk to him first."

Anyway I said, "No, I won't be uncomfortable. But thanks for asking." Then she said she'd maintain control of the class if anything should happen. I didn't know what she meant by that. I was like, Well, what's the worse that could happen? I was thinking, What are you going to do, write my name on the blackboard and point to it a lot? I guess I was worried she'd say, "For example, there's a gay student in this class right now and his name is Tristan and he's sitting right there," and point to me a lot. But I told her, "Okay. Sounds good." That's when she said, "Oh, I think it's great someone your age can be so comfortable in himself regardless of others and not hide it. You can count on me to lend you my support against anyone who'd give you a hard time, if you need it." I said, "Thanks." I thought she was very cool for A: undertaking that unit and B: for making sure it was okay by me. I thought it was the considerate thing to do.

Nothing actually did happen. The whole class was quite receptive to the unit. She started with this discussion about, "What do you think the causes of homophobia are?" and people said whatever. Fear. Prejudicial society . . . Pretty much just fear—that was the only thing they could come up with. Then she asked the question, "If one of your best friends came up to you and said they were gay, what would your reaction be? Would you be receptive? Understanding? Negative? Uncomfortable? Happy? Angry?" Whatever. And like all the girls said they would be receptive and understanding, but pretty much a higher—a much higher proportion of the boys said they would be uncomfortable but understanding. There were only one or two people who said, "I would burn them at the stake," and, you know, they were met with much name-calling and "How dare you!" and all that indignation. I guess one person thought he would be funny by saying, "Oh, I would hate him" nah-nah-nah-nah. And everyone turned around and they totally balled him out. "How dare you hate someone just because that's the way they are?" I think he was very embarrassed. And rightly so.

This idiot—let's call him Jeremy, because his name *is* Jeremy— started talking about how, you know, gays should be shot in the streets but lesbians are okay. I was like, "Do you think you're the only idiot with that opinion?" Other people just went, "Ahh," and rolled their eyes and stopped talking to him. The teacher was trying to be as impartial as possible, like showing him the most respect she had to by law. She said to him, "Well, I don't really think that's a valid point," and some other stuff. She was very diplomatic in the way she called him an idiot. But she let me have my peace at least. I told him that, you know, he basically should be ashamed of himself for hating something that he A: doesn't know and B: has no reason to hate. First I talked about the hypocrisy of his philosophy that lesbians are okay, but gay men are evil. And then I suggested perhaps *he* is gay since he fears them so much. I asked him, "Do you think you're prone to being gay, is that why you don't want them around? Are you worried you're going to be attracted to them and you won't be able to restrain yourself?" He kept saying, "No! No! That's sick!"

I said, "A-ha," and I very satisfiededly shuffled my papers and turned around. Another one for Tristan!

Everyone who was in on the discussion was on my side. After class a whole bunch of people were like, "Good job Tristan," you know, complimenting me for trying to defend my people from some guy who found his way into enriched English.

. . .

What else do you want me to say? Isn't that enough for today?

A week later . . .

I know I'm supposed to talk about my family and tell you all the dysfunctional details, but if it's all right with you, I'm really not in the mood. Since last time I told you about my teachers, I might as well tell you about my friends . . . or I can waste your time talking about the weather, if you want.

Yeah, it's the last week of school and everyone has graduation fever. My flock of friends are trying to figure out who's going in the limo with them. "Let's get Tristan, he'll be fun." I think it's a symptom of being gay—they think gays are more festive. They like the fact that they can, I guess, if need be, change in front of me without much hooting and hollering. It's every girl's dream to have a gay friend, so they kind of love you no matter what your personality is, so I have like this flock of girls by default to outweigh any enemies. Anyway, I'd rather have it this way than the straight way. You know, people who buy their wardrobe at Canadian Tire, with the chains, and then who like play hockey with their jock straps and, you know, testosterone and all that jazz.

I'm not even sure what the attraction is, but I guess gays tend to be funny and like . . . I don't know. Maybe it's the novelty that you can check out hot guys with a guy and, you know, go shopping with him slash me. Yeah, I admit it, sometimes I do indulge in grad dress shopping with my friends. I give them great advice. They need the help. I tell them they can't wear prints or plaid. Then I brush off my hands knowing my work here is done.

For this whole grad thing, I'm so disorganized, I haven't even thought about it. People are talking about reserving tables and I'm like, "I didn't know you had to reserve a table." I thought it was like, "Here's a table. Let's sit down." But, no, apparently that's not it. They're all urgent about it and they keep asking me, "You haven't reserved a table yet?" Graduation's next week and it's being held on some boat, so even if you're not having a good time you're sort of stuck on it.

At first I wasn't even going to go. People were like, "So are you coming to the grad?" And I was like, "No." And they were like, "Why?" And I said, "Because I like to hear the word 'why' shrieked at me repeatedly." But that didn't stop them, and people kept saying, "Oh, you should go. If you don't go then you'll regret it. What's the worse that can happen? So you'll have a bad time for a few hours, at least you'll know what it was like." So I said, "Fine," but I'm still not sure I'll show up.

I've only been to one school dance and it certainly was everything I anticipated and so much more in that it's like a bunch of teenagers, you know, twitching awkwardly. I went with this friend, Carly, and we went, you know, with the idea we were going to a zoo or a nature park or on safari. We sort of hid in the shadows and watched these gangly teenagers sort of jerking back and forth not even to the beat of the music. These other people kept trying to make me dance, and I sort of entertained them for a while until they eventually turned their backs and ran away.

We didn't stay long, though. Carly wanted to stay until the end but I told her I've seen *Degrassi* and I think I know what happens. Not the new one—I only like the old eighties one with Snake and Spike and the pregnant girls and the jean jackets. Sometimes it's better not to experience high school yourself when you can watch it on TV.

But for grad it's like the entire student body keeps encouraging me to bring a same-sex date. Well, some people have asked me, "So who's your date?" I tell them I don't have one anymore slash yet, and then they say, "Oh. So who do you want to bring?" I'm like, "I don't know yet."

I know what they're getting at—is it a boy or a girl? But I'm sort of making them beg. They keep telling me, "You should take one of your friends." That's what they say, "one of your *friends*." Well, how many do you think I have? I think they only want me to bring someone so they can take pictures and stuff. I expect autographs will be part of it as well.

I'm sure the student population would be overwhelming in favour, despite the horrified reactions of some. Like my Christian friend and I think my economics teacher would, you know, prefer if I took an opposite-sex date. Well, since the economics teacher is Greek Orthodox and doesn't want me to talk about it, I'm gonna hazard a guess she's more comfortable with straight relationships.

Yeah. Sarah's my sweet little Christian friend who's like, "Oh, my goodness," and all that stuff. She's devoutly Christian, you know, so by extension sort of anti-homosexual. She's not like, "Oh, I hate those fags." She's more like, "Well, it seems to me they're, you know, possessed by demons." She actually said that to me once and I was like, Oh, my God! When I told her, "You know, I'm gay," she was like, "Oh. Well. Okay." She tried to be very casual about it, right? Then she said to me, "Tristan, I think you have a problem." I was like, Oh, for Christ's sakes!

She brought me to her Christian youth group. She goes to Bible church, I'm not sure what brand it is, I can never get a straight answer out of anyone. I asked the priest or whatever, "So what type of Christian are you?" but he said, "We don't like to identify with any specific denomination." I was like, Hmmm. Two's company, three's a cult.

When she asked me to come with her to her Christian youth group, I said, "You're not going to make me your summer project, are you?" She was like, "Oh, Tristan. No." Then she whispered to me, "I only want you to be in a position where you can better see the light."

So I went and they didn't talk about homosexuality at all. So I was like, Well, why am I here then? They only talked about, you know, better living through Christ. This youth pastor put on this movie about some guy talking about how we don't need to be anything but be believers of Christ to get to Heaven. We can pretty much do anything we want as long as we love Christ in the end and we'll be okay, right?

When it was over the youth pastor told us he didn't really agree with that because he thought that was taking advantage of the system because it's still possible to get into Heaven even if you're a rapist or whatever as long as you believe in Christ.

They said nothing about being gay when I was there. Apparently the last time they did talk about it, so I missed out. I only went that once—it was just so boring—all the people there were so hypocritically nice. They were all nice and friendly and shiny on the surface and were like, "Hi! I'm—" whatever. I was like, "Hi. I'm Tristan," you know, relaxed, and they were like, "Okay, do you want to roast marshmallows now?" No matter what I'd say, they'd ask if I wanted more marshmallows. So. Anyway.

Now I find it sort of fun to shock Sarah. I think I'm working on showing her gays are not the Antichrist because she doesn't know anyone who's gay, so, I mean, all she knows is what her apparently biased teachings tell her. Obviously she's going to think that right? She doesn't bring my being gay up at all, she sort of does it indirectly. Like if a subject comes up like boys or something, she'll make a sly comment.

It's kind of difficult being friends with her because her parents don't let her have boys over to their house. Especially gay boys. I might, you know, bring down the property value.

All my friends that I used to have from my old school live near my mother, but when I moved out of my mother's house, I guess they sort of were alienated by my stress or whatever, even though I don't really think that was part of it. They all left my life in such a way that . . . well . . . now they hate me. I don't know. It's only been a few months—they've probably forgotten about me already. We don't go to the same school so I never have to see them. Anyway, the friends I have now through school are mostly girls. Who'd have guessed! They're my confidantes, but I don't see them out of school too often. We do the typical fag hag type things together.

My friends outside of school are mostly guys. Most of them are older, I guess like eighteen or nineteen. Gay, of course. I met most of them networking. Like you know one first and then they sort of introduce you to the other one, and then you become better friends with that person and you sort of leave out the guy who got you there. I could probably draw you the whole map on paper if you want. Usually we go downtown because I have this immense hatred for where I've grown up. I despise its neo-conservative suburban paradise status. So, yeah, most of the time I go downtown or just stay home and have various idle conversations on MSN. I have like sixty or so people on MSN. Most of them are random people who saw one of my, "Help me, I'm desperate and lonely" profiles on the Internet and have added me. And then there's whomever I know through whatever romantic interests I might have.

And, yeah, okay. Okay. Okay. On Monday I was in my chemistry class, right? And the teacher was talking about electrolytes or something, and I was experiencing this magnetic force between my head and . . . the . . . chemistry desk . . . like when he's talking. I was gazing out the door and this hot boy I like walked up and I was like, Oh, this is interesting. His locker's right across the hall from the classroom door and I was kind of staring for a while—I don't think he could see me. Then he started to get changed right there in the hallway—well like still in his boxers and stuff. I was like, Oh, this is way more interesting than electrolytes.

So he was getting changed and I was kind of staring and he was doing some kind of straight-guy deodorant thing or whatever. When I think of straight guys I always think of deodorant and hockey sticks. Whatever. So, anyway, I was like gazing at him and I think he saw me and I was like, Okay. Staring contest! I kept looking, wondering what would happen. My heart was like thump-thump-thump-thump-thump. He kind of smiled, and I was like, Oh yeah! Then he, I don't know, did some weird facial twitch thing that might have been a wink. I'm not sure. Anyway, he might not even be gay. He definitely has some gay qualities though. It's sort of like the thin, neat, single thing. He has a quality—I can't put my finger on it—he's tall and gawkish. I think he just doesn't know he's gay yet, but I wouldn't mind being the one to turn on a few light bulbs for him.

I heard from a few people that he has no life other than hockey because he's in the *sports études* programme. It was kind of exciting. He's not in any of my classes, but I see him all the time in the hallways. Normally he doesn't look at me, but my friend's boyfriend is friends with him, so I'm gonna have him do my bidding and find out if he's, whatever, interested. I feel like such a girl, but whatever. Just so I'm safely out of the school when he wants to beat me up or something. Well, even though I'm sure he won't beat me up, I'm sure he'd remember me. I just don't want it to be awkward. I don't want to have to look away when I see him. And my grad picture in the yearbook is really good, so I think I'll leave a positive impression on him.

Someone said he looks like me and I was like "Oh, my God!" except she said it in a sort of a negative way. She was making a face and saying, "You think he's hot? I think he looks like you." I totally missed the point and I was all excited: "You think he looks like me!" I thought she called me hot but she was really calling him ugly. Then she said, "It's like having a crush on yourself." I was like, "No it's not." Whatever. Taste the rainbow, bitch!

Well that's one bonus of being gay, you can totally check out the people who don't know without them clueing in. I can stare at, you know, guys without them thinking, "He must be checking me out." I don't know, maybe it *is* the first thing they think of, but I carry on under the assumption it isn't and gaze away. I've gotten a few uncomfortable looks, but I sort of giggle and look away.

I was seeing a guy for a while. I guess he was my first romantic interest, but it sort of sucked because he lives in Nevada. I used to work at Toys-R-Us and I met him there for like forty-five minutes. He was on a vacation of the Northeast with his family for some reason. I don't even know why he was at a suburban Canadian Toys-R-Us. Maybe he was looking for metric wrenches or beaver pelts or something—for kids. We were making eyes and such, and he asked me a question about something inane. I mean, it was sort of obvious—we danced the dance for a little bit—then I was very forward by saying, "Well, you know, I can take my lunch and we could go to Starbucks and get a coffee." He actually accepted. I was like, "Really!"

But he was leaving the next day, so Nevada boy and I had this relationship that after the initial meeting was actually virtual, you know. Like over the phone and on MSN and sending letters and e-mails with little pictures and all that good stuff. Like we kept up this constant volley. Then he decided, "Well, you know, I can't do this because of the distance," yadda, yadda, yadda. That was heart breaking for me—first love and all that jazz. I was like, "Just leave me alone and pass my Häagen-Dazs through the door." That type of thing.

So if it works out, I'll bring a date to grad. But, I mean, if I don't have a date or whatever I'm not going to sweat it. Anyway, I could always bring one of the flock of girls that hang around me. That's another thing about being gay, you get more popular. Well, I think *I've* gotten much more popular. Last year I didn't really know too many people and I was pretty much behind the scenes and nobody really knew me. The people who signed my yearbook last year wrote stuff like, "Dear Tristan. I don't know you, but you seem like a great guy. Have a great summer," and, "It's a shame I never got to know you, but you seem like a good person. Keep it up." But this year my yearbook is full and people are talking to me about actual things.

The only change I can see is I came out. This was last year, late December or early January. I think it was when I first got back from the Christmas break. It was sort of gradual. The first person I told was my friend Carly, over the Internet. I was talking to her on MSN and I told her I was chatting with Kalen, the Nevada boy, at the same time I was chatting with her, and I elaborated on the nature of the relationship. I think she already had her suspicions like I'm sure other people did. She was like okay, dot, dot, dot. Okay, dot, dot, dot, question mark. I actually got her to ask, "Are you gay," and I replied, "Yes," except I was more humourous than that. I was like, Well, haven't you figured it out? Well isn't it obvious? or something. Anyway, it was cutesy. She was like, "So you're attracted to boys?" and I was like, "Well, yeah," and then she was like, "So who do you think is hot in school?" Then we started to do all the gossip thing—sort of like girl talk. Now it's almost like we paint each other's nails and stuff.

I think she was sort of impressed actually. After all, gay students in high school are few and far between, you know—I mean people who actually admit it. I think she might have said, "Wow!" At least she acted impressed. She started to ask me all these questions, like silly things. I think it was more like a novelty for a while. It was kind of like a revelation for her, but she wasn't weird about it. It's not like she still asks questions. It was only for a few days after until she got used to it. She does still talk about how, you know, some people wouldn't take too kindly to my being gay, but she says if that happens, "I'll kick their asses."

I guess I decided I should just stop not talking about it. If it comes up, I'm not going to deny it. I sort of gave the push to the first few people and then they got the ball rolling and I was like, "Spread the word." Then everyone was like, "Wow, that's so cool," and they just sort of, you know, gathered around me and pretty soon I had this flock of people who were laughing and saying "Hi" to me in the halls. So now I have like this little posse of friends who I can pretty much train into my unholy army of the night. It's like, "Do my bidding." They're

all girls, so if any boys start trouble they can't fight back, so it's a perfect system I have.

Not that anyone would start something. At my school really noth-
ing more happens than, you know, "Oh, he's going to mean to me."
It's not like I have to watch my back or anything. But even if Andy
Auto-shop says, "You're a loser," my world doesn't screech to a halt.

I guess when it comes down to it the school's sort of ambivalent
about my being out. I haven't really faced any, you know, major controversy or like had my locker defaced or anything. Well, if I tried to
force myself on someone, maybe the guy would punch me, but I don't
think I would ever be attacked like Joe Rose was.

Anyway, by like about the fifteenth person, it wasn't really so much
spelling it out to them like, "P.S. I'm gay," as it was just talking about
the events of my life as if they already knew. It's gotten to the point
where it doesn't matter any more. Like if someone says, "Are you
gay?" I won't say, "No," but at the same time I take it like as if I were
Jewish. I wouldn't like come out as Jewish. I wouldn't say, "I'm Jewish,
hear me roar." But if someone asks, well I say, "Oh, yeah." When I
wasn't out and people asked me that, I'd make a cute comment to
confuse them like, "If I were, do you think I'd tell you?" Sometimes
they'd curse and make grumbling sounds. I was like, "Whatever. Why
don't you go make me a bird cage in wood shop."

Yeah, so the people I told responded rather anticlimactically. It's
like as if they were gearing up for this whole argument, right? But then
I totally took the wind out of their sails. It was really quite fun. They
were like, "Oh . . . Well carry on then."

It was pretty much the same when I told my parents. Well my father
and his wife. My mother's side doesn't know. That wouldn't be fun.
But my father's family, I guess, for the most part does. And it's pretty
big, so . . . Word flies pretty quickly in my mother's family, and although I don't know for sure, they probably already know, but they
don't care.

With my father and my stepmother I had tried to come out to them
in various subtle ways, and they kept retaliating with stuff like, "Well,
when you get married and have kids" and such. I was like, "Oh! Do
you *not* get it?" And they'd be like, "Get what?" I wasn't even that
subtle. When I was with them and I saw a hot guy I'd say, "Oh, he's
cute," and they so pretended not to get it.

Oh, oh! Okay. I was like seeing this college guy a few months ago and so I told them, "I'm going to have my friend sleep over tonight," and they said, "Okay." So I'm thinking, Oh that was easy. It was funny how we met. I went to an open house at the college I'm going to next year, this was in January, and I saw this one booth that was particularly festive, all colourful and stuff, and I was drawn like a moth to a flame. I figured what it was pretty quickly. Well, I mean, I put on my glasses and I said, "What's that?" There were banners and rainbows and stuff. And I was like, Oh! I know what that is. I mean, I checked to make sure first—it could have been the chess club that was feeling particularly celebratory. So I moseyed on over to see what was going on. There were a few people there, but I started talking to this one guy and he was like well . . . This is so embarrassing. He was like, "Well, I'm going to get going soon, do you want to come with me?"

When he came over we rented movies and stuff and then we fell asleep on the sofa together in such a way it was obvious he wasn't really just a friend. And then I woke up like at ten a.m., right? And I thought, Oh gee, they probably saw this, you know, considering someone had put a fresh load of laundry beside us.

Anyway. By the time I actually told my father and my step-mother, I was getting really pissed off, right? I was like, How can you *not* know? So again at supper the next day they were going on about, "Oh, when you settle down with a wife and kids" and whatever, and I said, "Yuck!" By that time I was really tired and I said, "You know, let's just cut the charade. In case you haven't noticed, I'm gay. Pass the salt."

They sort of needed coasters for their bottom lips, but aside from that little sulk, I guess it was fine. They weren't too surprised. They continued on with their inane conversation and whatever. Like moving right along . . .

Now they inquire about my various boyfriends as if they're my girlfriends. I mean, that's cool and all, but I'd rather not talk about it. I was thinking, Well, gee, what if I had girlfriends? I still wouldn't want to talk to them about it. So I guess it's the same thing. Then there was the whole condom talk with Dad, and that wasn't fun either. But in that respect, I can't fault them on their performance. They've been very cool about it. Everything's pretty much the same as it was before, only back then they didn't talk about it.

A few days later my father asked me why I told them. I guess he wanted me to say it was because we have such a close relationship or something. I didn't want to burst his bubble and tell him I did it just to stop the irritating marriage comments for once and for all and so I could maybe start to introduce my quote-unquote friends as who they really are. So it was, I guess, for simplicity.

There! You must be happy. I spoke about my family. Can I leave now?

Another week and then . . .

Yeah, so the grad was on the weekend, except everyone kept calling it "the prom," but I call it "the grad" because I think "prom" is an American-ism. Anyway, I'd say it had its ups and downs. I decided I'd go like the day before. There was a cocktail party beforehand, and from there everyone took their limousines or whatever to the pier since the grad was on some boat. I went with one of the flock and her date and his Mercedes, and I had to navigate him around Montreal because he didn't know where he was going. You could tell I was totally emasculating him because he had to keep asking me angrily, "Now where?"

When we finally got to the boat there were these little sailor people who you could tell were these seventeen-year-old French kids looking for a summer job and ended up having to wear these ridiculous outfits and do the whole stupid "welcome aboard" salute thing.

So we got on the boat and we passed a few, you know, skivvies or skippers or something, and we filed into the dining room. It was weird, the dining room was on a slope and rocking but it was a boat so I guess that should be expected. I was at a table with my flock—they all had dates but they didn't talk to them. I watched them, and their dates mostly spent their time elsewhere. Some of them didn't even go in the same limo. Well, there was one date who sat with us. He was having a great time, I could tell.

When I first got there a few people were like, "Hey, where's your date?" Wink, wink, wink, wink. "Like who did you bring?" And I would, you know, say some coy answer like, "My date's at home making me a pie," or something.

The meal was okay, but I had to eat everyone's salad because they didn't like it. It wasn't fennel, it was . . . I feel so uncultured forgetting the damn name of the weed. It was oval, soft velvet . . . expensive . . . anyway it was a good salad but it was too cultured or something for them. And then we had two brochettes and some wedge of a potato cake thing and beans and such. For dessert there was like a tiny piece of cake . . . and a strawberry.

When we finished eating we went out on the main deck for a too-lame-for-this-world dance. I spent most of my time up on the upper deck peering over the railing commenting on the obviously gay, but non-grad group of people who had accumulated on the deck below me. I was with Carly and her boyfriend—he's in the grade after us. Anyway, we were peering over and someone made some offhand comment about how obviously gay this one guy was because he had on like this weird Le Chateau puffy shirt unbuttoned scandalously low, and, you know, casual hair and tight jeans, and a friend with whom he seemed to be exceptionally close who was drinking red wine while everyone else was drinking beer. I don't know. I took that to mean something.

There were like four guys including one very hot polo-shirt guy. He was wearing a polo shirt, that's why I call him "polo-shirt guy." Go figure. Carly asked me if he was gay, you know like, "Is that guy gay?" She's so clueless sometimes. I said, "Yeah," and then we sort of stalked them, like watched to see what they would do to confirm our suspicions. We were so right. It was clinched when the Village People came on and they had their arms in the air and were making all the motions and stuff.

Carly was like engaging me in this stupid conversation about dandelions, but like really loudly, too. I could see them looking at me. No, sunflowers, because she won a sunflower award. It was like some gag prize thing to embarrass everyone involved. So polo-shirt guy looked at me weird after the whole dandelion slash sunflower thing, then him and his friends, you know, went somewhere else. "We have to go over here now."

Oh, oh, oh! After the stupid gag awards, this guy who doesn't go to our school—his girlfriend goes to our school—got up to the podium and he started to profess his undying love for her. Everyone was shouting out, "Don't do it! Don't propose!" because they knew what was going to happen. Did I tell you this already? He didn't seem to be discouraged although I really would have been. He did something that involved kneeling and a ring. I don't know if he actually proposed, or only, you know, gave her a ring on his knees because I fled as soon as I realized what was going down. They're like twelve. They haven't even graduated high school yet. Shouldn't they be saving up for a divorce?

Finally we de-boated at eleven and everyone had to rush back to the hotel and start on their unprotected sex as soon as possible, but I called an older gentleman friend and went to a club in the village with him. I actually met him on the Internet. Scandalous, isn't it?

I'd never been before. To a gay club I mean. I wasn't so impressed—it wasn't spectacular or anything. I mean, for starters the obese drag queen at the door sort of freaked me out. Then the noise! Noise! NOISE! kind of got to me after a while, and I had a very watered-down vodka and tomato juice. It wasn't great.

I just sort of, you know, hung around and tried to look as inconspicuous as I could. I didn't want to get separated from my friend though. God knows what would've happened. It was such a labyrinth and it was so confusing, I felt like an old person stepping out of his little apartment building and totally being in chaos in the world around him. I thought it wise to like find a corner and stick to it and sip my watered-down booze nervously.

I'd never been in a situation where there were all these men in one room—it was reminiscent of boy scouts. I'm kidding. It was okay. I mean, it's not like I had all of these fashion models around me. No, it was definitely *not* like I had all these models around me. They were either not my type or gross slash not my type. Except for one guy who sort of was reasonably to moderately cute . . . ish. He had these endearing glasses and I called him "grey-shirt guy" 'cause, you guessed it, he had on a grey shirt. This distinguished him from polo-shirt guy, because he was in the past now. I grieved. It was time to move on.

I spent most of the night sipping my tomato juice trying to, you know, explain to my friend and his friend why I didn't want to go to saunas. Well, it pretty much wasn't a coherent conversation—his friend was pretty busy trying to find his crystal meth so . . . He said to me, "Why don't you go to a sauna and get laid?" Well, he said something that sounded just as seedy. He thought that was the only way I could, I don't know, "get some," which A: isn't true and B: is quite insulting. I tried to convince him one can live all of one's childhood years without ever going to a gay sauna.

Out of the corner of my eye I kept watching grey-shirt guy and then I saw him like make some sort of facial distortion at me. It was, I don't know, I wouldn't really call it a wink because that would make it sound all seedy and gross when it was sort of cute actually. And then he like made the come-sit-down-next-to-me gesture, and I sort of giggled, you know, but didn't sit down. And then he passed by me incidentally, and made some other face, and I giggled some more. Well, I didn't really giggle as in "Tee-hee." I just sort of chuckled, I guess. I think I made him feel unloved. Anyway.

I saw him again outside the club as I was getting back into the car, and I actually got my friend to circle around that street, Amherst or not, and like spied on him to see what he was doing 'cause he was standing around outside. But by the time we circled around again, he was gone.

So that was that. I got home I'd say like two-ish.

I'd been to the gay village before, so it wasn't a big thrill or anything, but not to a gay club. I think its reputation as a festive place is completely erroneous. You go to the village and you don't see like rainbows and, you know, people dressed up as Dorothy and all that happy gay stuff. I mean, you imagine the yellow brick road and the gay pride parade and people in tank tops and roller blades, and a street car with hunky men leaning off of it. But it only seems to be a bunch of bars and T-shirt shops and, you know, immigrants who make pizza and stand outside their door in aprons and look at everyone really suspiciously. You see people in leather being taken around by leash, and people who are obviously stoned wandering around, and the street youth soliciting themselves on the corner of Champlain and St. Catherine Street. But I guess that's the fun part. It's not exactly as enchanting as some people think it is. I guess that's like a positive pre-conception about homosexuality that we have a happy-go-lucky little village. But, I mean, it can be quite grim.

That's probably the seedy underbelly of being gay, so I wouldn't say that's like as good as it gets or, you know, even the statistically mean atmosphere gay people provide.

Oh, my father and my stepmother were all excited I was going to the grad, they ended up giving me the money for my ticket actually. They're so looking forward to the ceremony in September they made me reserve tickets for them.

The money was a surprise since the situation with my father isn't ideal either—we're always engaged in this competitive relationship, except in most competitions you're like striving for something, and something good might happen to the winner. But, I mean, there's never a winner with us because it's never really ending—we're just going around in circles. Like we try to have dinner as a family, which I hate. Anyway, we're having dinner, and I'm sort of sitting very tensely waiting for something to happen. Then I'll have to break the news I need say a renewal on Zoloft, and then my father will challenge me by saying, "Well, why are you on Zoloft? You seen to be perfectly happy," and I try to explain to him in the calmest way possible that, "Gee, Dad! Maybe I'm happy *because* of the Zoloft and not *in spite* of it." And then, I don't know, he discounts that and says, "Well, just get your psychiatrist to write you a prescription and I'll buy it."

And oh, oh! He doesn't want me to see you anymore extensively because we're poor even though that's so not the case. He makes over six figures a year, and, I swear, all the time they talk about how they're going to lose that crappy little house of theirs. They keep saying it's money they don't have. I'm like, "Well, you know, it's point one percent of your salary," and he retaliates with, "We're spending twenty-five percent of our salary on your luxuries." I actually calculated it and it's like three percent, and those luxuries include such things as education and clothes and food and Zoloft. So everything pretty much to keep me alive is a luxury. Actually when he talks like this, I'd rather go without the luxury of staying alive. You know?

. . .

I kid. I jest. I hope you didn't take that seriously. Trust me, I'd have to cheer up first to kill myself.

My father's always on me for skipping school. I know I've done it a lot in the last few months, but it's not like I'm in danger of failing or anything. It's just at the end of the week I'm tired and disillusioned with the concept of education in the twenty-first century and I decide I don't want to go to my last fifteen minutes of wasted time where I'm supposed to be learning about something or other. So I will, you know, make a little note that says, "Please excuse Tristan at X hour," and I sign my father's name. I do it indistinguishably from him.

Then I go to the office and give it to the vice-principal and I'm like, "I have to go now," and she's like, "Oh. You'll be leaving us? Take care." She's such a perfect bitch to all the other students, but I'm just so nice to her. I'm very polite and animated and I actually take an interest and sympathize with her if I see she's had a rough day. I always say, "I can't imagine how you deal with this day-in and day-out." I strike a balance between saying something like, "I don't know why you get up in the morning," and, you know, not caring. I identify with her pain and she just can't hate me, so she always lets me go, no questions asked. I'm like, "And you have a great day now."

I feel slightly guilty, but that's only eclipsed by the thrill of like pulling yet another one over on the system. I call it "my mental health block" because they don't give us spare periods any more.

Anyhow. My father takes me on so many guilt trips I should be getting frequent flier points. But I guess it's still better than living with her.

. . .

Sorry. I'm not usually quiet like that.

. . .

Ever since I moved out of my mother's house, it's been sort of strange. I haven't really spoken to her for the last month. Before I moved out, my mother and father were surprisingly enough on friendly-ish type terms, but now she absolutely hates him and says she never wants to see him again and all these lovely things.

Anyway, this whole situation has been quite . . . emotionally taxing. She's been living with her boyfriend and his kids for about twelve years, and I basically felt like a third wheel there—*he* certainly didn't like me. For most of the twelve years he was quite the monster—at least a lot of the time—and what I found truly awful and the worse part about it was that it wasn't consistently awful. Like it wasn't a consistently abusive situation. I would say maybe five or ten percent of the otherwise quote-unquote normal existence I had there was awful. But, I mean, it only takes like five or ten percent, you know, peppered over the whole experience to make it unbearable.

And get this. Her boyfriend is vehemently anti-homosexual. Sometimes I think, Well, maybe I'm gay just to piss him off, because, I mean, it would *so* be worth it. He's anti-homosexual and anti-Semitic and racist . . . it's just so dumb. My mother never questions him or takes him to task on this in any way, shape, or form because I guess she thinks since she isn't gay or a Jew, what business is it of hers?

He's such a hypocrite. I mean, when he meets a Black or a Jew he's never anything other than like polite and friendly and like chummy. So I don't know even why he would say those things. I think it's to be shocking. I mean like after a few years of hearing about this every so often, I'd think, You aren't so much shocking as you are stupid. He'd say black people are inferior, yet he'd tell us that's okay to say because he has many black friends, even though he doesn't really have any black friends. So that's like a triple hypocrite.

As I grew older, I just became more and more disgusted by my mother's boyfriend's judgmental attitude and his hating people for no other reason than being born a certain way.

I mean he deserves what he gets, but . . . when this happened . . . It *is* a bit much, don't you think?

It's sort of a mock incest because they're not related by blood, but it's still grossly inappropriate. Like how do you forgive someone for that? It really doesn't make me happy—and my father wonders why I need Zoloft? Well, I'm still sort of disturbed by the fact she didn't hide it. I repeatedly saw them engaging in romantic activity.

I had my own room, but it was like I really lived in the den because that's where everything else happened to be—the computer, the TV—so there was often people in there. Despite my mother's claims I always had a place to myself, I never did. About two or three months before I actually moved out, I took to hiding in the bathroom and like reading or whatever. This went on until I, you know, completely ended the life I had with my mother.

Through all this I've tried to preserve my sense of sanity, which is often . . . not easy. "Keep laughing," I keep telling myself. "Keep laughing." But I know no amount of witty banter will help me deal with this shit. I guess that's where you come in.

So I don't know what's going on with her or who she's with now— the racist homophobic anti-Semite or his seventeen year old son, the son of the guy she's supposed to be with. Like my being gay is the problem—they should look at themselves and not look down their noses at me. *That's* what's so hard to deal with.

I mean, Hallmark doesn't make cards for something like this.

Rebel . . . Just Because
Evan's Story—Part II

THE DOOR to the principal's office is shut. I stand against the wall like I've been ordered to along with the usual suspects: the skinny kid who swears at teachers, using "fuck" as a noun, adjective, adverb, and preposition; the blond boy who by some bizarre coincidence is always in the same hallway where a fire alarm's been pulled; and the bored girl who's been found one too many times making out with some random guy. In a stairwell. Behind the school. In the boys' bathroom.

One of the secretaries smiles at me, the one who always sighs whenever I'm called down to the office.

"What did you do this time?"

I tell her tall tales of bomb threats and knife fights and white powder craftily planted to suddenly explode in the face of anyone who chances upon it. She laughs and shakes her head and sighs some more. Of course I'm innocent.

Sort of.

The kid who's constantly re-inventing the word "fuck" says to me, "Yo, man. I know your fucking secret. But, fuck, it's cool with me." The secretary gives him a warning look.

"Well," I reply, "first of all if you know it, it isn't much of a secret, is it? And, second, I honestly don't need your validation thank you very much."

"Evan!" the secretary says.

The "fuck" kid and I go back to standing in silence. I smile at the secretary and pantomime a last cigarette before the firing squad has its way with me. Blindfold and all. She laughs and the "fuck" kid rolls his eyes dramatically.

I never saw the kid before, some anonymous grade sevener,

although he could be the little brother of a girl in my French class. But I don't really talk to her, so why would I talk to her brother?

Since she's already in trouble and only standing at the wall outside the principal's office, the bored skanky girl decides now's as good a time as any to reapply her lip gloss. When she catches me looking at her, she sarcastically puckers her lips at me.

That's what's sad about my life—everybody knows me but I don't really know anybody. I guess that's the price you pay for being the only out gay student in the school—the price of fame I like to think.

I guess Ciaran did me a favour. He's the one who told everybody at school I'm gay after I told his sister, thinking it was in total confidence, of course. How dumb was I? My father warned me the only way someone will keep a secret is if they're dead. Even then.

Most people reacted really well when they found out. Lots of them said, "Oh. We knew," and, "Okay. So?" They were mature about it. But some people were like, "Oh, my God! You're gay?" I wasn't sure if that meant they wanted to celebrate or what. Evan's coming out party! I suppose they were shocked because I was only in grade eight and only fourteen years old. In a lot of people's minds that might be young.

When I came out I was flooded with questions, so all of a sudden I became the spokesman for homosexuality. When you come out, right away you're popular. People know you. Well, that's not always a plus, but you do get a lot of attention if that's what you like. I have to admit I like the attention.

Now I'm genuinely me; I'm not being something else; I'm not masking who I am and what I am to other people. I think I handled coming out relatively well. I suppose with time I'll learn more skills to deal with people—it's not everybody that has them, especially young gay people because they tend to be so much more introverted. At least the ones I've met.

I, on the other hand, don't keep quiet about it. Why should I?

Every year we have to do a public speech, and last year I did mine on same-sex marriage and how great it was the Canadian government finally recognized gay couples as couples and not as just two companions or two friends. It's an important issue. Personally I want to have the choice to get married, same as heterosexuals have the choice. Mind you, I don't see myself doing it any time soon, but I like having the option. Let's face it: people who are against same-sex marriages are homophobic. There are still lots of them around, so it's a cause worth standing up for. Not every student would do that.

The speech was good enough that I came in first in the class. The students got to vote. When it was over some of them told me I was courageous to have spoken in front of everyone like that. It's one thing when you're answering questions to a few chosen people in the hallway or outside on break, but it's another thing when you're standing in front of your English class doing a speech for marks. There's a risk of being booed off in front of everyone. You can be mocked. But everyone in my class was pretty much in agreement with me. I guess if I came in first it's because my arguments persuaded them enough to agree with me.

But there are some students in my school who are point-blank assholes. Both stupid and immature. I'm thinking of one in particular, a guy in my math class named Kurt. The biggest words in his vocabulary are "Shut up faggot," and after hearing that all day I'm like, "Oh! Ouch! That hurts." Totally sarcastic, if you can't tell. Once after he said, "Shut up faggot," I said, "Don't be jealous Kurt just because I can do the gay thing better than you can." When anyone calls me a faggot, I make it into my own joke: "You better *not* call me straight." Or something like that. Sadly all Kurt has as a comeback is, "Shut the fuck up faggot." As you can tell, he's not the coolest ice cube in the tray.

No one would believe this but I actually like school. Sometimes I even think I like my friends more than I do my family. My school's mostly an accepting place even if there's not that much diversity. Most of the students are white, but racism isn't a big problem. We don't have many black students, but the few black students that are there are some of the most popular kids in the school. Everybody's friends with them. We do have some French students and some bilingual students, like myself. We have a few Asians and some students from the Middle East. We have some foreign exchange students, too. From Mexico. From Hong Kong.

There's a dress code at our school—navy blue pants and white shirts—but the Muslim girls wear their veils over it. Even in gym class they're going to wear their veils. There are one or two boys who wear turbans. We have one guy in my grade who's growing a beard for religious reasons. It's been like an ongoing project for him.

Where there *is* a problem is with sexism. I notice guys are pretty chauvinistic to my female friends—it happens a lot. But most of them are going to hold back their comments when I'm there, because the girls may put up with it, but I won't. No one's going to call my best friend Sam a bitch. I have three older sisters and I was raised by women. After all, if anyone, *I* should understand what it's like to be oppressed.

I look around at the company I'm forced to keep as we wait for the principal to deign to see us. The "fuck" kid shoots angry looks at me, still broken up we didn't bond over my "secret." The bored promiscuous girl looks, well, bored as usual and as slutty as ever. Having to wait outside the principal's office clearly has taken a chunk out of her love life during the important peak school hours. You'd think she'd save a little something for the weekend. The blond pyromaniac-in-training has started to cry. He stands in silence with tears dribbling down his cheeks.

I almost feel sorry for this cast of characters lined up against the wall waiting execution. Well, as sorry as you can for the pathological. And as often as I've wanted to tell a teacher to fuck off, or set the school on fire, or make out with Pier-Luc Gagné in a storage room, apparently my crime today is far more serious, loathsome, and tragic. At least Jonathan Casey thinks so.

I guess he may have a point since it was his chest and abs I ran my hand down.

The door to the principal's office opens and Mr. Russell, the vice-principal, pokes his head out and grunts my name. I smile at the secretary and bid my fellow criminals "adieu." Their puzzled expressions confirm I'm swimming well beyond their feeding grounds. I'm making my way to the office when I hear the principal holler from inside, "Hurry up."

Now Mr. Pfeiffer's a cold, cold man. Whenever anybody lands up in his office, he always starts by saying, "I have work to do here," so you get the idea pretty quickly that you're intruding. I know if I'm in trouble, it's like Pfeiffer is saying, "Look Evan. Your homosexuality has gotten in the way of my work." Not that he'd ever use the word "homosexuality." The man has trouble saying the word "gay" or any variation of it. I know he's not at one with homosexuality because Tony Bianco, the teacher in charge of the variety show, told me Pfeiffer's homophobic. Tony's a good friend of Mr. Pfeiffer—it's probably the only reason he hasn't been fired.

"I'm not one hundred percent certain," he said. "It's not like it's written in stone or anything. It's only the impression I have."

"So Evan," Mr. Pfeiffer begins. He sits behind his desk where he can be found on any given day. Physically his shape reminds me of a vegetable. An onion. A Spanish onion. "Jonathan Casey has come to us with accusations of being sexually harassed by you. He's quite upset. Do you want to tell me about it?"

"It's funny the way you say it," I chuckle, but clearly they're in no mood to laugh. I quickly say, "Now before you jump to any ideas about me lurking in dark corners ready to pounce on poor unsuspecting Jon Casey, you've got to hear my side."

"We're waiting," Mr. Pfeiffer says. Already he's impatiently looking down at the papers on his desk.

"Well," I begin, "Jon was being sexually suggestive to Sam during math. You know, motioning to his penis. So Sam said to Jon, 'If you don't stop, Evan's going to hit on you.' And so he didn't stop. So I ran my hand down his chest, but I stopped at his belt. I know he's saying I grabbed his balls, but I *swear* I stopped at his belt. It was a joke. Ask Sam, she was there."

"Well, that's sexual harassment," Mr. Russell says. If Pfeiffer is an onion, Russell's a parsnip. "If Jonathan wants to he can file a formal complaint against you. The school board has a policy against harassment of any kind."

"It was a joke," I say again. "Jonathan Casey's such a drama queen. It's not like I haven't done stuff like this before. Everyone takes it as a joke."

Off the top of my head I can think of tons of examples—like there's the time I was waiting at the bus stop and David Longpré was there. I was having a smoke and he hates smokers, so he said to me, "The bus stop's a non-smoking zone."

"Well," I said, "does it have your name on it?"

"No, but . . ."

While he was still crying about his right to fresh air, I flicked my ash and I got some of it on his shirt. Accidentally. I swear! So I said, "Oh, please. Allow me to take it off," and I got a good feel of his abs.

"God, Evan! You have to do that?" he said, jumping back.

"Uh, Yeah."

Even Pier-Luc Gagné, my imaginary boyfriend, gets I'm only joking. Everybody knows I love him—I'm not quiet about it. Pier-Luc and his asshole best friend Dylan Phillips were sitting in the hall one recess, and I was passing by, and Dylan asked me, "Are you really attracted to Pier-Luc?" I just answered, "Yes," and kept on walking. Dylan yelled after me, "You know, Pier-Luc has a waterbed." I stopped right there and turned around and said, "No kidding? Well, he's just gotten a lot more interesting." I could see Pier-Luc turn red—beet red—he blushes so easily. Dylan was practically pissing himself laughing. But goddamn! It's Pier-Luc's own fault. If he weren't so hot, I wouldn't be so in love with him. He has this great black hair and amazing light brown eyes! His eyes! It's all about the eyes.

So, okay. I do push things over the limit sometimes. But it's nothing serious. People like Mr. Pfeiffer and Jonathan Casey need to lighten up. There are only two things you can honestly say about Jon: he's homophobic and not too bright. It's hard to believe he beat out a million other sperm. Oh, and he's a born-again Christian religious fanatic, and every day I have to hear him justifying his hate with religion. Well, the only thing he really says is "Leviticus 18 verse 22 prohibits homosexuality." So what? But I have to hear that over and over again.

Last year he gave me shit about that in math class, and Mr. Yamaguchi told him to stop it and to leave his religious convictions outside the classroom. So Jon started in on him: "Well, sir, don't you believe in God? Aren't you a Catholic? You believe in this, too, right sir?" Mr. Yamaguchi only said, "Jonathan. You don't want to argue with me. Trust me on that. Back to work." It was great. It pissed Jon off. It pissed him off and I have to admit I got a rise out of it pissing him off.

It's funny how his religious convictions don't stop him from calling me "fag." Yeah, *that's* what Jesus would do.

Of course none of that will help me out of *this* situation. It doesn't take a Jeopardy champion to know this trial isn't going my way. I know Pfeiffer and Russell are waiting for an apology. When they don't get one, Mr. Pfeiffer puts on his concerned pumpkin face and says, "How do you explain your behaviour, Evan? Is it because you're gay?"

"What the fuck is that supposed to mean? Would you ask Calvin Stevens if he's such an asshole because he's black?"

"Oh, well. I'm only asking," Pfeiffer says as though it's as trivial as asking for the time or if it's raining out. But I guess he's sorry he said it or else he'd have nailed me on the swearing.

"What I'm trying to get at, is in grade eight you basically came out and told everyone you're gay. I'm wondering if you're doing this to get attention."

I don't bother to answer—I don't see the point in dignifying *that* with a response. When they see I'm not speaking anymore, Mr. Pfeiffer says, "Well, we have to do *something* about this. When someone who's gay sexually harasses another guy, it's the same as when a girl sexually harasses a guy or—"

"Oh, God! Now are you calling me a girl?"

"I don't think you understand what I'm trying to say here."

"Well I do understand that if it was a girl who did what I did to Jon, he wouldn't complain. He'd love it. And if he did complain, I'm sure you'd brush it off as a joke."

That's when Pfeiffer gives me a three-day vacation, uh, suspension. All Mr. Russell does is shake his head at me like the dutiful sidekick he is.

Okay, I realize the school has to do something, but what kind of a punishment do you really give for this? It's more like it has to be perceived something's been done, whether it's justified or not or whether the person will truly learn a lesson. I mean, it's not as though I'm *not* going to do it again. I'll just do it with more style and to people I know won't run around filing complaints.

But what really pisses me off is what's not being said. Sexual harassment goes on all the time at this school. Guys are always hitting on girls. God! Jonathan Casey's always hitting on girls! If another guy had done this to Jon, it wouldn't have bothered him. Jon and his friends do worse to each other all the time like it's some big joke. When they see me, they grab each other's balls and hold each other around the shoulders in this mock affectionate way. They look right at me as if to say, "Oh, Evan, look at what we can do and you can't."

He complained because I'm gay and to him gay's bad. So the school prevented him from getting sexually harassed, but it's not as if they ever prevented *me* from getting harassed by *him*. Homophobia—isn't that harassment? Calling somebody a "faggot," isn't that harassment? No one's ever stopped Jon from calling me that. How many times does Kurt Mueller have to call me a fag before it's considered harassment?

I even get it from teachers from time-to-time. I'm thinking about this one teacher at my school—while I never had him I've spoken to him before because I speak to all the teachers. I always thought he was nice, but at the start of the year I was wearing a boy-boy pin on my shirt—you know, the symbol for the male that looks like an arrow. Well this one had two of them. So I was talking to Mrs. Hutchison, my English teacher, and he came up to ask her something. When he saw my pin he said, "Hey, that's the gay sign. You're not gay," and Mrs. Hutchison said, "Yes! He is!" Like, duh!

He quickly said, "Oh, that's cool with me. Oh, that's all right. I like gay people." Fuck you! Like I give a fuck what you think. Moron!

So I said to him, "Don't assume I'm straight and I won't assume you're an asshole," and walked away.

Why don't they do something about *him*? Where was the principal then?

Now that I've received my sentence, I leave without another word. Mr. Russell comes after me and stops me outside the main office.

"We're learning here," he tells me. "You're the first gay student we've had. Or at least that we've known about. We're trying to do our best here, what's right for everyone."

I grunt something non-committal so he'll leave me alone, then I walk away. What I should have said was: "Well, you're not learning fast enough."

As I reach my locker to get my backpack, Tony comes up and asks me how it went. I suppose the word is getting around about what happened with Jon, but I'm sure it's not like it's on CNN. I'm sure nobody except Pfeiffer takes Jon seriously. Everyone is probably like, "Oh, Evan hit on Jon. Whatever!" Yawn. Yawn squared.

"Suspended."

Tony scowls and shakes his head. "Will you be okay?"

"Sure. Why not?" I say, perhaps more abruptly than he deserves.

"Always taking the road less traveled, eh?" he says with a smile.

I could have taken that another way, but I know Tony's only being concerned—he's way cool; we all love him; he's friends with all the students. He doesn't sit in the staff lounge and gossip about the latest news turning our school into more of a soap opera than it already is. He's there for the students. It's not every school that has a teacher who genuinely gives a shit like Tony does. My school has a few good teachers who actually care, but the majority of our teachers really don't. The second we walk out of that classroom, they don't give a fuck whether we live or die.

"Nina wants you to come over for dinner this week."

I thought that was nice of her, even though I was in no mood to convey that to Tony. I met Tony's girlfriend Nina at the variety show. They were with Nina's best friend, Kenny, who was a student at my school a few years ago. He's gay, too, but he wasn't out or anything like me when he was at school. He's twenty-one now. Nina introduced us and we started this friendship. I think it's cool Tony and Nina have gay friends. I already had a lot of gay friends, people I met at Project 10, or through friends, or friends of friends, but one more couldn't hurt. Now Kenny and I talk on the phone all the time, and sometimes we meet for coffee.

Guess I'll have a lot of time to hang out with Kenny now that I have this unexpected holiday.

I'm back at school after spending three days sitting around the house with my parents' disappointment. They would have been a lot worse if I didn't pass off the principal's note home outlining my crime as over-exaggerated and a targeted injustice because of my sexual orientation. Frankly, I don't think my mother knew what to do about it. Luckily my relationship with my father's at such a precarious point at the moment he didn't dare punish me, especially over a touchy-touchy gay issue—in a manner of speaking. I mean, how do you punish your son for hitting on another boy? My mother told me I couldn't leave the house while I was suspended, but she was more worried my grandparents who live downstairs would see me and what they would think. We decided to tell them I wasn't at school because there was a school holiday. Ped days.

Not that I stayed home the entire time. I took house arrest as merely a helpful suggestion. After the first two days of finishing homework, reading a Stephen King novel, playing guitar, and listening to music— I'm retro like that—I had to get out. As much as I'm endeared to old school Eminem's vulgar outspokenness, there's only so much of his beats even I can listen to. On the third day when my mother went to work, I decided to catch a bus downtown and walk around the gay village. I hadn't been there for a couple of weeks.

I don't usually go to the village on weekdays, so I was surprised to find it pretty empty—there wasn't the usual rush of hot guys running from one club to another. One thing I did notice, though, while I was walking from one end of the village to the other, were the posters everywhere for a candlelight vigil. I stopped and read one, then ripped a small one down from a streetlight and stuffed it into my pocket. I knew Sam would go with me. There are some things you can't remain silent about.

At a bookstore I bought a book about the history of homosexuality and what it means to be gay today. It's about four inches thick. It's very educational. Not that you have to read a manual to know how to be gay. Just to balance out all that intellectual bias, I also bought an "All Boy XXX" magazine.

Before I caught the bus home, I stopped at a strip club. By law I'm not supposed to be there, but the several times I've gone nobody's carded me. Nobody's even questioned it. They make you buy a drink, but I don't drink alcohol so usually I get a Perrier or a Coke. It's pretty amusing when the strippers pay me a lot of attention because, well to be honest, I think they'd rather try to get me to buy a lap dance than some seventy-year-old, three-thousand-pound man. By the time my parents got home from work, I was sitting at the desk in my room hunched over my math book looking like I'm concentrating on polynomials.

Now that I'm walking through the school's front doors again, I can't help but wonder what everyone did without me? When I'm not there it's probably a lot less exciting. After all, without me the school's a wasteland of heterosexuality. Most of what my grade knows about homosexuality, I've told them. When I first came out I answered a lot of questions, and I can tell you a lot of people were very ignorant about it. They had this grade three concept: "It's when a guy loves another guy the way most guys love women." I kind of broadened a lot of perspectives. I pretty much educated the whole school.

I had a teacher come up to me a month ago, Mr. Lowell, and he told me that in his grade seven class one of his students is gay and he's being picked on. Well, he doesn't know for a fact the kid's gay, but he's like ninety-five percent sure. He didn't tell me who it is; I didn't ask. He wanted to know what he should do. I said he should let his students know right away he's not going to tolerate bullshit in his class. I told him to be sure to give the student space and time and compassion, because, God, that's what I would have wanted from people.

Anyway, I don't think that was quite the answer he hoped for. I think he was looking for a quick fix solution. Something he wouldn't have to put any effort into. But I didn't mind him asking. I honestly think it's up to me to make everyone realize it's not only a straight school.

I brought it up in biology class, but Mr. Côté didn't like it. He's a horrible teacher; he spits when he talks. I challenged him because I was certain I heard on the news they pinpointed a gay gene or a neurological difference or something in the chromosomes of homosexuals. So I asked him about it and he said, "That's nonsense. There's absolutely no difference." But I thought, You old coot. Fuck you went to university in like the seventies. What do you know? I don't think he totally agrees with my being gay. His daughter Karine was in my elementary school and I remember her saying homosexuality is wrong—like in grade three. I wonder where she got that.

Sometimes schooling these idiots is an uphill battle. Well, that's the burden of being the only out gay student in school.

As I walk into the school, thankfully Sam is waiting for me along with a few of our other friends. Sam and I have been best friends since grade eight. We know each other inside-out. Teachers hate having us in the same class, though. We talk a lot and get the giggles at least five times a day.

Everyone hugs me and laughs and says Jonathan Casey should consider himself lucky to be hit on by me.

"He's been going around telling everyone you grabbed his balls," Sam tells me. "But don't worry. Nobody's listening to him." Just like I thought.

I try to keep my head down for the rest of the day. "One day at a time," I keep telling myself. The rest of the day's like this: my friends supporting me; Jon sticking to his guns; and his friends keeping out if it. I suppose people who don't know me and only know I'm gay must think the worse about me and this whole ghastly affair. Damn hypocrites!

Anyway, I vow to myself over and over again to keep out of trouble for a while.

———

A few weeks pass and somehow I manage to avoid the pull of the black hole that's the principal's office. Don't get me wrong—this doesn't mean I've somehow laid down and died. I still give as good as I get. Maybe even better.

Just yesterday I asked someone in my French class how his weekend was, and he said, "Uh, pretty gay," so I said, "Yeah, it was a very homosexual weekend. My weekend was pretty faggy, too." I think he got the point.

And a week ago in Mr. Williams' class I was sick and tired of hearing Kurt say, "Shut up faggot," and having teachers do nothing about it, so I called out, "Sir, are you going to tolerate that in your class?" I've done it before, but this time I had the whole class's attention, and Williams was on the spot, so he had to do something. He told Kurt to step outside, and after a while he went out and spoke to him.

But despite what people might think of me, I have refrained from having my way with every boy I see, although Sam and I still go to the gym at lunch and sit on the stage and watch the hot boys play sports or whatever it is they're doing. They know we're checking them out, but it's all good. I suppose some of them are insecure about their sexuality and they might be bothered by it, but most of them don't care. Anyway, what am I going to do? Rape them? Surely they realize that.

School's over for another day. I'm heading out the door to catch my bus when I see Tony down the hall talking to his girlfriend Nina and my new friend Kenny. I walk up to them and they're with another guy who I assume is Kenny's twenty-six-year-old boyfriend, because as soon as he sees me he pulls Kenny closer to him. Kenny's told me about his boyfriend, but we've never met. Apparently he's jealous as hell and even abusive at times. I kiss Nina on both cheeks and I politely shake Kenny and the boyfriend's hands.

Nina, Tony, and I make small talk for a bit, until I hear the boyfriend say to Kenny loud enough so we all can hear, "*He's* the last person I want to see right now."

I look directly at him. "Well, by all means, leave then. No one's forcing you to be here."

Right away he steps towards me and leans in and says, "If I were you, I'd get out of my face right now."

"Fuck you!" I say. "This is my school. You leave!"

Suddenly the boyfriend goes into a jealous psycho rage and grabs my neck and pins me up against the locker. Just as quickly Tony hauls him off me.

There are a few other people in the hall witnessing this, like my English teacher, Mrs. Hutchison, this small little toothpick of a woman, and she runs up and starts giving Kenny's boyfriend shit. "You know, this isn't your school. You can't just barge in here and start fights with students. Leave at once!"

And then Mrs. Lehrer, the flashback hippy art teacher—God bless her soul—she comes up to me and takes me by the arm and says, "It's okay sweetie. It's going to be all right. Come on now, we're going to go to the office and make sure you're alright. It's okay now sweetie."

I don't appreciate all this "sweetie" stuff in front of everyone, but I go with her anyway.

All I can think is: I wish he would have done that right after the bell rang in a crowded hallway with all my friends there. I'd love to see that—a dozen girls ripping him to shreds.

While Mrs. Lehrer does her best to mother me, I tell her who Kenny is. She asks me how it all began, and I tell her, pouring everything out.

"You're sixteen and you slept with him?" she says shocked.

"Spare me please," I say. "I don't need a sermon right now."

"Okay. All right. I'm not going to moralize to you, but that's my opinion." She apologizes that it came out so bluntly. I continue telling her about the mess I've got myself into this time.

She nods and asks questions here and there, and smiles when I come to the conclusion I don't have that much invested in Kenny anyway, so whatever.

Mr. Russell comes in and asks if I want to speak to him. I thank Mrs. Lehrer for helping me out and follow him to his office. I'm rubbing my neck where, no doubt, I must have a nice war wound given how much it hurts.

"Are you okay?" he asks. I nod.

"Mr. Bianco has briefly filled me in on the details. Those young men have been escorted out of the building and won't be allowed back under any circumstances. I've made that crystal clear. It's up to you if you want to press charges. We'll support you either way."

I nod that I understand. I wait, wondering how this will be turned into another incident where it's all my fault. The gay problem child strikes again!

"I want you to know," Mr. Russell continues, "the school guarantees your safety. You can count on that. Especially now that we know about the situation. I'll be informing Mr. Pfeiffer about it, too. He's away at a meeting, but as soon as he gets back I'll let him know what happened." He goes on to tell me the school isn't going to tolerate someone coming in and attacking a student.

"I guess I've done it again, huh?" I say. "Created another big gay drama?"

But Mr. Russell says, "The fact is we have a gay student in our school, and I want you to know we're not going to overlook you if you have issues or complaints. The bottom line today is your safety—that's more important than anything else right now. It's not always about being gay, you know."

And I almost believe him.

An Open Letter to Out Gay Students
Pages from Joe Rose's Notebook

THE FIRST THING I'd say to you if you're gay and out in school is don't be affected by anything anyone says, unless it's good. In which case, be affected all you want. If it's bad, just carry on being who you are because it makes people more prone to respect you if they see you don't care what other people have to say. It also makes the person who's saying those things look dumb. When you come out, the first thing you have to do is learn how to be strong and to block out negative people and their words.

It's important to be yourself and be happy—know that you're fine the way you are. Feel inside pride for who you are, and no matter what people are going to say or do, don't let it change that feeling. Don't become an introvert, unless you're already that kind of person, because you'll need friends, and if your friends really are your friends, they'll accept you for who you are. True friends won't judge you.

There will be trials and tribulations when you're out, I won't lie, but there's always a light at the end of the tunnel. Wait it out and don't do anything drastic that you might regret.

If you're not out, take your time. First of all, make sure when you do come out you weren't pressured to do it and you're comfortable with it. Coming out is a leap of faith no matter what anyone says. Sometimes it's a hard decision to make. For some people, it's not something easy to live through. There might be harassment, that's true, so sometimes it's easier to be in the closet. But don't forget there are benefits of being out, the biggest one is you feel more accepting of yourself.

If you are being harassed, defend yourself. Don't just take it—it won't go away or get better. Find allies like a teacher, an administrator, or other students. Tell your parents. If you're being verbally harassed, think of a snappy comment. Don't only say, "Shut up," or something lame like that. Show them you won't remain silent. If you're being physically harassed, call the police.

If everything is going fine, then do what you want. But if you're being harassed for being gay anyway, and everyone's making fun of you, you might as well be yourself and come out. You have nothing to lose. Many of us think it's one of the more positive events in our lives.

It's your decision, but realize people are a lot more supportive than you know. You can talk to your friends. People are a lot more tolerant now. Many people are even accepting. Find them.

But above all, school is a time for having fun. So have fun.

And be yourself.

Pink hair cost gay man his life

4 youths held in Rose killing

Montreal – Early Sunday morning a local man was stabbed to death on a city bus by a gang of youths. Joe Rose, 23, was attacked by 15 or more assailants who jeered at him and shouted, "Faggot." The incident occurred at about 4:30 a.m. outside the Frontenac métro.

Witnesses to the attack say the youths beat him and stabbed him because his hair was dyed pink. The youths pulled off Rose's hat and started punching him, then pulled out hunting and kitchen knives and scissors and stabbed him repeatedly before fleeing the bus. A female bus driver who tried to intervene was struck but not seriously injured.

"I'm convinced it was because he's gay," said one witness who asked not to be identified. "There were a lot of people they could have singled out. Why him? He had pink hair and looked gay. They chose him."

A family spokesperson said Rose was returning home from a friend's house on the last bus. In college, Rose was the president of the gay and lesbian student group.

A 19-year-old and a 15-year-old will be charged later today with second-degree murder. Two juveniles, 14 and 15, who cannot be named under youth protection laws, will be charged as accessories after the fact.

About the Author

MICHAEL WHATLING grew up outside of Montreal, Canada. For a time he escaped and lived in London, Paris, and Tokyo. He holds a Ph.D. in education, and has taught at the elementary, secondary, and university levels. His writing includes short stories, novels, and screenplays. He now lives in the town where he grew up, tormented by intolerance, the need to write, and wild rabbits in his yard.

www.ingramcontent.com/pod-product-compliance
Lightning Source LLC
Chambersburg PA
CBHW020327110726
47898CB00003B/769